大修館
シェイクスピア双書
第2集

THE

TAISHUKAN

SHAKESPEARE

2nd Series

大修館書店

A

Moſt pleaſaunt and
excellent conceited Co-
medie, of Syr *Iohn Falſtaffe*, and the
merrie Wiues of *Windſor*.

Entermixed with ſundrie
variable and pleaſing humors, of Syr *Hugh*
the Welch Knight, Iuſtice *Shallow*, and his
wiſe Couſin M. *Slender*.

With the ſwaggering vaine of Auncient
Piſtoll, and Corporall *Nym*.

By *William Shakeſpeare*.

As it hath bene diuers times Acted by the right Honorable
my Lord Chamberlaines ſeruants. Both before her
Maieſtie, and elſe-where.

LONDON
Printed by **T. C.** for Arthur Iohnſon, and are to be ſold at
his ſhop in Powles Church-yard, at the ſigne of the
Flower de Leuſe and the Crowne.
1 6 0 2.

『ウィンザーの陽気な女房たち』初版本（1602 年）のタイトルページ

ウィリアム・シェイクスピア

ウィンザーの陽気な女房たち

William Shakespeare

THE MERRY WIVES
OF WINDSOR

竹村はるみ

編注

大修館シェイクスピア双書 第2集（全8巻）について

　大修館シェイクスピア双書 第一集（全12巻）の刊行が始まったのは1987年4月。その頃はシェイクスピア講読の授業を行う大学もまだ多く、双書はその充実した解説と注釈において（手頃な値段という点においても）、原典に親しむ学生の心強い味方となり、教員の研究・教育に欠かせないツールとなった。

　そうした時代に比べれば、シェイクスピアよりも実用英語という経済性偏重の風潮もあって、シェイクスピア講読の科目を有する大学は数えるほどになったが、双書が役割を終えたわけでは全くなかった。そのことは発行部数からもよくわかる。2010年代になっても双書のほとんどは継続的に増刷を続けており、例えば『ロミオとジュリエット』の総発行部数は15,000に届く勢いだ。英文学古典の注釈書としてはかなりの部数と言える。

　これは大学の教員や学生のみならず、多くの一般読者にも双書が届いているからに他ならない。実際、周囲を見回せば、通信教育、生涯学習講座、地域のカルチャー・センター、読書会や勉強会でシェイクスピアの原典を繙く人は少なくない。そういう読者に双書が選ばれているのだとすれば、その主な理由は第一集編集委員会の目指した理念が好意的に受け取られているからだろう。

　原文のシェイクスピアをできるだけ多くの人に親しみやすいものにすること。とは言え、入門的に平易に書き直したりダイジェスト版にしたりするのではなく、最新の研究成果に基づいた解説や注釈により、原文を余すところなく読み解けるようにすること。そのために対注形式を取り、見開き2ページで原文と注釈を収めて読みやすさを重視すること。後注や参考文献により学問的な質を高く保ちつつ、シェイクスピアの台詞や研究の面白さを深く理

解できるようにすること。こうした第一集の構想が、第二集においてもしっかりと受け継がれていることは言うまでもない。また、表記の仕方などを除いて、厳密な統一事項や決まりなどは設けず、編集者の個性を十分に発揮していただく点も第一集と同様である。

　一方、重要な刷新もある。第一集では Alexander 版（1951）のテクストを基本的にそのまま用いたが、当時と比べれば近年の本文研究は大きな進展をみせ、現在 Alexander 版は必ずしも使いやすいテクストではない。むしろ編者が初期版本の性質を見極めた上で、そこからテクストを立ち上げ、様々な本文の読みを吟味しつつ編集作業を行う方が（負担は増すものの）、意義ある取り組みになるのではないか。そうした考え方に基づいて第二集では大きく舵を切り、各編者がテクストすべてを組み上げた。そのため作品によっては本文編集に関する注釈を煩雑に感じる読者もおられようが、注釈に目を通していただくと、問題になっている部分が実は作品の読みを左右する要なのだとご納得いただけると思う。

　第二集の企画を大修館編集部の北村和香子さんにご検討いただいたのは 2017 年秋。無謀とも思える提案に終始にこやかかつ冷静沈着に耳を傾け、企画全体を辛抱強く推し進めて下さった。第二集 8 巻の作品選定は大いに悩んだが、第一集『ハムレット』で編者を務めた河合祥一郎氏からのご提言もいただき、喜劇・悲劇・歴史劇・ローマ劇・ロマンス劇からバランスよく作品を選ぶことができた。ご両名にこの場を借りて心から御礼を申し上げる。「さらに第 2 期、第 3 期と刊行をつづけ、やがてはシェイクスピアの全作品を網羅できれば」という初代の思いが次に繋がることを願いつつ、あとは読者諸氏のご支援とご叱正を乞う次第である。

　　大修館シェイクスピア双書　第 2 集　編集者代表　　井出　新

まえがき

　私が初めて原書でシェイクスピア劇を読んだのは、大学1回生の講読授業だった。1年かけて『マクベス』を講読した。え？結構読める！という嬉しい驚きが、新学期にテキストを開いた時の率直な感想だった。シェイクスピア劇が執筆されたのは16世紀から17世紀にかけての時期、400年以上前の時代である。国語の古文のようなものを想像していただけに、ところどころ見慣れぬ語はあるものの、全体的には現代英語とさして変わらないように思える英語にまずは心底感心した。そう、シェイクスピアは、中世ではなく、近代の劇作家なのだ。それは、シェイクスピアをとても身近に感じた瞬間だった。

　しかし、最初に感じたこの喜びは、無論最初だけである。近代は現代に近いと書いて近代であり、決して現代と同じではない。語学辞書には載っていない単語もあれば、現代英語とは意味が異なっている場合が多いので、そのまま辞書から字義をあてはめてもうまくいかない。単語レベルで既に手を焼くが、さらに難しいのが構文である。特に、韻律を整えるために倒置が頻繁に生じる韻文の読解の難しいこと。訳本を見ても、この英語がなぜそんな訳になるのかわからず、ふて腐れることがままあった。近くに感じたシェイクスピアの背中が果てしなく遠のいた時の落胆たるや、今思い出してもせつなくなる。

　人や物と付き合うにはある程度の時間と根気が必要だが、それは文学作品も同じである。辞書をひきつつ、注釈を頼りにたどたどしく読んでいるうちに、しだいに登場人物の声が自分の頭の中で聞こえるようになってくる。一言一句細かく読んでいるせいか、

ちょっとした比喩など、訳本を読んでいた時には見落としていた
ことに気づくこともある。決め台詞らしきものに出逢った時には、
なるほどこれがシェイクスピアか、と独りごちては、なんとなく
悦に入ったりもする。シェイクスピアが少しずつわかったような
気分になる頃には、イギリスへの尽きぬ興味の虜となっており、
２年後の夏休みには初めてイギリスに旅行し、『マクベス』の舞
台となったスコットランドを感無量の気持ちで訪れることとなる。

　韻文が極端に少ない『ウィンザーの陽気な女房たち』は、初め
て読むシェイクスピア劇にぴったりかと言えば、残念ながらそん
なことは全くない。この時代の散文は、韻文とはまた異なる手強
さがある。なぜそんなに怒っているのかよくわからない人物がの
っけから出てくる冒頭場面に困惑する読者もいるだろう。だが、
多少の戸惑いはあるにせよ、この作品は間違いなく、見るは勿論、
読むだけでも愉しいシェイクスピア劇であることに間違いはない。
フォルスタッフをはじめとして、シェイクスピア劇の醍醐味と言
っても過言ではない魅力的なキャラクターが充実しているからだ。
当時のイギリスの風俗への言及も多いので、イギリス好きな人に
は特におすすめしたい一作である。

　注釈を付すに際しては、あまり煩瑣になりすぎないよう心がけ
た。辞書をひかずとも読めるのはたしかに簡便だが、自分で意味
を探ることで得られる楽しみもたしかにあるからだ。複雑な構文
については極力説明しているが、もちろん手当たり次第というわ
けではない。ただし、どの場面から読んでも差し支えないように、
繰り返しになっても、都度注釈を付した箇所もある。注釈の分量
の塩梅はなかなかに難しいが、欲しいところに注がなく、不要な
ところばかりに注があるという事態はできるだけ避けたつもりで
ある。

　最後に、本書のおぼつかない進捗を辛抱強く見守って下さり、終始親身に助言を下さった大修館書店編集部の北村和香子氏には、心より感謝申し上げたい。氏と私には共通の趣味があり、その話が仕事上のやりとりに紛れ込むことがあったが、コロナ禍でとかく孤独を強いられがちな中、大いに心慰められた。

　2022 年秋

竹村はるみ

目次

挿絵リスト

凡例・略語表

1．凡例

（1）本文

　基本的に 1623 年に出版された『シェイクスピア全集』二つ折本に収録されている本文を底本とし、現代綴りへの変更、句読法の変更、ト書きの補足や整理、話者表示の統一といった、現代の編纂本に共通する修正を行った。

　修正に際しては、アーデン版、オックスフォード版、ケンブリッジ版を適宜参照した。各版の書誌情報については、次項（略語表）と参考文献解題を参照のこと。編集方針については、「解説」のテクストに関する項も参照されたい。なお、二つ折本については、*The Norton Facsimile of the First Folio of Shakespeare* への電子アクセスを含めて Stephen Greenblatt et al, eds, *The Norton Shakespeare*, Third edition（New York: Norton, 1997, 2008, 2016）に依拠した。

（2）登場人物一覧

　本作品の登場人物のリストは、四つ折本にも二つ折本にも掲載されていない。過去の版を参照しつつ、できるだけ見やすい配列を試みた。

（3）注釈

　見開きのページで確認できる対注形式となっており、見開きに収まらない場合のみ、後注に記載した。その場合は、対注の該当する箇所に「⇒後注」と記す。

　ト書き（Stage Direction）に関する注釈は、行数と共に SD と記す。

　注釈での幕・場・行数の表示にはアラビア数字を用いる。例えば 3.5.121 は、第 3 幕第 5 場 121 行を表す。

（4）ト書き

　二つ折本にないト書きで、編注者による補足は ［　］で記す。複数人物が入場・退場する場合の登場人物の並記順番は、入場の順番に拠る。

（5）解説

①シェイクスピア作品の作品名や登場人物名、その他英文学の作者名、作品名、文学用語（例：二つ折本）の日本語表記は、原則として『シェイクスピア辞典』（研究社）に拠る（『夏の夜の夢』のみ「大修館シェイクスピア双書第 1 集」タイトルに従った）。ただし、Falstaff に関しては、日本でより一般的に認知されていると思われる訳語に従い、「フォルスタッフ」と訳出する。

②英文学以外のヨーロッパ文学の作者名、作品名の日本語表記は、原則として『世界文学事典』（集英社）に拠る。

③行政関連用語の日本語表記は、原則として『英米史辞典』（研究社）に拠る。

④旧暦のユリウス暦が用いられた 16 世紀イングランドでは 3 月 25 日から年号が切り替わる一方で、1 月 1 日が元日として認識された。ただし、便宜上、本書で

は新暦で年号を記載する。

⑤一般に作品として認知される場合は、題名を『　』で記す。視覚芸術作品の題名は「　」で記す。

２．略語表

　注で用いた略語は以下の通りである。

Astington	John H. Astington, *Stage and Picture in the English Renaissance: The Mirror up to Nature* (Cambridge: Cambridge University Press, 2017)
Chambers	E. K. Chambers, *The Elizabethan Stage*, 4 vols (Oxford: Clarendon, 1923)
Craik	T. W. Craik, ed., *The Merry Wives of Windsor*, The Oxford Shakespeare (Oxford: Oxford University Press, 1990)
Crane	David Crane, ed., *The Merry Wives of Windsor*, The New Cambridge Shakespeare, Updated edition (Cambridge: Cambridge University Press, 2010)
Hibbard	G. R. Hibbard, ed., *The Merry Wives of Windsor* (Harmondsworth: Penguin, 1973)
Lindley	David Lindley, ed., *The First Quarto of The Merry Wives of Windsor*, The New Cambridge Shakespeare: The Early Quartos (Cambridge: Cambridge University Press, 2020)
Marsh	Christopher Marsh, *Music and Society in Early Modern England* (Cambridge: Cambridge University Press, 2010)
Melchiori	Giorgio Melchiori, ed., *The Merry Wives of Windsor*, The Arden Shakespeare, Third series (London: Bloomsbury, 2000)
OED	*The Oxford English Dictionary Online*
Oliver	H. J. Oliver, ed. *The Merry Wives of Windsor*, The Arden Shakespeare, Second series (London: Methuen, 1971)
Styan	J. L. Styan, *Shakespeare's Stagecraft* (Cambridge: Cambridge University Press, 1967)
Tilly	Morris Palmer Tilley, *A Dictionary of the Proverbs in England in the Sixteenth and Seventeenth Centuries* (Ann Arbor: University of Michigan Press, 1950)
Wiggins	Martin Wiggins, ed., *British Drama 1533-1642: A Catalogue* (Oxford: Oxford University Press, 2012-)

大修館シェイクスピア双書　第2集

ウィンザーの陽気な女房たち

THE MERRY WIVES OF WINDSOR

解　説

1．作品

　『ウィンザーの陽気な女房たち』は、異色のシェイクスピア喜劇である。シェイクスピアの作品群の中では一風変わった芝居で、シェイクスピアらしくない点が多々見受けられる。シェイクスピア喜劇の変わり種というのが本作品の最大の特徴であり、魅力でもある。いったいどんな点が他の喜劇作品と異なっているのか。以下順番にかいつまんで説明したい。

　まず目につくのは、場面設定の特異性である。イギリスの国民的作家でありながらも、実はイギリスを舞台にしたシェイクスピア劇は驚くほど少ない。イギリスの君主を主人公とする歴史劇の場合はもちろんイギリスが舞台となるが、それを除けば、ほとんどの劇が異国の地、あるいは『十二夜』や『お気に召すまま』のように、特にどことは特定できない架空の地が舞台となっている。『ウィンザーの陽気な女房たち』は、イギリスを真正面から描いた唯一のシェイクスピア劇なのである。

　具体的な地名がわざわざタイトルに盛り込まれているところを見ると、このイギリス色は当初から本作品の重要なセールスポイントだったに違いない。ウィンザー以外にも、イートンやフロッグモアやダチェットミードなど、ローカルな地名が頻出する。イギリス色はそれだけではない。熊いじめにグレイハウンドの競技会に鳥撃ちといった娯楽、ピピンと呼ばれるイギリス原産の林檎やシチューや鹿肉のパイにシェリー酒などの飲食物と、いかにもイギリスらしい事物への言及が多い。ヘンリー四世、あるいはヘンリー五世が統治した頃の時代が設定されてはいるものの、描か

れる風俗はまぎれもなくエリザベス朝イングランドのそれを想起させる。シェイクスピアの新作を楽しみにしていた当時のファンなら、待ってましたとばかりに、自分たちにとってはなじみ深い、しかしいつもとは違う設定に新奇な魅力を感じたはずである。

　このイギリス色満載の特徴は、本作品のもう１つの特異性と連動している。『ウィンザーの陽気な女房たち』の実質的な主人公であるフォルスタッフは、別のシェイクスピア劇の人気キャラクターなのだ。創作年代については後述するとして、フォルスタッフは、ほぼ同時期に執筆された歴史劇『ヘンリー四世　第一部・第二部』で、ヘンリー四世の息子である王子ハルの遊び仲間として登場する。後のヘンリー五世の不良時代の悪友フォルスタッフは、大酒飲みの大食漢で女好き、金に困れば追い剥ぎ稼業にも手を出す始末。嘘をつくことなど何とも思わず、戦場では他人の手柄を横取りする。道徳観念のかけらもないほら吹き騎士だが、名誉と王位をかけた戦いが繰り広げられる歴史劇の中で、そんなものは歯牙にもかけないフォルスタッフは強烈な個性を持つ。『ヘンリー四世』シリーズでは脇役であるフォルスタッフを主人公に据え、他にもピストル、ニム、クウィックリー、シャローら、複数の登場人物を再登場させた『ウィンザーの陽気な女房たち』は、人気を博した歴史劇のスピンオフ作品と言える。イギリスを舞台設定としているのは、歴史劇から喜劇へとジャンルを移したためであり、その特例を可能にしたのはフォルスタッフの破格のキャラクター性に他ならない。

　そもそもシェイクスピア劇の魅力は何かと問われれば、それは圧倒的な存在感を誇るキャラクターの魅力に尽きる。いわゆる四大悲劇として名高い『ハムレット』『マクベス』『オセロー』『リア王』の主人公が真っ先に思い浮かぶが、ロミオとジュリエットにクレオパトラと、他にも目白押しである。舞台上では強烈な個

性を放ち、芝居を見た後も忘れがたい印象を残す。あるいは、芝居を見たことがないのに、何となく姿形まで思い浮かべることができるほど、キャラクターがアダプテーションによって作品から遊離して一人歩きしている場合もある。そんな抗いがたい磁力を持ったシェイクスピアの人気キャラクターは、主人公とは限らない。ジュリエットの乳母、シャイロック、マルヴォーリオ、マクベス夫人、イアーゴー等々、主役を食う勢いで目立つ脇役も枚挙に暇がない。そんなシェイクスピア劇の名物キャラクターの中でおそらく五指に入ると思われるのが、本作品の主人公フォルスタッフである。複数の劇に登場するのはフォルスタッフだけであり、シェイクスピアにとっても相当お気に入りのキャラクターだった様子が窺える。

　『ウィンザーの陽気な女房たち』がフォルスタッフありきで執筆されたとなれば、この作品のもう1つの特異性にも合点がいく。『夏の夜の夢』『空騒ぎ』『お気に召すまま』『十二夜』等、シェイクスピアがその創作活動の初期・中期に執筆した喜劇は、若い男女が様々な障害や混乱を乗り越えてめでたく結婚へと至るまでの過程をメインプロットとする。これに対し、同じく中期に執筆された本作品では、フェントンとアンのロマンスはサブプロットとして用いられているにすぎず、しかもこの2人の恋愛感情はそれほど見えてこない。老境にさしかかった騎士が金銭目当てに人妻を誘惑しようと、勘違いも甚だしい恋文をしたためる第1幕で、それまでのシェイクスピア喜劇とはいささか異なる展開が待ち受けていることに観客は気づく。無論、老いてなお盛んなフォルスタッフを突き動かすのは恋愛感情などではなく、より本能的な欲望である。これを前にしては、若者の青臭いロマンスはすっかり隅へと追いやられてしまう。恋と結婚をめぐるてんやわんやを格好の喜劇的主題として描いたロマンティック・コメディとは違う

新たな路線を開拓している点において、本作はやはりかなりの異色作なのである。

　では、ロマンスをも遠くかすませるフォルスタッフの求心力はどこにあるのか。フォルスタッフのカリスマ的な魅力は、その抜群の言語表現力にあり、これはシェイクスピア劇を彩る名物キャラクターに共通する特性でもある。あまたの登場人物がいる中で、観客の脳裏にひときわ強い印象を残すのは、もちろんその役を演じる役者の技量もあるだろうが、その人物ならではの語り口、つまり言語的なスタイルを与えられているか否かにかかってくる。これでもかというほど比喩を駆使し、抒情性に溢れるロマンティックな台詞を語るロミオとジュリエット然り、舞台上で一人になるたびに深い内省に入り、不安定な心情を吐露する独白で観客を惹きつけるハムレット然りである。フォルスタッフもまた、そんな唯一無二の言語表現力を与えられており、それがただ者ではない雰囲気を醸し出す上で大きな効力を発揮しているのである。

　そして、フォルスタッフのこの特性は、『ウィンザーと陽気な女房たち』にこれまた重要な特異性をもたらすこととなる。韻文を基本とするシェイクスピア劇の中にあって、この作品はほとんど散文劇と呼んでも差し支えないほど、韻文が少ない。

　シェイクスピア劇を含むエリザベス朝演劇は、韻文による詩劇を原型としつつ、しばしば散文の場面がそこに挿入される。韻文と散文の切り替えは、それぞれの文体が有する演劇的効果と連動している。韻文、すなわち弱強五詩脚で脚韻をふまないブランク・ヴァース（無韻詩）の効果は、何と言ってもその音楽性が醸し出す高揚感であり、悲劇や歴史劇に向いている。例えば、『ジュリアス・シーザー』の第３幕で暗殺されたシーザーの死を悼むアントニーの台詞は、韻文ならではの鬼気迫る迫力で、広場の群衆はもちろん、劇場に集う観客の心をも鼓舞する。ヒロイックな格調

の高さが韻文の良さとすれば、散文の効果はその逆、地に足のついたリアリズムや諧謔《かいぎゃく》である。道化と酔っ払いはほぼ例外なく散文を語ることからもわかるように、散文は圧倒的に喜劇、あるいは悲劇や歴史劇の中の喜劇的場面で用いられることが多い。

　『ヘンリー四世』二部作においても、ヘンリー四世をはじめとする王侯貴族の台詞が韻文を基本とするのに対し、フォルスタッフは一貫して散文で語る。それは、『ヘンリー四世　第二部』の最終場面でも変わらない。ハル王子改め国王となったヘンリー五世は、かつての友人フォルスタッフをにべもなく拒絶する。フォルスタッフとヘンリー五世のやりとりは、それぞれ散文と韻文に分かれており、それが２人の決別を一層強く印象づける。もっとも、韻文と散文の分量のバランスに関しては、作品によって微妙な違いが存在する。特に、初期から中期にかけて執筆されたシェイクスピアの喜劇・歴史劇を辿ると、散文の分量は漸次増える傾向があり、それが頂点に達したのが本作品なのである。ボトム、シャイロック、ロザリンドと、散文の台詞で精彩を放つキャラクターは数あれど、フォルスタッフはその代表選手と言っても過言ではない。

　フォルスタッフの自由な言語感覚と鋭敏な機知が冴え渡るのは、悪口雑言である。他人を罵り、悪口をまくしたてるのに韻文がおよそ不向きであることは容易に想像がつく。では、フォルスタッフが語る散文はいわゆる普通の話し言葉かと言えば、実は必ずしもそうではない。脚韻や韻律こそないものの、軽快なリズムといい、巧みな比喩といい、個性的で凝った表現や語彙が用いられている。例えば、第２幕第２場に、ブルックという偽名を名乗って訪れたフォードを前に、正体を知らないフォルスタッフがフォードを「しょっぱいバターのように味気ない奴（mechanical salt-butter rogue）」とこき下ろす場面がある。塩気のあるバターと

は輸入物のバターを指し、イギリス原産のバターよりも風味が劣るとされていた。食い意地のはったフォルスタッフならではの比喩であり、奇抜だがわかりやすい。この悪口は、フォルスタッフを妻の愛人と信じこんでいるフォードをいたく悔しがらせ、観客はそんなフォードをも笑うことになる。夫人たちにまんまとだまされているという点ではフォルスタッフもフォードと同じく不利な立場にあるのだが、その卓抜した言語センスで観客をちゃっかりと味方につけてしまうのである。

　フォルスタッフの機知は、他人だけではなく自分をも笑いの対象とする。第4幕第5場に、夫人たちとの逢い引きに成功するどころか、洗濯かごに詰め込まれて川に投げ込まれたり、老女に変装させられてぶたれたり、と散々な目に遭った自身の失態がもしも宮廷の人間の耳に入ったら、とフォルスタッフが気を揉む場面がある。虚勢を張るが、実は臆病者で気が弱いのがフォルスタッフである。「あいつらは俺の脂肪を一滴一滴溶かして、その油で漁師の長靴を磨くだろう（they would melt me out of my fat drop by drop, and liquor fishermen's boots with me）」と嘆く台詞など、突飛でグロテスクな比喩の使い方が秀逸である。恥ずかしさの余りに冷や汗をかくというありふれた状況は、フォルスタッフの巨体が溶け出して、防水オイルに変じるというシュールな光景に転じ、絶妙なおかしみを生む。本作品のフォルスタッフは、別の登場人物が登場するまでのごくわずかな時間に短い独白を語ることが多く、この箇所もそうした独白の1つである。独白はそれを語る登場人物と観客の心理的距離を縮める機能を有しているが、逆境にあってもそれを笑い飛ばす余裕のあるフォルスタッフの遊び心に溢れた言語感覚は観客を魅了してやまない。

　ただし、悪口上手はフォルスタッフだけではない。妻を寝取られることよりも、寝取られ亭主として「ぞっとするような罵詈雑

言の集中砲火を浴びる（stand under the adoption of abominable terms）」ことをより恐れるフォードの不安が端的に示して
いるように、本作品にはやたらと悪態をつく人物が多数登場し、
悪口合戦といった様相を呈している。フォルスタッフが送りつけ
た恋文に呆れたペイジ夫人とフォード夫人が第2幕で語る台詞も、
ぽんぽん飛び出す毒舌が小気味よい。「まるでベルギー人のよう
な飲んだくれ（this Flemish drunkard）」、「あのソーセージみた
いな腹をした奴（as sure as his guts are made of puddings）」、
「お腹に油の大樽をしこたま仕込んだこの鯨（this whale, with
so many tuns of oil in his belly）」と、聞く者の五感を刺激する
巧みな比喩表現にかけては、フォルスタッフにひけをとらない。
あんな巨漢と浮気するぐらいなら、「巨人になって、ペリオン山
の下敷きになる方がまし（I had rather be a giantess and lie
under Mount Pelion）」と、きわどいジョークもお手のものである。
「機会さえあれば、あいつのアタマもタマも叩き潰してやる（I
will knog his urinals about his knave's costard when I have
good opportunities for the 'ork）」と口汚く罵るのが牧師のエヴ
ァンズなのだから、いやはや悪態をつくことにかけては、性別も
職業の貴賤も関係ない。

　こうした創造性に富む悪口雑言の数々は、この作品が執筆・上
演された1590年代後半、すなわちエリザベス朝末期における諷
刺文学の流行と無縁ではない。組織や階層やある特定のタイプの
人間を攻撃する諷刺文学は、誹謗中傷との線引きが時に曖昧とな
りやすい。そして、まさにそうした攻撃的な諷刺文学が台頭した
のが1590年代のイングランドなのだ。いち早くその危険性を察
知した当局が1599年に禁書令を出して、諷刺文学の取り締まり
に乗り出したほどである。シェイクスピアは、同時代の他の劇作
家、特にベン・ジョンソンやジョン・マーストンらジェイムズ朝

に活躍した劇作家と比べると、ユウェナリウス風と呼ばれる攻撃的な諷刺を回避する傾向が強い。それでも、現代人からすれば過度にも思える悪口はふんだんに盛り込まれている。本作品は、同時代のロンドンの劇場でたしかに生じていた新しい機知の文化を如実に反映しており、その点でも実にイギリスらしい喜劇なのである。

2．創作年代

　他の多くのシェイクスピア劇と同様、『ウィンザーの陽気な女房たち』の初演がいつだったのかは定かではない。ただし、本作品が宮廷で上演されたことは、シェイクスピア生前の 1602 年に出版された戯曲の表紙（本書口絵）に「宮内大臣一座によって女王陛下の御前で、あるいは他の場所で幾度も上演された」と記されていることからも明らかである。御前上演が宣伝文句として使われるのは、例えば現代のイギリス王室御用達商品のラベルに王室の紋章が誇らしげに印刷されるのに似る。ましてや、「処女王」としてカリスマ的な人気を誇ったエリザベス一世（図 1）である。女王陛下もご覧になった芝居というキャッチフレーズが作品の品質を保証する上で抜群の宣伝効果を発揮したことは、容易に想像できる。

図1　エリザベス一世の肖像画

　シェイクスピアが所属していた劇団は宮内大臣がパトロンであり、宮廷に呼ば

9

れて芝居を上演することは何ら珍しいことではない。舞踏会、花火、熊いじめ、馬上槍試合、晩餐会と並んで、芝居は宮廷における必須の余興だったからだ。宮廷祝典局なる専門の部署が設けられており、宮廷余興の一切合切を取り仕切った。ただし、『ウィンザーの陽気な女房たち』の宮廷上演に限っては、より直接的な女王との関係を示唆する都市伝説が18世紀以降まことしやかに囁かれるようになる。シェイクスピアがこの劇を執筆したのはフォルスタッフのファンだった女王の命令によるものであり、しかもわずか2週間で書き上げた、という逸話である。この逸話には何ら歴史的根拠はないのだが、妙に説得力があったのか、以後人口に膾炙することとなる。

　火のないところに煙は立たず。仮にこうした都市伝説が誕生するきっかけが作品内にあったとすれば、それはクウィックリー扮する妖精の女王が登場する最終場面ということになるだろう。妖精の女王はイギリスの民間伝承のストックキャラクターだが、エリザベス一世を妖精の女王グロリアーナになぞらえたエドマンド・スペンサーの叙事詩『妖精の女王』が1590年に出版されるなど、エリザベス一世を表現する格好の文学的モチーフとなった。妖精の女王が家臣の妖精をけしかけてフォルスタッフにお仕置きをする最終場面は、なるほど女王をはじめ宮廷人が喜びそうな趣向である。実際、似たような場面がジョン・リリーの喜劇『エンディミオン』にあり、1580年代後半に宮廷で上演されている。

　女王や宮廷との関係を匂わせる内証はまだある。同時代のイギリスを舞台にする喜劇であれば、普通はロンドンと相場が決まっているのに、なぜウィンザーなのか。ウィンザーと言えばウィンザー城、と言うくらい王室との縁が深い町である（図2）。テムズ川を眼下に見る高台に聳えるウィンザー城は、イギリス王室が所有する公邸の中でも随一の歴史と格式を誇る。特に有名なのが、

毎年イングランドの守護聖人である聖ジョージの祝日、すなわち
4月23日にウィンザー城の聖ジョージ礼拝堂で行われるガーター
ー騎士団の叙任式典である（図3）。ガーター騎士団は、1348年
にアーサー王の円卓の騎士団に倣ってエドワード三世によって創
設され、ガーター勲位は現在もイギリスの勲爵位の最高位として

図2　「テムズ川よりウィンザー城を望む」

図3　「ガーター騎士の行進」

知られる。ガーター亭なる宿屋をフォルスタッフの仮寓居と定め、ガーター騎士団への祝意を述べる台詞を最終場面で妖精の女王に与えるなど、本作品にはガーターが符合のように織り込まれているのである。

となると、この作品はもともとガーター騎士団の祝典の余興として上演されたのではないか、という推測が出てくるのは当然である。本作品の初演をガーター騎士団の関連行事に結びつける仮説もまた、先ほどの都市伝説と同様に18世紀から論じられていたが、それがにわかに有力な説となったのは、「文学探偵」の異名を持つレズリー・ホットソンが1931年に発表した論文による。ホットソンは、シェイクスピアの劇団のパトロンである宮内大臣のジョージ・ケアリーが1597年にガーター騎士団の勲位を叙勲されたことを突き止め、本作品は祝典の余興としてケアリーが劇団に発注したものであり、4月23日にロンドンのウェストミンスター地区にあったホワイトパレス宮殿で行われた祝典にて女王臨席のもとに上演されたという仮説を提唱した。1602年出版の版本の表紙が謳う「女王陛下の御前で」上演されたという惹句は、この機会を指すことになる。

この説の信憑性をさらに高めているのが、劇中やや唐突かつ断片的な形で挿入されているドイツ人貴族への言及である。1597年、ケアリーと共にドイツのビュルテンベルク公爵もガーター騎士に選出されている。外交的な理由から、他国の王侯貴族にガーター勲位を授けることはままあり、公爵の叙勲も海外貿易に絡む事情が背後にあったと推察される。結局ビュルテンベルク公爵はイングランドに来訪せず、式典にも欠席したが、この不在のドイツ人公爵への揶揄が、いわゆる時事ネタとして、ガーター亭の亭主の盗難騒ぎに関する場面に挿入されているという解釈には妥当性がある。

　1597 年 4 月 23 日初演という説は、状況証拠を重ねることで引き出されたに過ぎないものの、本作品が一連の歴史劇のスピンオフ作品として執筆されたという事情ともうまく合致する。フォルスタッフが初めて登場したのは『ヘンリー四世　第一部』であることはたしかで、この劇の初演は 1596 年から翌年にかけての冬と推定されている。『ウィンザーの陽気な女房たち』が執筆されたのは、『ヘンリー四世　第二部』の前なのか後なのか、それとも同時進行で執筆されていたのかは、決定しようがないのだが、文体の特徴などから、同時進行説が有力である。『ヘンリー四世　第二部』の初演がいつかは、『ウィンザーの陽気な女房たち』と同様にはっきりしないので、議論は堂々巡りを繰り返すものの、1597 年、あるいは 1598 年と推定されている。

　『ウィンザーの陽気な女房たち』の初演を 1597 年とする説については、新アーデン版（第 3 版）の編者ジョルジョ・メルキオーリが反論を述べるなど、必ずしも専門家の意見の一致をみているわけではない。とはいえ、1597 年初演説は今なお最も広く受け入れられている通説であり、前項の最後に述べた通り、諷刺的な誹謗中傷がやたらと熱を帯びた 1590 年代末期の風潮はたしかに本作品に色濃く漂っている。

3. 材源

　いわゆる種本が存在するシェイクスピア劇が多い中で、『ウィンザーの女房たち』にはなんら直接的な影響関係を示す作品は存在しない。とはいえ、妻に浮気をされているのではないかと悶々とする夫や、親に結婚を反対されている若い男女など、既視感を覚えるような、民話や滑稽譚でおなじみの類型化された登場人物が目立つ。天下無双に見えるフォルスタッフですら、古代ローマ喜劇やイタリア喜劇に登場する「ほら吹き隊長」と呼ばれるスト

ックキャラクターが原型となっている。つまり、ひとつ間違えば
いかにもありきたりの人物を寄せ集めただけの作品になりかねな
いのに、そうはならないどころか、個性溢れる多種多彩な人物が
登場する喜劇となっている。

　これという決まった材源はないとはいえ、あえて１つを挙げれ
ば、同時代のイタリアの散文物語集『愚か者（*Il Pecorone*）』に
なろう。セル・ジョヴァンニ・フィオレンティーノ（Ser
Giovanni Fiorentino）によるこの説話集は、1558 年にミラノで
出版された。英訳は存在しなかったので、シェイクスピアがどう
やってこの書物を知ったかどうかは不明だが、この本に収録され
ている物語の１つが『ヴェニスの商人』のメインプロットの材源
であることは明白なので、シェイクスピアが自分で読んだわけで
はないとしても、誰か第三者のインフォーマントを通して知って
いたことはたしかである。ノヴェラと呼ばれるイタリアの短編物
語集はシェイクスピアの重要な情報源だったので、作者は無名で
あるものの『愚か者』にも目が留まったのだろう。

　『ウィンザーの陽気な女房たち』との関連が指摘される物語は、
『愚か者』の１日目の第２話である。以下、あらすじを略述する。
学問の都ボローニャのとある大学生は、女性を誘惑する方法を教
授から伝授され、相手が教授の年若い妻であるとは知らないまま、
早速その技を試そうとする。一方、学生が誘惑しようとしている
のがどうやら自分の妻であるらしいことに薄々気づいた教授は、
こっそりと学生の後をつけ、逢い引きの現場を押さえようとする。
しかし、妻は学生を洗濯物の中に隠して夫の目を欺き、夫が再び
登校した隙に情事に及ぶ。翌日、何も知らない学生から事の顛末
を聞いた教授は内心怒り狂い、その夜も逢い引きの約束をしてい
ることを知って、再び家探しを始め、今度は洗濯物の山を切り刻
んだりするが、妻は別の方法で学生を脱出させる。最終的に学生

は密会の相手が師の妻であることを知り、罪の意識に駆られてボローニャを去る。

　両者を比較して気づくのは、些細な類似点よりも、大きな相違点である。洗濯物に紛れるといった細部は似ているものの、実際に情事が行われるか否かという点で、『愚か者』のこの挿話と『ウィンザーの陽気な女房たち』は全く異なっている。シェイクスピアは、若い妻の浮気を心配する夫と年老いた夫に辟易（へきえき）して若者との情事に耽（ふけ）る妻という、この種の説話集でおなじみの設定も切り捨てている。「陽気であっても、身持ちが堅い女房もいます（Wives may be merry, and yet honest too）」（第4幕第2場91行）——本作品の題名の由来になっているペイジ夫人の台詞は、艶笑譚にありがちなステレオタイプ化された女性観を否定する。この劇では、女性の機知は、間男気取りの勘違い男と異常なまでに嫉妬深い夫の双方に、笑いという名の鉄槌を陽気に振り下ろすのである。

　一見すると、年長の子供もいる中年主婦のペイジ夫人とフォード夫人はヒロインとはほど遠いと思われるかもしれない。しかし、機知に富んだ自由闊達（かったつ）なその精神において、2人はまさしくシェイクスピアのロマンティック・コメディのヒロインの系譜に位置づけられる。似て非なる材源との比較は、喜劇作家としてのシェイクスピアの並外れた技量のみならず、400年以上経っても衰えることのないシェイクスピアの人気の所以をも提示する。

4．批評史

　シェイクスピアの喜劇作品の中で、『ウィンザーの陽気な女房たち』に対するシェイクスピア研究者の評価は、お世辞にも高いとは言えない。シェイクスピア研究者の、とわざわざ断るのは、舞台上演での人気は一貫してとても高いからである。上演につい

ては次項で述べるとして、ここでは本作品をめぐる批評の変遷について概説する。

　『ウィンザーの陽気な女房たち』が批評家の関心をいまひとつ集めないのは、「作品」の項で述べたこと、すなわちこの劇がシェイクスピア喜劇としては異色の作品であることと関係がある。若い男女の求愛や結婚、あるいは生き別れになった家族の再会、といったシェイクスピアの喜劇の定石であるプロットや主題がこの劇では希薄なので、他の作品と関連づけて論じにくい。そのため、劇作家としてのシェイクスピアの発展や変化という、批評家好みの問題を扱うとなると、本作品は蚊帳（かや）の外に置かれることとなる。例えばそれは、シェイクスピア喜劇の名著として知られるC. L. Barber の *Shakespeare's Festive Comedy* で本作品が議論から漏れていることにも窺える。本書でバーバーは、シェイクスピアの喜劇の基本構造として、外の世界から闖（ちん）入した異分子によって引き起こされる混乱を経ることで硬直した価値観に変化が生じ、共同体が再生される過程を指摘している。『ウィンザーの陽気な女房たち』も、バーバーが「祝祭喜劇」と呼ぶこの型にぴたりと符合しているように思われるのだが、なぜか論じられていないのは、本作品が纏（まと）う異端性のせいかもしれない。

　シェイクスピアにしては異例の散文劇であるという点も、この劇の評価を下げる原因となった。特に、イギリスの国民的作家としてシェイクスピアの評価が高まった背景には、18世紀末から19世紀にかけてのロマン派によるシェイクスピア礼賛が大きく作用しているだけに、その評価はとかくシェイクスピアの詩人としての天賦の才に向けられがちである。国民的作家とは国民的詩人と同義であり、「シェイクスピア崇拝（Bardolatry）」と呼ばれる文化現象は、その語がいみじくも示す通り、「詩聖（the Bard）」としてのシェイクスピアを祭り上げる風潮を生み出した。

ロマン主義批評全盛期においては、『ウィンザーの陽気な女房たち』は不利にならざるをえない。散文の比率が圧倒的に高く、プロットの展開も主題も極めて散文的だからだ。ロマン派以前の時代では、本作品への評価は必ずしも悪くはない。例えば、シェイクスピア批評のはしりとも言えるジョンソン博士ことサミュエル・ジョンソンによる本劇の評価は上々で、特にメインプロットとダブルプロットを見事に融合させる最終場面の処理を絶賛している。ところが、続くロマン主義批評の到来により、そうした肯定的な評価はかき消され、詩情に乏しく、深みに欠ける作品と見なされるようになる。

　それに追討ちをかけたのが、この作品の成立背景をめぐる都市伝説である。この作品は女王の命令でたった2週間で執筆されたという逸話（「創作年代」参照）の出所は、実は比較的はっきりしている。1702年に『ウィンザーの陽気な女房たち』を書き直して『滑稽な色男』として上演したジョン・デニスが自作の宣伝として披露したのが発端である。ところが、この謳い文句は、こと文学作品としての質を問う批評家には、宣伝どころか作品の価値を貶める効果をもたらした。女王の指示という逸話は、シェイクスピアの内発的な創作意欲を疑問視させることとなり、2週間で完成という逸話も、性急に書かれた駄作という評価を誘発しやすい。上演の際の宣伝文句がこと文学批評ではマイナスに作用するというのは、この劇が批評史と上演史で対照的な扱いを受ける傾向があることと相俟って、なかなか興味深い問題を示唆している。

　批判は、フォルスタッフの人物造型にも向けられる。フォルスタッフの最大の魅力は、劇中の人物でありながらも、さながら劇世界に紛れ込んだ異分子のように、他の登場人物や劇中で生じている出来事に容赦なく皮肉を浴びせかけ、観客に複眼的な思考を

促す点にある。ところが、洗濯かごに押し込まれたり、こん棒で殴られたりと、派手なアクションが目立つ本作品の笑劇風の設定では、歴史劇のフォルスタッフが発揮するそうしたシニカルな諧謔精神は些_{いささ}か精彩を欠く。『ヘンリー四世　第一部』では死んだふりまでしてちゃっかり戦争を生き延びるフォルスタッフであるのに対して、『ウィンザーの陽気な女房たち』にはそうした抜け目なさは見られない。同じ文面の恋文を2人の女性に送るという、最初から失敗することが目に見えているようなお粗末な計略に始まり、3度も似たような手口で易々と騙されるフォルスタッフを、偉大な喜劇的ヒーローの凋落_{ちょうらく}として嘆く批評家は多い。シェイクスピアのキャラクター造型力に惚れ込んだロマン主義批評の泰斗ウィリアム・ハズリットですら、「フォルスタッフではなく、誰か他の人物が主人公だったら、この劇をもっと気に入ったのだが」と、いたく不満げである。[1]

　というわけで、『ウィンザーの陽気な女房たち』への研究者の評価は概ね低く、その批評的関心はフォルスタッフが登場する歴史劇との関連性や「創作年代」の項で述べた初演の状況をめぐる歴史的考察に向けられ、喜劇作品としてのこの劇の特性はなおざりにされる傾向があった。シェイクスピア喜劇の傍流に甘んじるそんな状況に変化が生じたのは、シェイクスピア以外の劇作家の作品が注目を集めるようになった1970年代以降のことである。特に、「市民喜劇（citizen comedy）」と呼ばれるジャンルへの関心は、本作品への注目度を俄然高めると共に、その評価をも押し上げることとなった。市民喜劇は、同時代のロンドンを舞台とし、王侯貴族ではなく中層階級の市民を主人公とする点に特徴がある。

---

[1] William Hazlitt, *Characters of Shakespeare's Plays*, in *The Complete Works of William Hazlitt*, ed. P. P. Howe (London: J. N. Fent, 1930), vol. 4, 349.

例としては、ベン・ジョンソンの『バーソロミューの市』、トマス・デッカーの『靴屋の祭日』、トマス・ヘイウッドの『チープサイドの貞淑な乙女』といった作品が挙げられ、16 世紀末から 17 世紀前半にかけてロンドンの劇場を席捲した。「悲劇は都市を好まない。これに対して、喜劇は都市を格好の舞台とする」とアン・バートンが指摘するように、都市に生きる人間の愚行は喜劇的な笑いとの相性が実によい。[2]『ウィンザーの陽気な女房たち』は、ロンドンが舞台ではないものの、中層階級の行動規範や理念を前景化している点で、まぎれもなく市民喜劇の関心や方向性を共有している。本作品は、シェイクスピアの珍しい市民喜劇として一躍脚光を浴びると共に、劇作家同士の影響関係を考察する上でも重要な作品として認識されるようになった。

　『ウィンザーの陽気な女房たち』の市民喜劇としての特性が注目を集めるようになると、宮廷上演という本作品の成立状況は、それまでとは異なる角度で論じられるようになる。いつ、どこで、どのように上演されたのかという歴史的考証よりも、作品における市民社会と宮廷社会の対置は何を意味しているのか、という点に関心が向けられる。騎士であるサー・ジョン・フォルスタッフは、周縁ではあるものの、宮廷側の人間として登場する。同じく、アンにひそかに求愛するフェントンもまた、階級こそ紳士だが、「身分が高すぎる」とペイジが難色を示すなど、フォルスタッフと同様に放蕩者の宮廷人の雰囲気を漂わせている。となると、フォルスタッフを徹底的に笑い物にし、ペイジ夫妻が娘とフェントンの結婚に断固反対するといったプロットには、市民階級の反宮廷主義とも言える意識や倫理観が読み取れる。ところが、その一

[2] Anne Barton, "London Comedy and the Ethos of the City," *The London Journal* 3-4 (1977-78), 160.

19

方で、ウィンザーの住人が総出でガーター騎士団を言祝ぐ最終場面では、この町とは切っても切れない深い縁で結ばれている王室に対する敬愛の念が示される。本作品における市民対宮廷の構図は、1980年代以降の文学批評を一新した新歴史主義批評の流行とも相俟って、活発な議論の対象となる。宮廷余興にして市民喜劇という稀有な立ち位置を有する本作品は、宮廷社会と市民社会が物理的にも心理的にも近接していたエリザベス朝ならではの特性を示している。女王も市民も同じ芝居を見て、笑い転げる——そんな夢のような空間が16世紀末のイギリスには存在していたのだ。

　批評理論の勢いが沈静化した今世紀のシェイクスピア批評で目を惹くのは、本作品の豊穣な言語世界に注目する研究である。シェイクスピアの時代は近代の始まりであり、英語が大きな転換点を迎えた時期である。宗教改革により、ラテン語訳聖書に代わって英訳聖書が礼拝で用いられるようになると、英語の格は飛躍的に上昇し、いわゆる「国語」に対する愛国主義も高まる。海外貿易の発展や科学・医学の進歩により、新しい言語が次々と流入し、創出される。1500年から1650年の間に生まれた新語は1万語を越え、中にはシェイクスピア劇が初出という語もある。[3] 発音も統語法も未だ流動的だった時代であり、英語は外から流入する語を取り入れ、自由自在に形を変える柔軟性を秘めていた。『ウィンザーの陽気な女房たち』では、そんな英語の国際性や可変性や多様性が如実に窺える。「俺は、英語を切り刻んで揚げ物にしちまうような奴にからかわれるために生きてきたんじゃない！」(第5幕第5場135-36) とエヴァンズのウェールズ訛りの英語を当

---

[3] Michael Mangan, *A Preface to Shakespeare's Comedies 1594-1603* (London: Longman, 1996), 6.

てこするフォルスタッフであるが、英語を鮮やかに「切り刻んで」独自の言語世界を構築するのは、シェイクスピアも同様である。本作品のイギリス色の最たる例をその言語的寛容性に見出し、国際言語としての一歩を歩み始めた時代ならではの英語の躍動感を指摘する批評家は多い。

5．上演史

　批評史においては長らく低空飛行を強いられた『ウィンザーの陽気な女房たち』だが、上演史では打って変わって常にシェイクスピア喜劇の人気演目としての地位を保っている。批評史と上演史における評価の二極化は、本劇の娯楽性もさることながら、読まれるためではなく見られるために執筆されている、という重要な、しかしえてして忘れられやすいシェイクスピア劇の本質をも考えさせる。

　初演当時から本作品が人気を博したことは、1602年に出版された初版の表紙（本書口絵参照）に「「宮内大臣一座によって女王陛下の御前で、あるいは他の場所で幾度も上演された」と記されていることから推測できる。こうした宣伝文句はある程度定型化していたので、必ずしも額面通りに受け取ることはできないとしても、1604年にジェイムズ一世のために、1638年にはチャールズ一世のためにと、ステュアート朝になってからも宮廷で上演されており、安定した人気ぶりを見せている。

　1602年の初版本が掲げる宣伝文句からは、この劇の人気がキャラクターの人気に負うところが大きかった様子も窺える。「サー・ジョン・フォルスタッフとウィンザーの陽気な女房たちの世にも楽しく素晴らしい喜劇」とあり、主人公はフォルスタッフであることが明確に打ち出されている。タイトルに続く箇所では、「ウェールズ人騎士サー・ヒュー・エヴァンズ、シャロー判事、

その甥のスレンダーの多彩で愉快な気質、ピストル旗手とニム伍長の大言壮語もあります」とあるところを見ると、一部は歴史劇にも登場するこれらの人物が人気キャラクターとして期待されていたのだろう。「気質（humours）」とは、強いて訳せば「性癖」のような意味で用いられた流行語で、様々な性癖を類型化された登場人物によって戯画化する演劇スタイルが台頭していた。「気質喜劇（comedy of humours）」と総称されるこの種の喜劇の原型はベン・ジョンソンによって確立されるが、変なキャラクターが入れ替わり立ち替わり登場する気質喜劇としての側面は、本作品のセールス・ポイントだったようである。キャラクターの充実がヒットの法則であることは、今も昔も変わりはない。ともあれ、牧師のエヴァンズを騎士として取り違えるといった錯誤はあるものの、初版の表紙は、本作品の初演当時の雰囲気を今に伝える貴重な史料である。

　内乱期と共和制時代の劇場閉鎖を経て、1660年の王政復古と共に劇場が再開された際に、『ウィンザーの陽気な女房たち』は真っ先に上演された演目の１つだったことからも、いかにこの作品が演劇愛好家にとって愛すべき作品だったかがわかる。芝居通の海軍省書記官サミュエル・ピープスは、1660年12月５日の日付で観劇記録を日記に残している。劇に対する全体的な評価は芳しくなかったようだが、日記によると、1661年、1667年と繰り返し観劇しており、その度に書き付けた文句とは裏腹に、わりと気に入っていたのではないかとすら思えてくる。

　演劇の様式も観客の嗜好も革命前とは様変わりした王政復古時代において、シェイクスピア劇はしばしば大胆な改作を施した上で上演された。悲劇『リア王』がハッピーエンドに変更されたり、ロミオが息を引き取る前にジュリエットを目覚めさせるなど、大幅な改変はつきものだったが、『ウィンザーの陽気な女房たち』

の場合は、あまり大きな修正は好まれなかったようである。「批評史」の項で言及したジョン・デニスによる改作劇『滑稽な色男』は作品としてのみならず興業的にも失敗するが、原作の『ウィンザーの陽気な女房たち』は継続的に上演され、フォルスタッフは、トマス・ベタートン（図４）やジェイムズ・クウィンといった王政復古時代の錚々（そうそう）たる役者によって演じられた。特に1720年に若干27歳という若さでフォルスタッフ役に抜擢されたクウィンは、1751年に引退するまで150回以上の公演でこの役を演じ続け、文字通りの当たり役となった。批評家には愛されなくとも、役者や興行主や観客の人気は常に滅法高いのが、『ウィンザーの陽気な女房たち』のフォルスタッフなのである。

　王政復古時代から現代に至るまで、この作品が時代

図４　トマス・ベタートンの肖像画

図５　トゥリー演じるフォルスタッフとエレン・テリー演じるペイジ夫人

23

を超えて愛される理由の1つは、そのイギリス色にあったのかもしれない。エリザベス朝イングランドの風俗を生き生きと描いた本作品は、後世の観客にとっては「古き佳きイングランド」を偲ぶよすがとなる。1902年のエドワード七世の戴冠式を祝う特別公演として本作品に白羽の矢が立った背景には、そうした配慮があったのかもしれない。この公演では、イギリス演劇史に名女優として名を残すエレン・テリーがペイジ夫人を、ハーバート・ビアボーム・トゥリーがフォルスタッフをエリザベス朝の衣装で演じ、記念碑的な公演として人気を博した（図5）。

　20世紀に入ると、アンがフェントンのバイクの後ろに乗って登場したり、ペイジ夫人とフォード夫人が電話でやりとりしたりといった演出で観客を驚かせたオスカー・アッシュによる公演（1929年）など、現代風の衣装や小道具を用いた演出も見られるようになるものの、こうした演出は原作の台詞や場面設定にそぐわないことも多く、実験性は評価されても、全体的な劇評は否定的なものが目立つ。現代色を出し過ぎると、第1幕の決闘騒ぎや最終場面におけるウィンザーの森での幻想的でフォークロア的な雰囲気の効果がそがれることになりかねないからだ。

　最後にアダプテーション作品にも簡単に触れておきたい。映画化・テレビドラマ化もされているが、特筆

図6　ヴェルディのオペラ『ファルスタッフ』のリブレット

すべきは歌劇で、『ウィンザーの陽気な女房たち』を元にして少なくとも 10 のオペラが執筆され、そのうちの 4 作品は現在も上演されている。中でも、ヴェルディの『ファルスタッフ』(1893 年)は、特に名高い（図 6）。台本を執筆したアルリーゴ・ボイトは、80 歳を目前にしてなお創作意欲衰えぬヴェルディが新領域であるオペラ・ブッファ（喜劇的オペラ）に果敢に取り組もうとしていることを知って、本作品を巨匠に薦めたらしい。『ファルスタッフ』は、『ヘンリー四世　第一部』の場面も適宜活用することで、時に『ウィンザーの陽気な女房たち』よりもシェイクスピアらしいと言わしめるほど、フォルスタッフのカリスマ的な求心力を表現することに成功している。ヴォーン・ウィリアムズのオペラ『恋するサー・ジョン』は、エリザベス朝イングランドを意識したバラッド風の楽曲をちりばめることで、ヴェルディとはまた異なる魅力を創出した。2006 年には、グレゴリー・ドラン潤色のミュージカルがロイヤル・シェイクスピア・カンパニーによって上演されるなど、音楽劇へのアダプテーションの試みが続いている。

　そして、「歌うフォルスタッフ」ならぬ「謡うフォルスタッフ」を生み出し、『ウィンザーの陽気な女房たち』の斬新なアダプテーションとして高い評価を受けているのは、高橋康也作・野村万作演出の狂言『法螺侍』である。これは、1991 年に国際シェイクスピア学会が日本で開催された際に、*The Braggart Samurai* という英訳題名を付して上演された。喜劇が扱う笑いは、悲劇が扱う悲しみや怒りといった感情に比べると、文化的な制約を受けやすい。悲劇とは異なり、喜劇は時代や国境を越えない、と言われるのはこのためである。しかし、『ウィンザーの陽気な女房たち』は、そんな喜劇のジンクスもはねのけて、時代を超え、国境を越えて、フォルスタッフを名実共にシェイクスピアが生んだ偉大なキャラクターとして知らしめることに貢献しているのである。

6．テクスト

　シェイクスピア劇の刊本は、実に悩ましい問題である。複数の異なる刊本が存在する上に、公演に応じて修正が生じる演劇というジャンル特有の性格もある。

　『ウィンザーの陽気な女房たち』が初めて出版されたのは 1602年、シェイクスピアがロンドンの演劇界で活躍し、その人気も実力も頂点に達していた時代である。この刊本は四つ折本（Quarto）の形態で出版された。四つ折本とは、文字通り 1 枚の紙を 4 つに折って作られた本を指す。シェイクスピア死後の 1619 年にも、別の印刷業者によって四つ折本が出版されるが、これは最初の四つ折本（以下第 1 四つ折本）の再版であり、大きな違いはない。次いで本作品が出版されたのは 1623 年、シェイクスピア初の作品集『シェイクスピア全集』（以下二つ折本）である。この作品集は二つ折本として出版され、シェイクスピアの肖像画を掲げた表紙、喜劇・歴史劇・悲劇に分類した目次、シェイクスピアの同僚役者による献辞、宮内大臣一座の役者 26 名の名前を列挙した主要俳優一覧と共に、36 篇の作品を収録している。

　『ウィンザーの陽気な女房たち』の重要な刊本は、第 1 四つ折本と二つ折本ということになる。両者には大きな違いがあるのだが、そしてそれは本作品のテクストを編集する際に諸々の悩ましい問題を生じさせることとなるのだが、編者には実はあまり選択肢はない。というのも、第 1 四つ折本は極端に短く、二つ折本の半分ほどの分量しかないからだ。四つ折本は、作者ではない第三者、おそらくは出演者の記憶に基づいて再生されたものと推測され、不確かな箇所が多い。ガーター亭の亭主の台詞が最も安定しているので、この出版に関与したのは亭主の役を演じた俳優ではないかと推測する批評家は多い。これに対し、二つ折本は、シェイクスピアの下書き原稿に基づいて印刷されたと推測されるだけ

あって、テクストとしての信憑性ははるかに高い。したがって、本作品を編集する際には、当然二つ折本を底本とすることになるわけだが、ことほどさように簡単ではない。第1四つ折本には、二つ折本にはない貴重な情報が多々含まれているからである。

　込み入った話になるので、詳細な比較は割愛するが、一例を挙げれば、フォードが用いる偽名である。妻の不貞を疑うフォードが変装してフォルスタッフの元を訪れる際に名乗るのが、第1四つ折本ではブルック（Brook）であるのに対し、二つ折本ではブルーム（Broom）となっている。ブルックは小川（brook）の意味があり、川や浅瀬（ford）を意味するフォードの偽名としてより相応しい上に、フォルスタッフが地口として用いる台詞もある。第2幕第2場、フォードがまずはサックワインを送り届けて、フォルスタッフに面会を請う場面で、酒飲みのフォルスタッフが嬉しげに語る台詞である。二つ折本では、「酒を流し込んでくれるブルームならいつでも大歓迎だ（Such Brooms are welcome to me, that o'erflows such liquor）」となっているが、四つ折本のブルックの方が洒落の意味が生きる。そのため、現代版では、二つ折本と四つ折本を融合する形で、ブルックを採用することが多く、本書もそれに倣っている。なぜ第1四つ折本のブルックが二つ折本ではブルームになったのか。その理由については、後注で解説を付している。

　他にも二つ折本と四つ折本には様々な異同があり、両者を突き合わせることで状況が明確になる場合もある。かつては、二つ折本の権威を重視し、対する四つ折本を粗悪な不完全版とする風潮があったが、近年の研究では異なる見方が強まっている。公演に応じて微妙に変化する台本の場合、何をもって決定版とするかを判断するのはそもそも不可能だからだ。[4]

　『ウィンザーの陽気な女房たち』についても、すっきりと簡潔

な四つ折本の方が上演に向いており、公衆劇場ではこちらが使用された可能性を指摘する編者もいるほどである。[5] 二つ折本にあって四つ折本にないのは、冒頭のシャローの紋章をめぐる議論、ペイジ夫人の息子ウィリアムがラテン語のレッスンを受ける場面、そして第5幕第5場でクウィックリー演じる妖精の女王がガーター騎士団への祝意を表する台詞など、いずれも教養がある上流階層の観客を想定した場面ばかりである。しかし、公衆劇場での公演と宮廷での上演をあまりに分けて考えるのは、下は徒弟から上は王侯貴族まで、他の時代に比してはるかに様々な階層の観客を有していたエリザベス朝の劇場文化を考察する上で適切とは言えない。たしかなことは、ただ1つ。その時々で台詞の変更や場面の割愛といった修正を施しながら上演する——本作品の刊本はそうした柔軟な芝居のあり方を如実に示しているという点である。

---

[4] シェイクスピア作品の本文批評が辿る推移については、金子雄司『シェイクスピアの「原作」——20世紀シェイクスピア本文批評の歴史』、人文研ブックレット31（中央大学人文科学研究所, 2014）がわかりやすい。

[5] Giorgio Melchiori, ed., *The Merry Wives of Windsor*, The Arden Shakespeare, Third series (London: Bloomsbury, 2000), 31-42; David Crane, ed., *The Merry Wives of Windsor*, Updated edition, The New Cambridge Shakespeare (Cambridge: Cambridge University Press, 2010), 164.

参考文献解題

1．テクスト

　シェイクスピア劇の精読には、学術的な解説と注釈が充実している アーデン版（Melchiori）、オックスフォード版（Craik）、ケンブリッ ジ版（Crane）が最も有用。ペンギン版（Hibbard）はこの3シリー ズに比べると注釈は簡易だが、読みやすいという利点がある。以上4 冊の書誌情報については、「凡例・略語表」を参照のこと。初学者向 けのテクストとしてはシグネット版（William Green, ed., *The Merry Wives of Windsor*, Signet Classic Shakespeare, 1965; 2006）もある。 編注者によって解釈や見解が異なるので、必要に応じて比較すると興 味深い知見が得られる。ケンブリッジ版には参考文献表が、ペンギン 版とシグネット版には参考文献解題が付されている。

2．邦訳

　シェイクスピア作品には良質の翻訳が数多く存在する。その中から、 文庫本で入手しやすく、現代的な日本語で読みやすい以下の2冊を挙 げる。それぞれ解説（松岡訳には注と日本における上演の年表も）が 付されている。
⑴　小田島雄志訳『ウィンザーの陽気な女房たち』（白水社 , 1983年）
⑵　松岡和子訳『ウィンザーの陽気な女房たち』（筑摩書房 , 2001年）

3．辞典

　シェイクスピア劇を原書で読むには、『オックスフォード英語大辞 典（*Oxford English Dictionary*）』、通称 *OED* が不可欠である。語学関 連の辞書以外にも、用途に応じて以下の辞典を活用されたい。特に⑴ は必須。個々のシェイクスピア作品の詳細な解説はもちろん、シェイ

クスピアと同時代の演劇に関するありとあらゆる情報が網羅されている。年表、イギリス王室の系図、シェイクスピアの時代のロンドンの地図、シェイクスピア研究のための詳細な文献解題も付されており、この種の書物として驚異的な完成度の高さを誇る。(2)は、例えば騎士（Knight）や星室庁（Star Chamber）など、当時の身分や組織や社会制度についてさらに調べる際に有益。

⑴　高橋康也、大場建治、喜志哲雄、村上淑郎編『研究社シェイクスピア辞典』（研究社, 2000年）

⑵　松村赳、富田虎男編『英米史辞典』（研究社, 2000年）

⑶　ジャン＝クロード・ベルフィオール著、金光仁三郎主幹『ギリシア・ローマ神話大事典』（大修館書店, 2020年）

⑷　Morris Palmer Tilley, *A Dictionary of the Proverbs in England in the Sixteenth and Seventeenth Centuries*（復刻版：名著普及会, 1982年）

4．材源

　シェイクスピア劇の材源研究については、以下2点を挙げる。(1)は、シェイクスピア劇の直接の材源や何らかの影響を与えたと思われる作品の該当箇所の抜粋を収録している。英語以外の文献の場合は英訳が掲載されている。全8巻から成り、『ウィンザーの陽気な女房たち』は第2巻1 -57頁で扱われている。(2)は、個々の作品の材源の概説。

⑴　Geoffrey Bullough, ed., *Narrative and Dramatic Sources of Shakespeare*, 8 vols（London: Routledge and Kegan Paul, 1957-75）

⑵　Kenneth Muir, *The Sources of Shakespeare's Plays*（New Haven: Yale University Press, 1977）

5．批評

　「解説」の批評史の項を併せて参照されたい。以下、難易度の低いものから順に挙げる。初学者の場合は、この順番で徐々に理解を深めることを勧める。間違っても、いきなり1980年代以降の文学批評理論

から入らないこと。文学批評は進化論的に発展するわけではなく、初期の批評の方が作品の全体像を理解する上で役立つことが多い。

　(16)(17)はシェイクスピア喜劇への導入を目的とする入門書。(31)は初学者向けの本作品の概説書。

　シェイクスピア喜劇の構造や主題や作劇術に関しては、やはり古典的な名著(1)(6)(7)(20)(28)が最も有益。ロマン主義的性格批評の一例として(10)を挙げる。ロマン主義批評は20世紀後半に批判に晒されるも、近年静かに再評価される傾向がある。エリザベス朝喜劇の形成と発展を時系列で論じた(3)は、シェイクスピアを同時代の喜劇作家と比較する上で参考になる。古代ギリシャ・ローマ喜劇や中世演劇など、ヨーロッパの演劇がシェイクスピア喜劇に与えた影響については、(24)に詳しい。エリザベス朝市民喜劇に関しては(2)(15)があり、特に本作品の市民喜劇としての特性については(2)が秀逸。本作品における古代ギリシャ・ローマ神話のモティーフを分析した(26)も示唆に富む。

　歴史劇の副産物として執筆され、著しく異なる四つ折本と二つ折本が存在する本作品については、その成立状況をめぐる研究が活発である。ここでは、特に代表的な(9)(12)(18)(19)(21)(23)(25)を挙げる。

　1980年代から世紀末にかけての文学批評では様々な批評理論が勃興し、シェイクスピア批評は最も熱い議論が展開された領域の１つとなった。(4)(11)(22)はフェミニズム批評、(5)(13)(14)は新歴史主義批評、(8)はクィア批評、(29)はマルクス主義批評。いずれも、性や権力をキーワードとしながら、男性と女性、市民社会と宮廷社会、といった社会的な対置構造を作品に読み取り、拮抗するイデオロギーを解明する点に特色がある。

　(27)(30)(32)は本作品の言語的特性を文化史的な視点から論じた好論で、ポスト批評理論と言われて久しい時代におけるシェイクスピア批評の新たな方向性を感じさせる。

⑴　C. L. Barber, *Shakespeare's Festive Comedy: A Study of Dramatic*

Form and its Relation to Social Custom (1959; Princeton: Princeton University Press, 2012)

(2) Anne Barton, "Falstaff and the Comic Community", in *Shakespeare's 'Rough Magic': Renaissance Essays in Honour of C. L. Barber*, ed. Peter Erickson and Coppélia Kahn (Newark: University of Delaware Press, 1985), 131-48.

(3) M. C. Bradbrook, *The Growth and Structure of Elizabethan Comedy*, rev. edn (London: Chatto and Windus, 1973)

(4) Sandra Clark, " 'Women may be merry and yet honest too': Women and Wit in *The Merry Wives of Windsor*", in *'Fanned and Winnowed Opinions': Shakespearean Essays Presented to Harold Jenkins*, ed. John W. Mahon and Thomas A. Pendleton (London: Methuen, 1987), 249-67.

(5) Peter Erickson, "The Order of the Garter, the Cult of Elizabeth, and Class-Gender Tension in *The Merry Wives of Windsor*", in *Shakespeare Reproduced: The Text in History and Ideology*, ed. Jean E. Howard and Marion F. O'Connor (New York: Methuen, 1987), 116-42.

(6) Bertrand Evans, *Shakespeare's Comedies* (Oxford: Clarendon, 1960)

(7) Northrop Frye, *A Natural Perspective: The Development of Shakespearean Comedy and Romance* (New York: Columbia University Press, 1965)

(8) Jonathan Goldberg, "What Do Women Want?: *The Merry Wives of Windsor*", *Criticism* 51 (2009), 367-83.

(9) William Green, *Shakespeare's Merry Wives of Windsor* (Princeton: Princeton University Press, 1962)

(10) William Hazlitt, "*The Merry Wives of Windsor*", in *Characters of Shakespeare's Plays*, in *The Complete Works of William Hazlitt*, ed. P.

P. Howe (1817; London: J. M. Dent, 1930), vol. 4, 349-51.

⑾   Lisa Hopkins, *The Shakespearean Marriage: Merry Wives and Heavy Husbands* (London: Macmillan, 1998)

⑿   Leslie Hotson, *Shakespeare versus Shallow* (London: Nonesuch, 1931)

⒀   Rosemary Kegl, " 'The adoption of abominable terms': Middle Classes, Merry Wives, and the Insults That Shape Windsor", in *The Rhetoric of Concealment: Figuring Gender and Class in Renaissance Literature* (Ithaca: Cornell University Press, 1994), 77-125.

⒁   Mary Ellen Lamb, *The Popular Culture of Shakespeare, Spenser, and Jonson* (New York: Routledge, 2006)

⒂   Alexander Leggatt, *Citizen Comedy in the Age of Shakespeare* (Toronto: University of Toronto Press, 1973)

⒃   Alexander Leggatt, *The Cambridge Companion to Shakespearean Comedy* (Cambridge: Cambridge University Press, 2002)

⒄   Michael Mangan, *A Preface to Shakespeare's Comedies 1594-1603* (London: Longman, 1996)

⒅   Leah S. Marcus, *Unediting the Renaissance: Shakespeare, Marlowe, Milton* (London: Routledge, 1996)

⒆   Giorgio Melchiori, *Shakespeare's Garter Plays: Edward III to 'Merry Wives of Windsor'* (Newark: University of Delaware Press, 1994)

⒇   Kenneth Muir, *Shakespeare's Comic Sequence* (Liverpool: Liverpool University Press, 1979)

㉑   J. M. Nosworthy, *Shakespeare's Occasional Plays: Their Origins and Transmission* (London: Edward Arnold, 1965)

㉒   Anne Parten, "Falstaff's Horn: Masculine Inadequacy and Feminine Mirth in *The Merry Wives of Windsor*", *Studies in Philology* 82 (1985), 184-99.

㉓   Jeanne Addison Roberts, *Shakespeare' English Comedy: The Merry*

Wives of Windsor in Context（Lincoln: University of Nebraska Press, 1979）

⑷　Leo Salingar, *Shakespeare and the Traditions of Comedy*（Cambridge: Cambridge University Press, 1974）

⑸　Alice-Lyle Scoufos, *Shakespeare's Typological Satire: A Study of the Falstaff-Oldcastle Problem*（Athens, Ohio: Ohio University Press, 1979）

⑹　John M. Steadman, 'Falstaff as Actaeon: A Dramatic Emblem", *Shakespeare Quarterly* 14（1963）, 231-44.

⑺　Margaret Tudeau-Clayton, *Shakespeare's Englishes: Against Englishness*（Cambridge: Cambridge University Press, 2020）

⑻　Brian Vickers, *The Artistry of Shakespeare's Prose*（London: Methuen, 1968）

⑼　Wendy Wall, "Why Does Puck Sweep?: Fairylore, Merry Wives, and Social Struggle", *Shakespeare Quarterly* 52（2001）, 67-106.

⑽　Wendy Wall, *Staging Domesticity: Household Work and English Identity in Early Modern Drama*（Cambridge: Cambridge University Press, 2002）

⑾　R. S. White, *The Merry Wives of Windsor*, Twayne's New Critical Introductions to Shakespeare（Boston: Twayne's Publishers, 1991）

⑿　Adam Zucker, *The Places of Wit in Early Modern English Comedy*（Cambridge: Cambridge University Press, 2011）

6．上演史

　(1)は、例えば韻文をどう語るかといった、シェイクスピアの戯曲を上演する際に重要となる点について論じた古典的名著。本作品の上演への言及はほとんどないものの、巻末に付された上演研究の手引き

も含めて有用。同様の批評的関心は(3)にも通底し、20世紀半ばから後半にかけてのイギリスにおける様々な上演が引証され、シェイクスピアの作劇術が具体的な演劇的効果や観客反応という視点で解説されている。(8)は、本作品を狂言に翻案した『法螺侍』について、作者による英訳と解説を収録している。

⑴ John Russell Brown, *Shakespeare's Plays in Performance* (1966; Harmondsworth: Penguin Shakespeare Library, 1969)

⑵ Russell Jackson, ed., *The Cambridge Companion to Shakespeare on Screen* (Cambridge: Cambridge University Press, 2000)

⑶ Richard David, *Shakespeare in the Theatre* (Cambridge: Cambridge University Press, 1978)

⑷ Peter Holland, *English Shakespeares: Shakespeare on the English Stage in the 1990's* (Cambridge: Cambridge University Press, 1997)

⑸ Nancy A. Mace, "Falstaff, Quin and the Popularity of *The Merry Wives of Windsor* in the Eighteenth Century", *Theater Survey* 31 (May 1990), 55-66.

⑹ George C. D. Odell, *Shakespeare from Betterton to Irving* (New York: Charles Scriber's Sons, 1920)

⑺ Kenneth S. Rothwell, *A History of Shakespeare on Screen: A Century of Film and Television* (Cambridge: Cambridge University Press, 2004)

⑻ Takashi Sasayama, J. R. Mulryne, and Margaret Shewring, eds, *Shakespeare and the Japanese Stage* (Cambridge: Cambridge University Press, 1998)

⑼ J. C. Trewin, *Shakespeare on the English Stage 1900-1964* (London: Barrie and Rockliff, 1964)

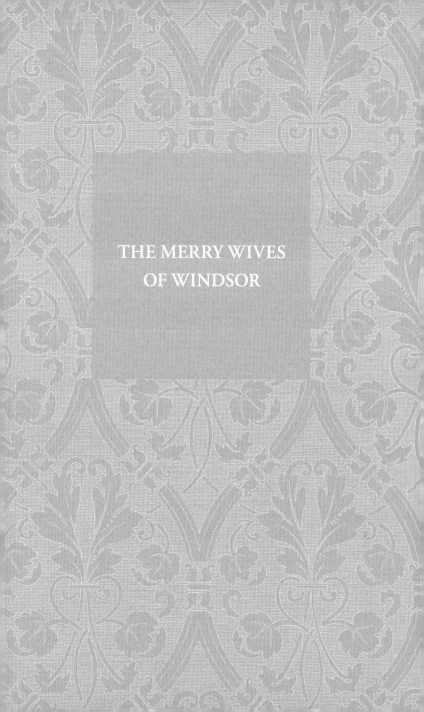

THE MERRY WIVES
OF WINDSOR

The Characters of the Play

Sir John FALSTAFF	a knight
BARDOLPH	
PISTOL	his followers
NIM	
ROBIN	his page
Master Francis FORD	a citizen of Windsor
MISTRESS Alice FORD	his wife
JOHN	their servants
ROBERT	
Master George PAGE	a citizen of Windsor
MISTRESS Margaret PAGE	his wife
ANNE Page	their daughter
WILLIAM Page	their son
Master Robert SHALLOW	a Justice of the Peace
Master Abraham SLENDER	his nephew
Peter SIMPLE	Slender's servant
Doctor CAIUS	a French doctor
Mistress QUICKLY	his housekeeper
John RUGBY	his servant
Master FENTON	a young gentleman
Sir Hugh EVANS	a Welsh parson and schoolmaster
The HOST of the Garter Inn	
Children of Windsor	

登場人物

サー・ジョン・フォルスタッフ	騎士
バードルフ	
ピストル	フォルスタッフの子分
ニム	
ロビン	フォルスタッフの小姓
フランシス・フォード	ウィンザーの市民
フォード夫人（アリス）	その妻
ジョン	
ロバート	フォード家の使用人
ジョージ・ペイジ	ウィンザーの市民
ペイジ夫人（マーガレット）	その妻
アン・ペイジ	ペイジ夫妻の娘
ウィリアム・ペイジ	ペイジ夫妻の息子
ロバート・シャロー	治安判事
エイブラム・スレンダー	その甥
ピーター・シンプル	スレンダーの使用人
キーズ	フランス人の医師
クウィックリー	キーズ家の家政婦
ジョン・ラグビー	キーズ家の使用人
フェントン	若い紳士
サー・ヒュー・エヴァンズ	ウェールズ人の牧師・教師
宿屋ガーター亭の亭主	
ウィンザーの子供達	

[Act I, Scene I]

Enter Justice Shallow, Slender, [and] Sir Hugh Evans

SHALLOW   Sir Hugh, persuade me not. I will make a Star Chamber matter of it. If he were twenty Sir John Falstaffs, he shall not abuse Robert Shallow, Esquire.

SLENDER   In the County of Gloucester, Justice of Peace and Coram.   5

SHALLOW   Ay, cousin Slender, and Custalorum.

SLENDER   Ay, and Ratolorum too; and a gentleman born, Master Parson who writes himself 'Armigero' in any bill, warrant, quittance, or obligation — 'Armigero.'

SHALLOW   Ay, that I do, and have done any time these three   10
hundred years.

SLENDER   All his successors gone before him, hath done't, and all his ancestors that come after him may. They may give the dozen white luces in their coat.

SHALLOW   It is an old coat.   15

EVANS   The dozen white louses do become an old coat well. It agrees well passant. It is a familiar beast to man, and signifies love.

SHALLOW   The luce is the fresh fish; the salt fish is an old coat.

SLENDER   I may quarter, coz.   20

SHALLOW   You may, by marrying.

EVANS   It is marring indeed, if he quarter it.

SHALLOW   Not a whit.

EVANS   Yes, py'r Lady. If he has a quarter of your coat, there is but three skirts for yourself, in my simple conjectures. But   25
that is all one. If Sir John Falstaff have committed disparagements unto you, I am of the Church, and will be glad to do my benevolence to make atonements and compromises between you.

SHALLOW   The Council shall hear it; it is a riot.   30

〔1. 1〕あらすじ……………………………………………………………………

治安判事のシャローはフォルスタッフを訴えると息巻いている。ウェールズ出身の牧師エヴァンズはシャローをなだめつつ、シャローの甥スレンダーと裕福なペイジの娘アンの縁組みを提案する。一行はペイジ家を訪れ、そこに来合わせていたフォルスタッフとその仲間と対峙する。

……………………………………………………………………………………

1. Sir Hugh ⇒後注

1-2. Star Chamber matter 「星室庁裁判所の案件」星室庁裁判所（Star Chamber）では、国民の訴えに基づき民事事件や刑事事件が処理された。裁判所の名称は、ウェストミンスター宮殿の「星の間」と呼ばれる天井に星が描かれた部屋で開廷されたことに由来する。

3. Esquire = squire 「郷士」 ⇒後注

5. Coram ラテン語の quorum が訛ったもの。justice of the quorum は特定治安判事の意。法曹用語にはラテン語が多用された。

6. cousin 現代とは異なり、親しみをこめて呼びかける際に用いられた。ただし、シャローはスレンダーと縁戚関係にあるらしいことが3. 4. 41からわかる。

6. Custalorum ラテン語の custos rotulorum（州首席治安判事）が訛ったもの。続くスレンダーの台詞の Ratolorum も同じ言葉の後半部が訛ったもの。

8. writes himself 「署名する」署名（サイン）には肩書きが付された。

8. Armigero Armiger が訛ったもの。Armiger は Esquire のラテン語訳で、紋章（arms）を有する身分の者に使用が許可された敬称。

9. quittance 「負債免除状」

13. give 「示す」紋章の図柄として用いること。

14. luces 「カワカマス」淡水魚の一種で、河川に生息する。 ⇒後注

14. coat = coat of arms「紋章」

16. become 「〜に似合う」次行の agree も同じ意味。

17. passant 「非常に（passing）」と紋章学用語の「歩いている状態（passant）」の洒落。獅子や豹の紋章図形は、passant や rampant（左後脚で立ち上がった状態）で描かれることが多い。

19. salt fish 「塩漬けの魚」シャローは、「淡水魚（freshwater fish）」と「新鮮な魚」をかけて fresh fish とした上で、古い紋章には「塩漬けの魚」が似合うと軽口を叩いている。

20. quarter 紋章学用語で「4分割する」盾の紋章を4つのスペースに分割して、それぞれに意匠を凝らすこと。

24. py'r Lady 「マリア様にかけて（by our Lady）」エヴァンズのウェールズ方言では、b は p の音になる。Lady は聖母マリアを指す。

25. skirts スリットで分かれたコートの裾の部分。coat と coat of arms の洒落。

30. Council 「国王評議会」1-2 行目の星室庁裁判所と同義。

EVANS   It is not meet the Council hear a riot. There is no fear
of Got in a riot. The Council, look you, shall desire to hear
the fear of Got, and not to hear a riot. Take your vizaments
in that.

SHALLOW   Ha! O' my life, if I were young again, the sword   35
should end it.

EVANS   It is petter that friends is the sword and end it. And
there is also another device in my prain, which peradventure
prings goot discretions with it. There is Anne Page, which is
daughter to Master George Page, which is pretty virginity.   40

SLENDER   Mistress Anne Page? She has brown hair, and speaks
small like a woman.

EVANS   It is that fery person for all the 'orld, as just as you will
desire. And seven hundred pounds of moneys, and gold, and
silver, is her grandsire upon his death's-bed — Got deliver to   45
a joyfull resurrections! — give, when she is able to overtake
seventeen years old. It were a goot motion if we leave our
pribbles and prabbles, and desire a marriage between Master
Abraham and Mistress Anne Page.

SLENDER   Did her grandsire leave her seven hundred pound?   50

EVANS   Ay, and her father is make her a petter penny.

SLENDER   I know the young gentlewoman. She has good gifts.

EVANS   Seven hundred pounds, and possibilities, is goot gifts.

SHALLOW   Well, let us see honest Master Page. Is Falstaff
there?   55

EVANS   Shall I tell you a lie? I do despise a liar as I do despise
one that is false, or as I despise one that is not true. The
knight Sir John is there; and I beseech you be ruled by your
well-willers. I will peat the door for Master Page. [*He knocks
on the door*] What ho! Got pless your house here!   60

PAGE   [*Within*]   Who's there?

EVANS   Here is Got's plessing and your friend, and Justice
Shallow, and here young Master Slender, that peradventures

32. Got God が訛ったもの。エヴァンズのウェールズ方言では、d は t で発音される。

33-34. Take your vizaments in that 「それについてはよく考えろ」vizaments は、エヴァンズが advicement を訛って発音したもの。

40. virginity 「独身のお嬢さん」

41-42. speaks small like a woman 「女らしい優しい声で話す」small は副詞で「小さな声で優しく」の意。

43. fery これもエヴァンズのウェールズ方言で、v が f の音になっている。

43. for all the 'orld 「まさにどこから見ても」'orld ＝ world で、エヴァンズの発音通りに最初の文字が省略されている。

47-48. leave our pribbles and prabbles 「つまらない言い争いをやめる」pribbles and prabbles は「無駄話、つまらない言い争い」を意味する成句。(*OED*)

51. is make her a petter penny 「もっと大金を遺すつもりだ」b が p の音になるエヴァンズの方言に注意。better penny はさらに多くの金を意味する慣用表現。is ＝ is to

52. gifts スレンダーはおそらくアンの人間的な「魅力」を意味しているが、文脈からは「贈り物」、すなわちアンが相続することになっている遺産も連想される。

53. possibilities 「もっと多くの金額をもらえる見込み」文脈から考えて、金銭的な可能性に関する言及と推測できるため。

58-59. be ruled by your well-willers 「あなたのためを思う人間の言うことを聞きなさい」well-willer は well-wisher（他人の幸せを願う人）と同じ意味。一般論として語っているものの、エヴァンズは自分のことを言っている。

59. peat the door ＝ beat the door で、「ドアを叩く」。

for は願望や期待を示す前置詞。

59 SD. [*He knocks on the door*] 二つ折本にないト書きで、編注者による補足は［ ］で記す。

shall tell you another tale if matters grow to your likings.

[*Enter Page*]

PAGE   I am glad to see your worships well. I thank you for my   65
venison, Master Shallow.

SHALLOW   Master Page, I am glad to see you. Much good do it
your good heart! I wished your venison better; it was ill
killed. How doth good Mistress Page? And I thank you
always with my heart, la, with my heart.   70

PAGE   Sir, I thank you.

SHALLOW   Sir, I thank you; by yea and no I do.

PAGE   I am glad to see you, good Master Slender.

SLENDER   How does your fallow greyhound, sir? I heard say he
was outrun on Cotsall.   75

PAGE   It could not be judged, sir.

SLENDER   You'll not confess, you'll not confess.

SHALLOW   That he will not. 'Tis your fault, 'tis your fault. [*To
Page*] 'Tis a good dog.

PAGE   A cur, sir.   80

SHALLOW   Sir, he's a good dog and a fair dog. Can there be
more said? He is good and fair. Is Sir John Falstaff here?

PAGE   Sir, he is within; and I would I could do a good office
between you.

EVANS   It is spoke as a Christians ought to speak.   85

SHALLOW   He hath wronged me, Master Page.

PAGE   Sir, he doth in some sort confess it.

SHALLOW   If it be confessed, it is not redressed. Is not that so,
Master Page? He hath wronged me; indeed he hath; at a word
he hath. Believe me. Robert Shallow, Esquire, saith he is   90
wronged.

[*Enter Sir John Falstaff, Bardolph, Nim, and Pistol*]

PAGE   Here comes Sir John.

64. tell you another tale 「あなたに別の件もお話しする」

64. if matters grow to your likings 「もしもその件があなたのお気に召せば」
先にエヴァンズが話していたスレンダーとアンの縁談の件を指す。複数形が用
いられているのは、エヴァンズの方言の可能性がある。

67-68. Much good do it your good heart! 「あなた様のお役に立てば幸いで
す！」定型の丁寧な挨拶で、構文は祈願文。good はここでは名詞で、do (a
person) good で「（人）のためになる」の意。your good heart は、敬愛を
こめた呼びかけ。

68-69. I wished your venison better; it was ill killed. 「もっと良い肉だったら
よかったのですが。あれは仕留め方がまずかったものですから」牛肉、鶏肉、
豚肉、子羊とある中で、鹿肉はご馳走の部類に入る。血抜きの案配を指してい
るのか、ill killed の詳細は不明。

70. la 「とても、ほんとうに」強意を表す単語で、本作品に頻出する。

72. by yea and no 「たしかに」同じく強意を表す単語。

74. fallow 「ベージュ色の」

74-75. I heard say he was outrun on Costall. 「コッツウォルズの競争で負け
たと耳にしました」he は、前文で言及されているグレイハウンドを指す。
Cotsall は、コッツウォルズの丘陵地帯を意味する地元の言葉。グレイハウン
ドの猟犬としての資質を競う競技が開催されたものと推測される。

77. confess 「事実だと認める」

78. 'Tis your fault 「お前が間違っている」at fault には、狩猟用語で「獲物の
臭跡を失う」という意味もある。この台詞は、スレンダーに向けられたもの。
シャローは、ペイジをかばい、甥の軽口をたしなめている。

80. cur 「雑種犬」ことさらに貶める意はないが、普通の犬だと謙遜している。

82. good / fair どちらも似たような意味。good and fair は、良い猟犬を形容
する際に用いられた慣用的な表現。シャローは冗長な言い回しを好む傾向があ
る。

83. do a good office 「尽力する、役に立つ」ペイジは、シャローとフォルス
タッフの間で生じている諍(いさか)いを知った上で、仲裁を申し出ている。

87. in some sort 「ある程度」

88. If it be confessed, it is not redressed. 「罪を認めても、償ったことにはな
らない」if は even if 「たとえ〜としても」の意。「罪を認めれば、半分謝った
ようなもの（Confession of a fault is half amends）」という諺が逆の意味
に転用されている。

89. at a word ＝ in a word 「要するに」

FALSTAFF Now, Master Shallow, you'll complaine of me to the King?

SHALLOW Knight, you have beaten my men, killed my deer, 95 and broke open my lodge.

FALSTAFF But not kissed your keeper's daughter?

SHALLOW Tut, a pin! This shall be answered.

FALSTAFF I will answer it straight. I have done all this. That is now answered. 100

SHALLOW The Council shall know this.

FALSTAFF 'Twere better for you if it were known in counsel. You'll be laughed at.

EVANS *Pauca verba*, Sir John, good worts.

FALSTAFF Good worts? Good cabbage! Slender, I broke your 105 head. What matter have you against me?

SLENDER Marry, sir, I have matter in my head against you, and against your cony-catching rascals, Bardolph, Nim, and Pistol.

BARDOLPH You Banbury cheese! 110

SLENDER Ay, it is no matter.

PISTOL How now, Mephostophilus?

SLENDER Ay, it is no matter.

NIM Slice, I say *pauca, pauca*. Slice, that's my humour.

SLENDER Where's Simple, my man? [*To Shallow*] Can you tell, 115 cousin?

EVANS Peace, I pray you. Now let us understand. There is three umpires in this matter, as I understand: that is, Master Page, *fidelicet* Master Page; and there is myself, *fidelicet* myself; and the three party is lastly, and finally mine host of the 120 Garter.

PAGE We three to hear it, and end it between them.

EVANS Fery goot. I will make a prief of it in my notebook, and we will afterwards 'ork upon the cause with as great discreetly as we can. 125

94. the King フォルスタッフが登場する歴史劇『ヘンリー四世』二部作のいわばスピンオフとして執筆された本作品は、ヘンリー四世あるいはヘンリー五世の時代に設定されている。 ⇒後注

96. lodge 「森の番小屋」番小屋は、次行で言及される猟場番人（keeper）が暮らす小屋。猟場番人は、主人が所有する狩猟場の管理を任されていた。

98. Tut, a pin! 「ふん、くだらんことを（言うやつめ）!」a pin は、「（小さなピンほどの価値もない）つまらないもの」という意で、否定的に用いられる。

102. in counsel 「内緒で、秘密に」同音の council と counsel をかけている。

104. *Pauca verba* 「言葉を控えなさい」pauca verba は、ラテン語で「少ない言葉（が一番）」の意。

104. worts 「言葉」エヴァンズのウェールズ方言では、d が t の音になる。wort はキャベツの一種なので、フォルスタッフに揚げ足を取られる。

106. matter 「訴え」法律用語で訴訟を起こすための基礎事実を指す。

107. Marry 「なんだと」驚きや怒りなど、強い感情を示す言葉。

108. cony-catching 「詐欺師の」cony はウサギの一種。文字通り訳すと「ウサギを狩る者」となる cony-catcher は、詐欺師を意味した。詐欺師にだまされる人をおとなしい小動物の典型であるウサギに喩えた表現。

110. Banbury cheese 「オックスフォード州のバンベリーで作られるチーズのように薄っぺらい（as thin as Banbury cheese)」という慣用表現があった。スレンダーの痩せた姿形（と色白の肌）が揶揄されている。

112. Mephostophilus 正しくは Mephostophilis で、同時代の劇作家クリストファー・マーロウ（Christopher Marlowe）の悲劇『フォースタス博士（*The Tragical History of Doctor Faustus*)』に登場する悪魔の名前。

114. Slice, I say *pauca, pauca* 「問答無用で薄切りにするぞ」pauca, pauca は Pauca verba（1. 1. 104）と同じ。チーズの比喩がまだ続いている。

114. humour 「気質」humour は4つの体液（血液、粘液、黄胆汁、黒胆汁）を意味し、その配合が人間の性質を決定すると考えられた。気質は当時の流行語となり、同時代の演劇作品でも人気の主題となった。ニムはこの語が気に入っているらしく、多用する傾向がある。

119. *fidelicet* ラテン語の videlicet（「すなわち」）がエヴァンズ流に訛り、v が f の音で発音されている。

121. the Garter 「ガーター亭」宿屋の名前 ⇒後注

123. prief brief（要約）がエヴァンズ流に訛り、b が p の音で発音されている。エヴァンズはここで手帳を取り出して、要件を書きとめている。

FALSTAFF   Pistol!

PISTOL   He hears with ears.

EVANS   The tevil and his tam! What phrase is this? 'He hears with ears'? Why, it is affectations.

FALSTAFF   Pistol, did you pick Master Slender's purse?   130

SLENDER   Ay, by these gloves did he — or I would I might never come in mine own great chamber again else — of seven groats in mill-sixpences, and two Edward shovel-boards that cost me two shilling and twopence apiece of Yead Miller, by these gloves.   135

FALSTAFF   Is this true, Pistol?

EVANS   No, it is false, if it is a pickpurse.

PISTOL   Ha, thou mountain-foreigner!
Sir John and master mine,
I combat challenge of this latten bilbo.   140
Word of denial in thy *labras* here!
Word of denial! Froth and scum thou liest!

SLENDER   [*Pointing at Nim*]   By these gloves, then 'twas he.

NIM   Be advised, sir, and pass good humours. I will say 'marry trap' with you, if you run the nuthook's humour on me. That   145
is the very note of it.

SLENDER   By this hat, then, he in the red face had it. For though I cannot remember what I did when you made me drunk, yet I am not altogether an ass.

FALSTAFF   What say you, Scarlet and John?   150

BARDOLPH   Why, sir, for my part, I say the gentleman had drunk himself out of his five sentences.

EVANS   It is his 'five senses'. Fie, what the ignorance is!

BARDOLPH   And being fap, sir, was, as they say, cashiered. And so conclusions passed the careers.   155

SLENDER   Ay, you spake in Latin then, too. But 'tis no matter. I'll ne'er be drunk whilst I live again, but in honest, civil, godly company, for this trick. If I be drunk, I'll be drunk

128. The tevil and his tam! 「なんてことだ！」エヴァンズの訛りで、d が t の音になっている。The devil and his dam (＝ mother)! は、強い驚きや嫌悪を表す慣用表現で、文字通りの意味ではない。

129. affectations 「気取った言い方」牧師であるエヴァンズは、ピストルの台詞を勝手に聖書の引用と解釈している可能性がある。「神よ、我らはこの耳で聞いています（We have heard with our ears）」（「詩篇」44 章 1 節）参照。

132. great chamber 「大広間」現代の家屋であれば居間に相当か。

132. else 「もしそうでなければ」

132-33. seven groats in mill-sixpences 「6 ペンス紙幣で 28 ペンス」1 グロートは 4 ペンス銀貨。mill は貨幣用印刷機で、mill-sixpence は 6 ペンス紙幣。28 ペンスは 6 で割り切れないので、スレンダーの計算はおかしい。

133. two Edward shovel-boards 「銭当てゲーム用のエドワード六世時代の 1 シリング金貨 2 枚」1 シリングは 12 ペンスに相当。shovel board は、数字が記された盤上で硬貨をはじいて点数を競う盤ゲーム。大きめのエドワード六世時代の硬貨が重宝された。

134. Yead Miller 「エドワード・ミラー（の店）」Yead は Edward を略した愛称。

138. mountain-foreigner 「山奥から出てきた異人」ウェールズ出身のエヴァンズを田舎者として揶揄している。

140. I ... latten bilbo 「このど素人に決闘を挑みますぞ」倒置に留意。challenge が述語動詞で、combat（戦い）を目的語とする。散文から韻文への転換が示すように、ピストルは大仰にすごんでみせている。スレンダーは「薄いブリキのビルボー剣」すなわち安っぽい飾り物の剣に喩えられている。

141. Word of denial in thy *labras* here! 「貴様の口に否と言ってやる！」labra は、「唇」を表すラテン語。ピストルの芝居がかった調子に留意。

142. Froth and scum thou liest! 「このカス野郎が嘘ついてらあ！」froth も scum も似たような意味で、ビールなどの液体に浮くアクやかすを指す。

144-45. 'marry trap' with you 「痛い目に遭うぞ！」罵り言葉であることはたしかだが、意味不明。marry は、by Mary（聖母マリア様にかけて）に由来し、何かをきっぱりと言う際に用いる強意表現。

145. if ... me 「もし俺に対して警官まがいのことを言えば」nuthook は、警官の隠語。humour については、114 行目の注参照。ニムはこの語を多用する。

150. Scarlet and John 「赤ら顔の相棒」ロビン・フッドの仲間のウィル・スカーレットとちびのジョンにかこつけて、赤ら顔と言われたバードルフに呼びかけている。scarlet には深紅の意もある。

154. cashiered 「（店から）追い出された」

155. conclusions passed the careers 「あっという間の結末というわけだ」乗馬用語の「全力で疾走する（pass a career）」を踏まえた比喩。

with those that have the fear of God, and not with drunken
knaves.   160

EVANS   So Got 'udge me, that is a virtuous mind.

FALSTAFF   You hear all these matters denied, gentlemen. You
hear it.

[Enter Anne Page with wine]

PAGE   Nay, daughter, carry the wine in; we'll drink within.

[Exit Anne Page]

SLENDER   Oh heaven, this is Mistress Anne Page!   165

[Enter Mistress Ford and Mistress Page]

PAGE   How now, Mistress Ford?

FALSTAFF   Mistress Ford, by my troth you are very well met.
By your leave, good mistress.

[He kisses her]

PAGE   Wife, bid these gentlemen welcome. Come, we have a
hot venison pasty to dinner. Come, gentlemen, I hope we   170
shall drink down all unkindness.

[Exeunt all except Slender]

SLENDER   I had rather than forty shillings I had my book of
songs and sonnets here.

[Enter Simple]

How now Simple, where have you been? I must wait on
myself, must I? You have not the book of riddles about you,   175
have you?

SIMPLE   Book of riddles? Why, did you not lend it to Alice
Shortcake upon Allhallowmas last, a fortnight afore
Michaelmas?

161. So Got 'udge me 「神よどうかご覧ください」God が訛って発音されて
いる。'udge ＝ judge。 me は聞き手の関心をひくために挿入された虚辞（心
性的与格）で、特に意味はない。

166. Mistress Ford 「フォード夫人」少なくとも 18 世紀までは、Mistress（略
語は Mrs）は未婚・既婚の区別なく用いられた。

168. By your leave 「失礼して」leave は、許可を意味する名詞。

168. SD 女性の手に接吻するのは正式の挨拶であり、特に疚しい意味はない。

170. to dinner 「夕食には」to ＝ for

172-73. my book of songs and sonnets 「僕の恋愛詩集の本」『トッテル詞華集
（*Tottel's Miscellany*）』という通称で知られるリチャード・トッテルが編纂し
た『ソングとソネット（*Songs and Sonnets*）』は、サリー伯やトマス・ワイ
アットら廷臣の恋愛抒情詩を収録し、1557 年の初版以来何度も版を重ねるほ
どの人気を博し、その題名はいわゆる恋愛詩集の代名詞となった。

175. the book of riddles 「なぞなぞの本」特定の本を指しているわけではない。

178-79. upon Allhallowmas last, a fortnight afore Michaelmas? 「この間の
万聖節の時、ミカエル祭の 2 週間前に」万聖節（Allhallowmas ＝ All Saints'
Day）は 11 月 1 日、ミカエル祭（Michaelmas Day）は 9 月 29 日なので、
シンプルの計算は主人スレンダーの金額計算（132 行目 -）と同様に間違って
いる。

[*Enter Shallow and Evans*]

SHALLOW Come, coz. Come, coz, we stay for you. A word   180
with you, coz. Marry, this, coz: there is, as 'twere, a tender, a
kind of tender, made afar off by Sir Hugh here. Do you
understand me?

SLENDER Ay, sir. You shall find me reasonable. If it be so, I
shall do that that is reason.   185

SHALLOW Nay, but understand me.

SLENDER So I do, sir.

EVANS Giue ear to his motions, Master Slender. I will
description the matter to you, if you be capacity of it.

SLENDER Nay, I will do as my cousin Shallow says. I pray you   190
pardon me. He's a Justice of Peace in his country, simple
though I stand here.

EVANS But that is not the question. The question is concerning
your marriage.

SHALLOW Ay, there's the point, sir.   195

EVANS Marry, is it, the very point of it, to Mistress Anne
Page.

SLENDER Why, if it be so, I will marry her upon any reasonable
demands.

EVANS But can you affection the 'oman? Let us command to   200
know that of your mouth, or of your lips, for divers
philosophers hold that the lips is parcel of the mouth.
Therfore, precisely, can you carry your good will to the maid?

SHALLOW Cousin Abraham Slender, can you love her?

SLENDER I hope, sir, I will do as it shall become one that would   205
do reason.

EVANS Nay, Got's lords, and his ladies, you must speak
possitable if you can carry her your desires towards her.

SHALLOW That you must. Will you, upon good dowry, marry
her?   210

180. stay for you 「お前を待っている」stay ＝ wait

181. Marry 「いいか」＝ by Mary（聖母マリア様にかけて）に由来し、何か
をきっぱりと言う際に用いる強意表現。

181. as 'twere ＝ as it were「いわゆる」

181. tender 「申し出」

182. afar off 「遠回しに、それとなく」

184. reasonable 「世間の道理をわきまえている」スレンダーは、フォルスタッ
フらと和解することを勧められていると思っている。

188. his motions 「叔父さんが仰ること」

188-89. I will description the matter to you 「私がこの件についてあなたに説
明しましょう」名詞 description が動詞として用いられているのは、エヴァン
ズの方言による。

191-92. simple though I stand here 「僕は平凡な人間だけど」though I stand
here ＝ even though I am

200. can you affection the 'oman? 「あの女性を愛せますか」1. 1. 189 と同様、
エヴァンズの方言により、愛情を意味する名詞 affection が動詞として使用さ
れている。'oman ＝ woman

201. of your mouth 「あなたの口から」

202. parcel 「部分」

203. can you carry your good will to the maid? 「あのお嬢さんに求愛できる
か」good will は「好意」、carry は「伝える」の意。

205. become 「〜にふさわしい」

207. Got's lords, and his ladies 「だめですなあ」エヴァンズ独特の言い回し
で、他の文献には見られない表現。スレンダーの煮え切らない返事に業を煮や
したエヴァンズが発する軽いののしりの言葉と思われる。Got's は、God's が
訛って発音されている。

208. possitable これもエヴァンズ独特の言い回しだが、おそらく「積極的に
（positively）」を意味していると推測される。

209. upon good dowry 「持参金がたっぷり入るという条件で」upon ＝ on the
promise of

SLENDER   I will do a greater thing then that, upon your request, cousin, in any reason.

SHALLOW   Nay, conceive me, conceive me, sweet coz. What I do is to pleasure you, coz. Can you love the maid?

SLENDER   I will marry her, sir, at your request. But if there be   215
no great love in the beginning, yet heaven may decrease it upon better acquaintance, when we are married and have more occasion to know one another. I hope upon familiarity will grow more content. But if you say 'marry her', I will marry her. That I am freely dissolved, and dissolutely.   220

EVANS   It is a fery discretion answer, save the fall is in the 'ord 'dissolutely'. The 'ort is, according to our meaning, 'resolutely'. His meaning is good.

SHALLOW   Ay, I think my cousin meant well.

SLENDER   Ay, or else I would I might be hanged, la!   225

[*Enter Anne Page*]

SHALLOW   Here comes fair Mistress Anne. Would I were young for your sake, Mistress Anne.

ANNE   The dinner is on the table. My father desires your worships' company.

SHALLOW   I will wait on him, faire Mistress Anne.   230

EVANS   'Od's plessed will, I will not be absence at the grace.

[*Exeunt Shallow and Evans*]

ANNE   Will't please your worship to come in, sir?

SLENDER   No, I thank you, forsooth, heartily. I am very well.

ANNE   The dinner attends you, sir.

SLENDER   I am not a-hungry, I thank you, forsooth. — Go,   235
sirrah, for all you are my man, go wait upon my cousin Shallow.

[*Exit Simple*]

213. conceive me 「私の言っていることを理解しろ」

214. pleasure 「喜ばせる」動詞で用いられている。

215. if = even if

216. decrease 「少なくする」本来は「増す（increase）」が正しいが、スレンダーは言い間違えている。マラプロピズム（malapropism）と呼ばれる、シェイクスピア劇に見られる言葉遊びの一種。似たような音だが、意味が全く違う言葉を間違って言うことで笑いが生じる。

218. upon familiarity 「お互いをよく知るようになれば」I hope に続く節の中の述語動詞 grow に対する主語は content。倒置に留意。

220. That I am freely dissolved, and dissolutely　これもスレンダーのマラプロピズム。resolved（決心する）と言うべきところを dissolved（溶ける）と言い間違い、resolutely（強い意志をもって）のつもりで間違って dissolutely（みだらに）と言ってしまっている。

221. fery = very で、エヴァンズの発音の訛り。

221-22. save the fall is in the 'ord 'dissolutely' 「「みだらに」という語が間違っている以外は」'ord = word。fall は fault が訛ったものである可能性があり、ここでは「間違い」の意。

222. 'ort = word　同じくエヴァンズの方言

228-29. your worships' company 「皆さんがいらっしゃること」worship は、所有格の人称代名詞と共に用いると、「あなた様」「貴殿」といった敬称を表す。

231. 'Od's plessed will 「これはありがたい」'Od's = God's、plessed = pleased で、「神のよき思し召し」が直訳だが、ここでは感謝の意を表す表現。

231. grace 「食前の祈り」

232. Will't please your worship to come in 「恐れいりますが、家の中にお入り下さいますか」Will't = Will it で、it は to come in を指す。

235-36. Go, sirrah 「こらっ、行け」もちろんアンではなく、召使いのシンプルに対する台詞。

236. for all = although

A Justice of Peace sometime may be beholding to his friend
for a man. I keep but three men and a boy yet, till my mother
be dead. But what though? Yet I live like a poor gentleman   240
born.

ANNE   I may not go in without your worship; they will not sit
till you come.

SLENDER   I'faith, I'll eat nothing. I thank you as much as
though I did.   245

ANNE   I pray you, sir, walk in.

SLENDER   I had rather walk here, I thank you. I bruised my
shin the other day with playing at sword and dagger with a
master of fence — three veneys for a dish of stewed prunes
— and, by my troth, I cannot abide the smell of hot meat   250
since. Why do your dogs bark so? Be there bears i'th' town?

ANNE   I think there are, sir. I heard them talked of.

SLENDER   I love the sport well, but I shall as soon quarrel at it
as any man in England. You are afraid if you see the bear
loose, are you not?   255

ANNE   Ay, indeed, sir.

SLENDER   That's meat and drink to me now. I have seen
Sackerson loose twenty times, and have taken him by the
chain. But I warrant you, the women have so cried and
shrieked at it that it passed. But women, indeed, cannot abide   260
'em. They are very ill-favoured rough things.

[Enter Page]

PAGE   Come, gentle Master Slender, come. We stay for you.

SLENDER   I'll eat nothing. I thank you, sir.

PAGE   By cock and pie, you shall not choose, sir. Come, come.

SLENDER   Nay, pray you lead the way.   265

PAGE   Come on, sir.

SLENDER   Mistress Anne, yourself shall go first.

ANNE   Not I, sir. Pray you, keep on.

238-39. be beholding to his friend for a man 「召使いのことで親戚に感謝する」be beholding (beholden) to A for B は「B について A の世話になる」friend は「親戚」の意。

240. what though 「それがなんだと言うのです」what though = what of that

244. I'faith = In faith「実のところ」

248. playing at sword and dagger 「長剣と短剣の二刀流の試合をしていて」右手に長剣を、左手に短剣を持って戦うフェンシングがジェントルマンの間で流行した。安全のために、剣には刃留めが施された。

249. master of fence 「剣術の先生」

249. three veneys 「3回勝負」

250. hot meat 「あたたかい料理」meat は、肉だけではなく、食事や料理も意味した。ここでは、後者。

251-52. ロンドンで人気のあった熊いじめ（bear baiting）を想定したやりとり。熊いじめは、闘牛のようなアニマル・スポーツの一種で、杭に繋いだ熊にたくさんの猟犬を放ち、熊と猟犬が殺し合う様を見物する競技。16 世紀から17 世紀にかけてのイングランドで流行した。

253. quarrel at it 「競技を見ながら（興奮のあまり他の観客と）喧嘩してしまう」

257. That's meat and drink to me 「僕は大好き」meat and drink は「大好物」を意味する慣用句。

258. Sackerson サザックの熊いじめ場で特に人気のあった熊の名前。

260. that it passed 「信じられないぐらいに」it passed = it passed belief で、「理解を超える」の意。

261. 'em = them　ここでは熊を指す。

261. ill-favoured 「見るも恐ろしい」favour は「容貌」を意味した。

264. By cock and pie 「ぜったいに」きっぱりと断言する際に用いる表現。cock は、God の婉曲表現として用いられた。(*OED*)

SLENDER Truly, I will not go first, truly, la! I will not do you
    that wrong. 270

ANNE I pray you, sir.

SLENDER I'll rather be unmannerly than troublesome. You do
    yourself wrong indeed, la!

Exeunt

[**ACT I, SCENE II**]

    Enter Evans and Simple

EVANS Go your ways, and ask of Doctor Caius' house, which
    is the way. And there dwells one Mistress Quickly, which is in
    the manner of his nurse, or his dry nurse, or his cook, or his
    laundry, his washer, and his wringer.

SIMPLE Well, sir. 5

EVANS Nay, it is petter yet. Give her this letter, for it is a 'oman
    that altogethers acquaintace with Mistress Anne Page, and
    the letter is to desire and require her to solicit your master's
    desires to Mistress Anne Page. I pray you be gone. I will
    make an end of my dinner; there's pippins and cheese to 10
    come.

Exeunt

[**ACT I, SCENE III**]

    Enter Falstaff, Host, Bardolph, Nim, Pistol, [and Robin]

FALSTAFF Mine host of the Garter!

HOST What says my bully rook? Speak scholarly and wisely.

FALSTAFF Truly, mine host, I must turn away some of my
    followers.

HOST Discard, bully Hercules, cashier. Let them wag. Trot, 5
    trot.

FALSTAFF I sit at ten pounds a week.

272-73. You do yourself wrong 「自分で自分を貶めている」do (a person) wrong は「（人に対して）ひどいことをする」の意。

〔1. 2〕あらすじ••

　エヴァンズは、スレンダーの召使いシンプルをフランス人医師キーズの家に向かわせ、アンと親しいキーズ家の家政婦クウィックリーにスレンダーとアンの縁組みへの助力を頼む書簡を言付ける。

••

2. the way 「（キーズ医師の家への）行き方」

2-3. in the manner of his nurse 「彼の家政婦のようなもの」manner は「種類、たぐい」の意で、dry nurse 以下の名詞も manner of にかかる。

3. dry nurse 「お世話係」wet nurse は授乳も行う乳母を指すのに対して、dry nurse は授乳はしない世話係を指す。ここでは、子供の養育係ではなく、家政婦の意味で用いられている。

4. laundry 「洗濯女」laundress と言うべきところを言い間違えている。

4. his washer, and his wringer 「洗濯物を洗う係（washer）」と「洗濯物を絞る係（wringer）」

7. altogethers acquaintance with 「〜とよくつきあいがある」名詞を動詞のように使うのはエヴァンズの方言にしばしば見られる用例。altogethers は意味を強める副詞。

8. solicit 「伝える」

10. pippins 林檎（の種類）。林檎とチーズはデザートの定番だった。

〔1. 3〕あらすじ••

　金欠のフォルスタッフは、フォード夫人とペイジ夫人に言い寄り、それぞれが管理する夫の金を手に入れようと画策する。早速2人の女性に宛てた恋文をしたためたフォルスタッフは、それを手下のピストルとニムに届けさせようとするも断られ、逆上して2人を解雇し、小姓のロビンを使いに出す。一方、ニムとピストルは、フォルスタッフの計画をペイジとフォードに知らせる計画を立てる。

••

2. bully rook 「よう、相棒」bully は親しみを表す呼びかけ。rook は仲間の意。

3. turn away 「暇を出す」

5. Hercules ギリシャ・ローマ神話の英雄ヘラクレス。勇猛果敢な偉丈夫。

5. cashier 「追い出す」

5. wag 「立ち去る」

7. sit 「（ガーター亭に）逗留している」

Host Thou'rt an emperor: Caesar, Kaiser, and Pheazar. I will
entertain Bardolph: he shall draw; he shall tap. Said I well,
bully Hector?   10

Falstaff Do so, good mine host.

Host I have spoke. Let him follow. [*To Bardolph*] Let me see
thee froth and lime. I am at a word. Follow.

                                                                                        [*Exit*]

Falstaff Bardolph, follow him. A tapster is a good trade. An
old cloak makes a new jerkin; a withered servingman a fresh   15
tapster. Go, adieu.

Bardolph It is a life that I have desired. I will thrive.

                                                                                        [*Exit*]

Pistol O base Hungarian wight, wilt thou the spigot wield?

Nim He was gotten in drink. Is not the humour conceited?

Falstaff I am glad I am so acquit of this tinderbox. His   20
thefts were too open. His filching was like an unskilful singer:
he kept not time.

Nim The good humour is to steal at a minute's rest.

Pistol 'Convey', the wise it call. 'Steal'? Foh, a *fico* for the
phrase!   25

Falstaff Well, sirs, I am almost out at heels.

Pistol Why then, let kibes ensue.

Falstaff There is no remedy: I must cony-catch; I must shift.

Pistol Yong ravens must have food.

Falstaff Which of you know Ford of this town?   30

Pistol I ken the wight. He is of substance good.

Falstaff My honest lads, I will tell you what I am about.

Pistol Two yards and more.

Falstaff No quips now, Pistol. Indeed I am in the waist two
yards about, but I am now about no waste. I am about thrift.   35
Briefly. I do mean to make love to Ford's wife. I spy
entertainment in her. She discourses, she carves, she gives the
leer of invitation. I can construe the action of her familiar

8. Caesar, Kaiser, and Pheazar Caesar と Kaiser はどちらも皇帝を意味するが、Pheazar は不明。単なる語呂合わせか。

9. entertain 「雇う」

9. draw / tap 「酒樽から酒を汲む」/「酒樽の栓（tap）をひねって酒を汲む」

10. Hector ギリシャ・ローマ神話に登場するトロイの大将ヘクトル。

13. froth 「ビールの泡を立てる」

13. lime 「ワインにライム汁を加える」古くなったワインの酸味をごまかすためにライム汁を絞って給仕する酒場があった。

13. I am at a word. 「わかったな」言うべきことを言ったという意味。

14-15. An old ... jerkin. 「古い上着が流行最先端のベストになる」jerkin は、男性用の上着で、丈が短く、身体にフィットさせたデザイン。

18. Hungarian wight 「飢えたる者」Hungarian は国名ではなく、hungry の意。韻文になり、芝居がかった大仰な言い回しで語られる。

18. spigot 「酒樽の栓」「（武具などを）ふるう」を意味する動詞 wield の目的語としてはミスマッチだが、ピストルのふざけた意図には適っている。

19. He was gotten in drink 「父親が酔っ払っている時にもうけた子だ」gotten ＝ begotten

19. Is ... conceited? 「気の利いた気質じゃないかい？」根っからの酒好きで、喜んでバーテンダーになるバードルフを揶揄している。conceited は witty（機知に富んでいる）の意。

20. I am so acquit of this tinderbox 「あのキレやすい男をこんな風にお払い箱にした」tinderbox は点火に用いる火口箱で、怒りっぽい人間の比喩。

22. he kept not time 「タイミングを見極めることをしなかった」

23. at a minute's rest 「一瞬の隙に」

24. Convey 「失敬する」「盗む」の婉曲表現として用いられた。

24-25. a *fico* for the phrase! 「そんな言葉はクソ食らえだ！」fico はイタリア語で「イチジク（fig）」A fig for ～は、侮蔑を表す表現。

26. out at heels 「一文無し」慣用句だが、ピストルはこの表現を「かかとがむき出しになっている」とわざと文字通りに解釈し、続く台詞を語る。

28. shift 「なんとかやりくりする」

29. Yong ＝ Young　　**31. ken** ＝ know　　**31. He is ... good** 「彼は資産家だ」

32. what I am about 「俺が今からやろうとしていること」1. 3. 27 に続き、次行でピストルはフォルスタッフの台詞をわざと文字通りに解釈する。

37. entertainment 「誘うような雰囲気」

37. carves 「気のある素振りを見せる」意味不明だが、carve は食卓で肉を切り分けて客人に給仕する動作を意味するので、誘うような仕草を指すと思われる。　　**38. familiar** 「なれなれしい」

style; and the hardest voice of her behavior, to be Englished
rightly, is 'I am Sir John Falstaff's'.   40

PISTOL   He hath studied her will, and translated her will out of
honesty into English.

NIM   The anchor is deep. Will that humour pass?

FALSTAFF   Now, the report goes she has all the rule of her
husband's purse; he hath a legion of angels.   45

PISTOL   As many devils entertain, and 'To her, boy!', say I.

NIM   The humour rises; it is good. Humour me the angels.

FALSTAFF   I have writ me here a letter to her. And here another
to Page's wife, who even now gave me good eyes too, examined
my parts with most judicious œillades. Sometimes the beam   50
of her view gilded my foot, sometimes my portly belly.

PISTOL   Then did the Sun on dunghill shine.

NIM   I thank thee for that humour.

FALSTAFF   O, she did so course o'er my exteriors, with such a
greedy intention, that the appetite of her eye did seem to   55
scorch me up like a burning-glass. Here's another letter to
her. She bears the purse too. She is a region in Guiana, all
gold and bounty. I will be cheaters to them both, and they
shall be exchequers to me. They shall be my East and West
Indies, and I will trade to them both. [*To Nim*] Go, bear thou   60
this letter to Mistress Page; [*To Pistol*] and thou this to
Mistress Ford. We will thrive, lads, we will thrive.

PISTOL   Shall I Sir Pandarus of Troy become,
And by my side wear steel? Then Lucifer take all!

[*He gives back the letter*]

NIM   I will run no base humour. Here take the humour-letter.   65
[*He gives it back*] I will keep the haviour of reputation.

FALSTAFF   [*To Robin*]   Hold, sirrah, bear you these letters
tightly;
Sail like my pinnace to these golden shores.

39. the hardest voice of her behavior 「彼女の行動の意味深長な様子」

41-42. translated ... English 「貞節（という見かけ）から彼女の真意を英語に訳出した」honesty はジェンダー化されて用いられ、女性の場合は貞淑の美徳を意味した。

43. Will that humour pass? 「その性質はうまくいくかな？」humour は、自分に都合のよいように解釈するフォルスタッフの気質を指すと思われる。

45. a legion of angels 「たくさんのエンジェル金貨」大天使ミカエルの図柄が刻印されていることからこの名で呼ばれた。

46. As many devils entertain 「お前さんはたくさんの悪魔を抱え込んでいるんだから」フォードが「エンジェル」金貨を豊富に持っていることにかけている。entertain は「迎え入れる」の意。

47. The humour rises 「気分が乗ってきたぞ」

47. Humour me the angels 「ほらほら、エンジェル金貨もその気にさせろ」humour は動詞で使われており、「機嫌をとる、へつらう」の意。me は、聞き手の関心をひくために挿入される虚辞（心性的与格）で、ここでは「さあ」という程度の意味。

50. judicious œillades 「意味ありげな流し目」œillades はフランス語。judicious は知的な判断力を示す形容詞。

51. view 「眼力」

54. course o'er = course over 「〜の上を通り過ぎる」まだ視線の比喩が続いている。

56. burning-glass 「凸レンズ」太陽光線を集めるのに用いられた。

57. a region in Guiana 「ギアナの土地」ギアナは南アメリカのアマゾン川流域の熱帯地域で、「エルドラド」と呼ばれる黄金郷があると考えられていた。1595 年にサー・ウォルター・ローリーが探検航海を試みるも失敗。

63. Pandarus ギリシャ・ローマ神話のトロイの武将パンダラス。シェイクスピアの『トロイラスとクレシダ』では、トロイの王子トロイラスを自分の姪クレシダに紹介する俗っぽい恋の取り持ち役として登場する。

64. by my side wear steel 「武具を身にまとう」再び韻文調で芝居がかった台詞になっている点に注意。

65. I will run no base humour 「そんな卑しい気質じゃないぞ」

65. humour-letter 「気質の丈をこめた手紙」意味不明の表現だが、humoured letter として訳出した。

66. I will keep the haviour of reputation 「しかるべき体面は維持するつもりだ」haviour = behaviour で、態度や振る舞いを意味する。

Rogues, hence, avaunt! Vanish like hailstones, go!
Trudge, plod away o'th' hoof, seek shelter, pack!   70
Falstaff will learn the humour of the age:
French-thrift, you rogues, myself and skirted page.

[*Exeunt Falstaff and Robin*]

PISTOL Let vultures gripe thy guts! For gourd and fulham
  holds,
  And high and low beguiles the rich and poor.
  Tester I'll have in pouch when thou shalt lack,   75
  Base Phrygian Turk!

NIM I have operations, which be humours of revenge.

PISTOL Wilt thou revenge?

NIM   By welkin and her star!

PISTOL With wit or steel?

NIM   With both the humours, I.
  I will discuss the humour of this love to Ford.   80

PISTOL And I to Page shall eke unfold
  How Falstaff, varlet vile
  His dove will prove, his gold will hold,
  And his soft couch defile.

NIM My humour shall not cool. I will incense Ford to deal   85
  with poison. I will possess him with yellowness, for the revolt
  of mine is dangerous. That is my true humour.

PISTOL Thou art the Mars of malcontents. I second thee.
  Troop on.

                                                  Exeunt

[ACT I, SCENE IV]

Enter Mistress Quickly [and] Simple

MISTRESS QUICKLY What, John Rugby!

[*Enter Rugby*]

70. Trudge ... o'th' hoof 「とぼとぼ歩いて、失せやがれ」o'th' hoof = on the hoof で、hoof はひづめを意味するため、動物を追い立てる様子が連想される。

70. pack 「出て行け」荷物をまとめて立ち去ることを意味する動詞。

72. French-thrift 「フランス流の倹約生活」フォルスタッフが考え出した悪態で、根拠はない。バードルフに加えてピストルとニムも解雇したことを指す。

72. skirted page 「長い上着を着た小姓」skirt はウェストを絞ったコート。

73. gripe 「つかみ取る」

73. gourd and fulham holds 「いかさま用のサイコロはうまくいく」gourd も fulham も決まった数が出るように細工を施したサイコロ。hold = hold good

74. high and low 「(大きな数も小さな数も思うがままに出せる)いんちきなサイコロ」

75. Tester 「6 ペンス硬貨」pouch は金を入れる巾着袋。

76. Base Phrygian Turk! 「畜生め！」Phrygian（フリギア人の）もここでは「トルコ人の」という意味で悪態として用いられている。base は「卑劣な」を意味する形容詞。

77. operations 「計画」

78. By welkin and her star 「天と星にかけて」welkin は空を意味する詩語。

79. steel 「剣」 I = Aye「そうだな」

80. discuss ... to Ford discuss は「知らせる」の意。 ⇒後注

81. eke 「同じように」

83. His dove will prove 「ペイジの女房にちょっかいを出す」prove は「試す」の意味で、性的な意を含む。主語は前行のフォルスタッフ。my dove（いとしい人）のように、dove は所有格と共に用いると、恋人（恋女房）を意味する。

84. couch 「寝床」

86. possess him with yellowness 「フォードを嫉妬でいっぱいにする」黄色を嫉妬の意で用いるのはシェイクスピアの造語。

88. the Mars of malcontents 「まさに不平分子の大将マルスってところだな」マルスはギリシャ・ローマ神話の軍神。malcontent は何かにつけて不機嫌で、世の中に不満がある不平分子を指す。

88. second 「応援する」Troop on までで弱強七詩脚の韻文になっており、芝居がかった調子で場面が終わる。

〔1. 4〕あらすじ・・・
　　アンのことが好きなキーズは、エヴァンズがスレンダーとアンの縁談を進めようとしていることを知って怒り狂い、牧師への果たし状を届けさせる。クウィックリーは、フェントンからもアンへの求婚の助力を依頼される。
・・・

I pray thee go to the casement and see if you can see my master, Master Doctor Caius, coming. If he do, i'faith, and find anybody in the house, here will be an old abusing of God's patience and the King's English.   5

RUGBY   I'll go watch.

MISTRESS QUICKLY   Go; and we'll have a posset for't soon at night, in faith, at the latter end of a sea-coal fire.

[*Exit Rugby*]

An honest,willing, kind fellow, as ever servant shall come in house withal, and, I warrant you, no tell-tale, nor no breed-   10
bate. His worst fault is that he is given to prayer. He is something peevish that way, but nobody but has his fault. But let that pass. Peter Simple you say your name is?

SIMPLE   Ay, for fault of a better.

MISTRESS QUICKLY   And Master Slender's your master?   15

SIMPLE   Ay, forsooth.

MISTRESS QUICKLY   Does he not wear a great round beard, like a glover's pairing-knife?

SIMPLE   No, forsooth. He hath but a little wee face, with a little yellow beard, a Cain-coloured beard.   20

MISTRESS QUICKLY   A softly-sprighted man, is he not?

SIMPLE   Ay, forsooth. But he is as tall a man of his hands as any is between this and his head. He hath fought with a warrener.

MISTRESS QUICKLY   How say you? Oh, I should remember   25
him. Does he not hold up his head, as it were, and strut in his gait?

SIMPLE   Yes, indeed does he.

MISTRESS QUICKLY   Well, heaven send Anne Page no worse fortune! Tell Master Parson Evans I will do what I can for   30
your master. Anne is a good girl, and I wish —

RUGBY   [*Within*]   Out, alas! Here comes my master!

MISTRESS QUICKLY   We shall all be shent. Run in here, good

4-5. here ... English 「手当たり次第に悪口雑言を浴びせることになる」old ＝ lots of で、of God' patience ... は「神様の堪忍袋であろうがきちんとした英語であろうがおかまいなしに」という意味。標準英語という意味に加えて（イギリス）英語へのプライドをも含意する King's English という語が初めて用いられたのはエリザベス朝で、この箇所は極めて初期の使用例。

7. posset 「ミルク酒」ワインやエールを入れてプリンのように凝固させ、スパイスや砂糖を加えたデザート風のホットミルク。

7. for't ＝ for it で、「見てきてくれたら（その御礼に）」

7-8. soon at night 「夜にならないうちに」soon は「〜前に早く」を意味する特殊な用法。

8. at the latter end of a sea-coal fire 「石炭をくべた暖炉の端に座って」石炭は、鉱山があるイングランド北東部から海路で運ばれたことから sea-coal と呼ばれた。木炭よりも良質の燃料だった。

9-10. as ever servant shall come in house withal 「およそ考えられる使用人のだれよりも」＝ as any servant you will have in a house

10-11. breed-bate 「もめ事を起こす人」

11. given to prayer 「お祈りに夢中になる」give oneself to ... で「…に没頭する」の意。

12. peevish 「融通がきかない、頑固な」

14. Ay, for fault of a better 「いかにもさようで」for fault of ＝ for lack of で、直訳すると「他によい名前がないので、そのとおり」となるが、当時の慣用表現。

18. glover's pairing-knife 「皮革職人が使うナイフ」三日月の形状をしていた。

19. wee 「小さな」

20. Cain-coloured 「黄色の」聖書の「創世記」で言及される兄弟殺しの罪を犯すカインは黄味を帯びた髪で絵画に描かれることが多かったことに因む。

21, softly-sprighted ＝ softly-spirited 「穏やかな気性の」

22-23. as tall a man of his hands as any is between this and his head 「ここらあたりの誰よりも腕っぷしが強い」a tall man of his hands は「喧嘩が強い勇ましい男」、between this and his head は「このあたり」を意味する決まり文句。

24. warrener 「猟場番人」

25. How say you? 「おや、そうなのかい？」相手の話に驚いた時に発する言葉。

25-26. I should remember him 「今思い出した」

33. be shent 「叱られる」shent は、shend（叱る）の過去分詞。

young man; go into this closet. He will not stay long. [*Simple goes into the closet*]   What, John Rugby? John! What, John, I say! 35

[*Enter Rugby*]

Go, John, go enquire for my master. I doubt he be not well that he comes not home.

[*Exit Rugby*]

[*Sings*]   'And down, down, adown-a', *etc.*

[*Enter Doctor Caius*]

CAIUS   Vat is you sing? I do not like dese toys. Pray you go and 40 vetch me in my closet *une boîte en vert*: a box, a green-a box. Do intend vat I speak? A green-a box.

MISTRESS QUICKLY   Ay, forsooth. I'll fetch it you. — [*Aside*] I am glad he went not in himself. If he had found the young man, he would have been horn-mad. [*She goes to fetch the box*] 45

CAIUS   *Fe, fe, fe, fe! Ma foi, il fait fort chaud. Je m'en vais voir à le court la grande affaire.*

MISTRESS QUICKLY   [*Returning, she shows him the box*]   Is it this, sir?

CAIUS   *Oui, mette-le au mon* pocket. *Dépêche*, quickly. Vere is dat 50 knave Rugby?

MISTRESS QUICKLY   What, John Rugby! John!

[*Enter Rugby*]

RUGBY   Here, sir.

CAIUS   You are John Rugby, and you are Jack Rugby. Come, take-a your rapier, and come after my heel to the court. 55

RUGBY   'Tis ready, sir, here in the porch.

CAIUS   By my trot, I tarry too long. 'Od's-me! *Que ai-je oublié?* Dere is some simples in my closet, dat I vill not for the varld I shall leave behind. [*He goes into the closet*]

34. closet 「部屋」戸棚の可能性も全くないわけではないが、通常は小さな私室を意味した。

37-38. I doubt he be not well that he comes not home 「まだ帰らないなんて、お加減が悪いんじゃないかしらね」I doubt ＝ I fear

39. 'And down, down adown-a', etc. バラッド（ballad）のリフレインと思われる。バラッドとは、中世以降大衆によって歌い継がれる形で各地に伝わった口承詩の総称。通常は作者不詳の形で伝承されたが、近代初期以降は作者名を出す創作バラッドも登場し、流行歌としての側面も有した。歌詞の内容は、恋愛、冒険、戦い等多岐に亘るが、簡素な言葉と詩形で素朴な感情を物語形式で歌うものが多く、リフレインが多用される。クウィックリーがここで歌っているのは、バラッドでよく用いられたリフレインの典型。

40. Vat is you sing? 「何を歌ってる？」エヴァンズと同様、キーズも独特の英語を話す。キーズのフランス語訛りの英語では、w は v の音に、th [ð] が d の音に、f が v の音になる。英語もフランス語も文法のミスが多い。

41. *une boîte en vert* フランス語で「小さな緑の箱」

42. intend フランス語の entendre（聞く）を英語風に発音している。

45. horn-mad 「怒り狂って」horn は雄牛や牡鹿が怒って角で突く行為を意味する動詞で、ここでは「角で突かんばかりに」と「激怒して」（mad）を強めている。

46-47. *Ma foi ... affaire* ＝ By my faith, it is hot. I am going to the court, important business 「なんて、暑いんだ。これから大事な用で宮廷に出かけるのに」

50. *Oui, mette-le au mon* ＝ Yes, put it in my

54. Jack Rugby ジャックはジョンの愛称だが、ここでは特に身分の低い者を侮蔑する意味もある。

55. come after my heel 「私のすぐ後についてこい」キーズ特有の言い方。

57. By my trot ＝ By my troth「断じて」

57. 'Od's-me ＝ God's me (God save me)「ああ神様」

57. *Que ai-je oublié?* ＝ What have I forgotten?

58. simples 「薬」simple は1種類の薬草だけで作られた薬を意味するが、もちろん隠れているシンプルを観客に連想させる効果がある。

MISTRESS QUICKLY   [*Aside*]   Ay me, he'll find the young man   60
  there, and be mad.

CAIUS   [*Within*]   O, *diable*, *diable*! Vat is in my closet? Villany!
  Larron! Rugby, my rapier!

MISTRESS QUICKLY   Good master, be content.

CAIUS   Wherefore shall I be content-a?   65

MISTRESS QUICKLY   The young man is an honest man.

CAIUS   What shall de honest man do in my closet? Dere is no
  honest man dat shall come in my closet.

MISTRESS QUICKLY   I beseech you, be not so phlegmatic. Hear
  the truth of it. He came of an errand to me from Parson   70
  Hugh.

CAIUS   Vell?

SIMPLE   Ay, forsooth, to desire her to —

MISTRESS QUICKLY   Peace, I pray you.

CAIUS   Peace-a your tongue. [*To Simple*] Speak-a your tale.   75

SIMPLE   To desire this honest gentlewoman, your maid, to
  speak a good word to Mistress Anne Page for my master in
  the way of marriage.

MISTRESS QUICKLY   This is all indeed, la! But I'll ne'er put my
  finger in the fire, and need not.   80

CAIUS   Sir Hugh send-a you? Rugby, *baillez* me some paper.
  [*To Simple*]   Tarry you a little-a while.

[*Rugby brings paper. Caius writes*]

MISTRESS QUICKLY   [*Aside to Simple*]   I am glad he is so quiet.
  If he had been throughly moved, you should have heard him
  so loud, and so melancholy. But notwithstanding, man, I'll   85
  do your master what good I can. And the very yea and the no
  is, the French doctor, my master — I may call him my master,
  look you, for I keep his house, and I wash, wring, brew, bake,
  scour, dress meat and drink, make the beds, and do all
  myself —   90

60 SD [*Aside*]　傍白（aside）。独白（soliloquy）とは異なり、他の登場人物が舞台上にいるが、その人達には聞こえていないという設定で語られる台詞。この後の 91 行目のシンプルのように、特定の人物に向けてひそひそとかわされる場合もある。いずれにせよ、ひとりごとのように呟かれることが多いが、観客には明瞭に聞こえる必要があるので、役者の技量を要する。一般的に独白は一定の長さを有するのに対して、傍白は短い。傍白は、独白と同様、登場人物が知らない情報を与えることで、観客を有利な状況に置く演劇的仕掛けである。本作品では、フォルスタッフをはじめ、様々な人物が騙されるプロットが展開するが、意外にも傍白の数は少ないという特徴がある。ただし、本作品の場合もそうだが、シェイクスピアの時代に出版された版本には傍白も含めてト書きが記されていないことが多く、編集の段階で挿入される。そのため、果たして傍白なのかどうかはもちろん、それがひとりごととして語られるのか、あるいは聞かせる相手が舞台上にいるのかどうか、といった様々な解釈上の問題が浮上する。

63. *Larron* 　フランス語で「泥棒」

69. phlegmatic 　「冷静な」文脈に合わないが、おそらくクウィックリーは、choleric（怒りっぽい）と言うべきところを言い誤っている。どちらも気質（humour）の類型を表す用語。

74. Peace, I pray you 　「お願い、黙って」

79-80. I'll ne'er put my finger in the fire, and need not 　諺で「やらないで済むなら、危険なことに首をつっこむことはしない」and = if

81. *baillez* 　フランス語で「持ってくる」

84. If he had been throughly moved 　「すごく怒ったら」throughly = thoroughly「完全に」

85. melancholy 　「陰鬱な」69 行目の phlegmatic と同様に、文脈に合わない。クウィックリーは、またも choleric（怒りっぽい）と取り違えている。

86. the very yea and the no 　「いいかい」何かを強い調子で断言する時に使う言い回し。

88. brew 　「自家製のビールなどを醸造する」

89. scour 　「床を磨く」

89. dress meat and drink 　「食事や酒の準備をする」

SIMPLE   [*Aside to Mistress Quickly*]   'Tis a great charge to come
  under one body's hand.

MISTRESS QUICKLY   [*Aside to Simple*]   Are you advised of that?
  You shall find it a great charge, and to be up early and down
  late. But notwithstanding — to tell you in your ear; I would   95
  have no words of it — my master himself is in love with
  Mistress Anne Page. But notwithstanding that, I know
  Anne's mind. That's neither here nor there.

CAIUS   [*Giving a letter to Simple*]   You, jack'nape, give-a this
  letter to Sir Hugh. By gar, it is a shallenge. I will cut his troat   100
  in de Park, and I will teach a scurvy jackanape priest to
  meddle or make. You may be gone. It is not good you tarry
  here. By gar, I will cut all his two stones. By gar, he shall not
  have a stone to throw at his dog.

[*Exit Simple*]

MISTRESS QUICKLY   Alas, he speaks but for his friend.   105

CAIUS   It is no matter-a ver dat. Do not you tell-a me dat I
  shall have Anne Page for myself? By gar, I vill kill de jack
  priest. And I have appointed mine host of de Jarteer to
  measure our weapon. By gar, I will myself have Anne Page.

MISTRESS QUICKLY   Sir, the maid loves you, and all shall be   110
  well. We must give folks leave to prate. What the good-year!

CAIUS   Rugby, come to the court with me. [*To Mistress Quickly*]
  By gar, if I have not Anne Page, I shall turn your head out of
  my door. — Follow my heels, Rugby.

MISTRESS QUICKLY   You shall have An — [*Exeunt Caius and*   115
  Rugby] — fool's head of your own. No, I know Anne's mind
  for that. Never a woman in Windsor knows more of Anne's
  mind than I do, nor can do more than I do with her, I thank
  heaven.

FENTON   [*Within*]   Who's within there, ho?   120

MISTRESS QUICKLY   Who's there, I trow? Come near the house,
  I pray you.

91. charge　「責任」

93. Are you advised of that?　「そう思うだろう？」be advised of ＝ be aware of

95-96. I would have no words of it　「普通はこのことは言わないんだけど」

98. That's neither here nor there　「ともかくそれは置いておいて」

99. jack'nape ＝ jackanape「小僧」侮蔑的な呼び方。

100. By gar ＝ By God「絶対に」以後、キーズの台詞に頻出する。

100. shallenge　「決闘の果たし状」キーズのフランス語訛りの英語では、c が s になっている。

100. troat ＝ throat

101. scurvy jackanape priest　「卑しいごろつき牧師」

102. meddle or make　決まった言い方で、どちらの語も「首をつっこむ、干渉する」の意。

103. stones　「睾丸」

105. but ＝ only

106. It is no matter-a ver dat　「それはどうでもいい」ver は for が、dat は that がそれぞれ訛って発音されたもの。

107-08. jack priest　「ごろつき牧師」jack は 99 行目の jack'nape に同じ。

108. Jarteer　Garter（ガーター亭）がフランス語風に（jarretière）訛って発音されている。

109. measure our weapon　文字通り訳すと「（決闘の際に不正がないように）剣の重さを量る」だが、「決闘の立会人を務める」の意味。

111. give folks leave to prate　「皆に言いたいことを言わせる」leave は許可を意味する名詞、prate は「べらべらと噂話をする」の意。

111. What the good-year!　「なんてことだい！」由来ははっきりしないが、My Goodness! といった程度のスラング。

115. An　「アン（Anne）」と言いかけたが、キーズが出て行ったのを見届けると、本音が出て、冠詞の an に言い換えられる。ass-head（fool's head と同じく「お馬鹿さん」の意）に続けようとした可能性がある。

121. I trow ＝ I wonder

121. Come near　「入る」

[*Enter Fenton*]

FENTON   How now, good woman? How dost thou?

MISTRESS QUICKLY   The better that it pleases your good
   worship to ask.   125

FENTON   What news? How does pretty Mistress Anne?

MISTRESS QUICKLY   In truth, sir, and she is pretty, and honest,
   and gentle, and one that is your friend — I can tell you that
   by the way, I praise heaven for it.

FENTON   Shall I do any good, think'st thou? Shall I not lose my   130
   suit?

MISTRESS QUICKLY   Troth, sir, all is in His hands above. But
   notwithstanding, Master Fenton, I'll be sworn on a book she
   loves you. Have not your worship a wart above your eye?

FENTON   Yes, marry, have I. What of that?   135

MISTRESS QUICKLY   Well, thereby hangs a tale. Good faith, it is
   such another Nan! But, I detest, an honest maid as ever
   broke bread. We had an hour's talk of that wart. I shall never
   laugh but in that maids company. But, indeed, she is given
   too much to allicholy and musing. But for you — well, go   140
   to —

FENTON   Well, I shall see her today. Hold, there's money for
   thee. Let me have thy voice in my behalf. If thou seest her
   before me, commend me.

MISTRESS QUICKLY   Will I? I'faith, that we will. And I will tell   145
   your worship more of the wart the next time we have
   confidence, and of other wooers.

FENTON   Well, farewell. I am in great haste now.

MISTRESS QUICKLY   Farewell to your worship.

                                                        [*Exit Fenton*]

   Truly an honest gentleman. But Anne loves him not. For I   150
   know Anne's mind as well as another does. — Out upon't!
   What have I forgot!   *Exit*

124-25. The better that it pleases your good worship to ask 「おかげさまで元気です」定型の挨拶文。your good worship あるいは your worship は「あなた様」の意。

127. honest 「身持ちがよい」男女によって違う意味で用いられた honest の用法については、1. 3. 41-42 注参照。

128. gentle 「育ちがよい」

128. your friend 「あなたのいい人」friend には恋人の意味もあった。

130. do any good 「成功する、うまくいく」

130-31. lose my suit 「求婚に失敗する」

132. Troth 「まったく」

132. His = God's

133. I'll be sworn on a book 「聖書にかけて誓う」on a book = on the Bible

136. thereby hangs a tale 「それにはちょっといい話があるんです」慣用的な成句。

136-37. it is such another Nan 「アンは特別なお嬢さんですよ」Nan は Anne の愛称。such another は「この上ない」を意味する決まり文句（Tilley）。

137. detest protest（断言する）と言うべきところを detest（毛嫌いする）と言い間違っている。マラプロピズムの例。

137-38. an honest maid as ever broke bread 「本当にいいお嬢さんなんです」break bread は直訳すると「パンをちぎる」だが、「聖餐式に与る」の意。broke は break の古い過去分詞で、全体としては、「今まで聖餐式に与った誰よりも身持ちのいい娘」となる。正直者をほめる一種の諺（Tilley）。

140. allicholy 「憂鬱（melancholy）」の言い間違え。

140-41. go to 「この話はもう終わり」

143. voice 「口添え、支持」

144. commend me 「僕からよろしくと伝える」

147. confidence 「打ち明け話」

150. honest 127 行目とは若干意味が異なり、男性に使うと「立派な」といった意味で honourable や respectable に近い。

151. Out upon't = Out upon it で、驚いた時に使う言葉。「あらやだ」

[ACT II, SCENE I]

Enter Mistress Page [with a letter]

MISTESS PAGE   What, have I 'scap'd love-letters in the holiday
time of my beauty, and am I now a subject for them? Let me
see. [*She reads*] 'Ask me no reason why I love you, for though
Love use Reason for his precisian, he admits him not for his
counsellor. You are not young; no more am I. Go to, then,   5
there's sympathy. You are merry; so am I. Ha, ha, then,
there's more sympathy. You love sack, and so do I. Would
you desire better sympathy? Let it suffice thee, Mistress Page
— at the least if the love of soldier can suffice — that I love
thee. I will not say pity me — 'tis not a soldier-like phrase —   10
but I say, love me. By me,
    Thine own true knight,
    By day or night,
    Or any kind of light,
    With all his might,   15
    For thee to fight,
                John Falstaff.'
What a Herod of Jewry is this! O, wicked, wicked world! One
that is well-nigh worn to pieces with age to show himself a
young gallant! What an unweighed behaviour hath this   20
Flemish drunkard picked — with the devil's name — out of
my conversation, that he dares in this manner assay me? Why,
he hath not been thrice in my company. What should I say to
him? I was then frugal of my mirth. Heaven forgive me! Why,
I'll exhibit a bill in the parliament for the putting down of   25
men. How shall I be revenged on him? For revenged I will be,
as sure as his guts are made of puddings.

[*Enter Mistress Ford*]

MISTRESS FORD   Mistress Page! Trust me, I was going to your

　ペイジ夫人とフォード夫人は、フォルスタッフの求愛に、しかも同じ文面の恋文を 2 人に送ってきたことに怒り、思い上がった騎士にひと泡吹かせるべく一計を案じる。一方、ニムとピストルは、ペイジとフォードにフォルスタッフの計画を密告する。ペイジがこれを一笑に付するのに対して、フォードは妻への猜疑心に駆られる。フォードはガーター亭の亭主に頼み、ブルックという偽名を用いてフォルスタッフに探りを入れることを決意する。

……………………………………………………………………………………………………

1. 'scap'd = escaped「逃す」

1-2. holiday time 「最上の時、盛り、旬」

4. Love / Reason 抽象名詞が擬人化されているので大文字で始まっている。

4. precisian 「ピューリタン的な指南役」ピューリタンは、その禁欲主義的傾向のために、お説教好きの堅物として揶揄された。

6. sympathy 「類似点」

7. sack 「サックワイン」スペインやカナリア諸島で生産されたシェリー酒で、アルコール度数を強めた白ワイン。食前酒や食後酒として飲まれることが多い。

15. might 「力」

18. a Herod of Jewry 「まるでユダヤの民のヘロデ王のよう」ヘロデは、キリストの誕生を恐れて、ベツレヘムの 2 歳以下の幼児の虐殺を命じた暴君で、中世の聖史劇に悪役として登場した。

19. well-nigh worn to pieces 「ぼろぼろになりかけている」be worn to pieces で「やつれ果てる」の意。nigh = near

20. unweighed 自分の重さがわかっていないことから、「身のほど知らずの」。

21. Flemish drunkard 「フランダース人みたいな酔っ払い」フォルスタッフはイングランド人だが、酒飲みが多いとされたフランドル人に喩えられている。フランダースは、オランダ南西部、ベルギー西部、フランス北部にわたる地域。

21. with the devil's name 嫌悪や怒りを示す間投詞で「いまいましいったらありゃしない」。

22. conversation 「振る舞い」

22. assay 「言い寄る」

22. Why 何かを強い調子で主張する時に使う表現で、「だってほら」。

25. exhibit a bill 「法案を提出する」

25. putting down 「排除、撤廃」

27. puddings 「詰め物」現代のイギリス英語では、pudding はデザート菓子を指すのに対して、16 世紀のイングランドでは、ハーブを混ぜてこねた挽肉を豚や羊の内臓に詰めて焼いた料理を指した。

house.

MISTRESS PAGE   And trust me, I was coming to you. You look   30
very ill.

MISTRESS FORD   Nay, I'll ne'er believe that. I have to show to
the contrary.

MISTRESS PAGE   Faith, but you do, in my mind.

MISTRESS FORD   Well, I do, then. Yet I say I could show you to   35
the contrary. O Mistress Page, give me some counsel.

MISTRESS PAGE   What's the matter, woman?

MISTRESS FORD   O woman, if it were not for one trifling
respect, I could come to such honour.

MISTRESS PAGE   Hang the trifle, woman; take the honour.   40
What is it? Dispense with trifles. What is it?

MISTRESS FORD   If I would but go to hell for an eternal
moment or so, I could be knighted.

MISTRESS PAGE   What? Thou liest! Sir Alice Ford? These
knights will hack, and so thou shouldst not alter the article   45
of thy gentry.

MISTRESS FORD   We burn daylight. Here, read, read. Perceive
how I might be knighted. [*She gives a letter to Mistress Page*] I
shall think the worse of fat men, as long as I have an eye to
make difference of men's liking. And yet he would not swear,   50
praised women's modesty, and gave such orderly and well-
behaved reproof to all uncomeliness, that I would have sworn
his disposition would have gone to the truth of his words. But
they do no more adhere and keep place together than the
Hundredth Psalm to the tune of 'Greensleeves'. What   55
tempest, I trow, threw this whale, with so many tuns of oil in
his belly, ashore at Windsor? How shall I be revenged on
him? I think the best way were to entertain him with hope till
the wicked fire of lust have melted him in his own grease. Did
you ever hear the like?   60

MISTRESS PAGE   Letter for letter, but that the name of Page

32-33. show to the contrary 「その逆だということを教える」顔色の悪さを心配するペイジ夫人に対して、（恋文をもらうぐらいに）むしろ顔色は冴えていることを示唆している。

38. if it were not for 「～がなければ」

39. come to such honour 「とても名誉のある身分になる」

40. Hang the trifle 「ささいなことなんてどうでもいいわよ」Hang は何かを強く否定する際に用いられた決まり文句。

45. hack = hackney で、「売春宿に通う」の意。女性関係のトラブルを起こしやすいことが示唆されている。

46. gentry 「ジェントリー階級」

47. burn daylight 日中に明かりをともすことから、諺で「時間を無駄にする」。

50. make difference of 「区別する、しっかりと品定めする」

50. liking 「体型」

52. uncomeliness 「見苦しい振る舞い」

53. his disposition would have gone to the truth of his words 「彼の性格は話す事と一致している」フォルスタッフは自分で言う通りの人間に違いないということ。disposition は「気質」、go to は「～と一致する」の意。

54. they 前行の his disposition と his words を指す。

55. Hundredth Psalm 「詩篇の 100 番」「詩篇」は旧約聖書に収められた書の 1 つで、150 篇の詩で構成される。 ⇒後注

55. Greensleeves 現在も有名なフォークソング「グリーンスリーブス」は 16 世紀に流行したバラッド（民謡）で、1580 年に書籍商リチャード・ジョーンズによって出版登録されている。かつての恋人である「緑の袖の貴女（Lady Greensleeves）」をいつまでも忘れられない男性が歌う失恋ソングで、哀切な旋律が特に有名で愛唱された。バラッドについては、1. 4. 39 注参照。

56. I trow = I wonder

58. entertain him with hope 「彼に希望を持たせる」

60. the like 「こんな話」

61. Letter for letter 「一字一句同一の手紙」letter には「文字」と「手紙」の両方の意味が掛けられている。

and Ford differs. [*She shows her own letter from Falstaff*] To thy
great comfort in this mystery of ill opinions, here's the twin-
brother of thy letter. But let thine inherit first, for I protest
mine never shall. I warrant he hath a thousand of these   65
letters, writ with blank space for different names — sure,
more, and these are of the second edition. He will print them,
out of doubt, for he cares not what he puts into the press,
when he would put us two. I had rather be a giantess and lie
under Mount Pelion. Well, I will find you twenty lascivious   70
turtles ere one chaste man.

MISTRESS FORD   Why, this is the very same: the very hand, the
very words. What doth he think of us?

MISTRESS PAGE   Nay, I know not. It makes me almost ready to
wrangle with mine owne honesty. I'll entertain myself like   75
one that I am not acquainted withal; for, sure, unless he know
some strain in me that I know not myself, he would never
have boarded me in this fury.

MISTRESS FORD   'Boording' call you it? I'll be sure to keep him
above deck.   80

MISTRESS PAGE   So will I. If he come under my hatches, I'll
never to sea again. Let's be revenged on him. Let's appoint
him a meeting, give him a show of comfort in his suit, and
lead him on with a fine-baited delay till he hath pawned his
horses to mine host of the Garter.   85

MISTRESS FORD   Nay, I will consent to act any villainy against
him, that may not sully the chariness of our honesty. O that
my husband saw this letter! It would give eternal food to his
jealousy.

[*Enter Ford with Pistol, and Page with Nim*]

MISTRESS PAGE   Why, look where he comes, and my goodman   90
too. He's as far from jealousy as I am from giving him cause,
and that, I hope, is an unmeasurable distance.

63. ill opinions 「見くびられていること」既婚者であるにもかかわらず、自分に気があるとフォルスタッフに思われていることを指す。

66. writ = written

68. puts into the press 「出版する」press は印刷機を意味するが、押しつけるという性的な意味も含まれている。

69. when he would put us two 「私たち2人を一緒にするとは」

70. Mount Pelion 「ペリオン山」ギリシャ・ローマ神話で、オリュンポスの神々に反逆した巨人族が天の頂きに上ろうとして積み上げた山の名前。巨人達は天罰としてその山の下に埋められた。

71. turtles = turtle-doves「キジバト」キジバトは誠実な恋人の象徴なので、lascivious（淫らな）という形容詞とは不一致。矛盾した語をあえて並べるオクシモロン（oxymoron）の用例。一見誠実そうに見えても実は浮気な男性が多いということを揶揄している。

72. hand 「筆跡」

75. wrangle 「葛藤する」

75. honesty 「貞節の美徳」

75. entertain 「思い込ませる」

76. I am not acquainted withal 「私が貞節の美徳をわかっていない(とでも)」withal = therewith「それに」で、「それ」とはこの場合前行の honesty を指す。

77. strain 「気質、傾向」

78. boarded 「攻撃をしかけてきた」board は敵方の船に乗り込んで攻撃することを意味する。続くフォード夫人の台詞も含め、海事の比喩が続く。

78. in this fury 「こんなに激しい様子で」

79-80. keep him above deck 「甲板の上に留めておく（それ以上は先に進ませない）」

81. hatches 「（船室へと続く）船の昇降口」

83. show of comfort 「見込みがありそうな様子」

84. fine-baited 「おびき寄せるためのわなを仕掛けてじらすこと」

84-85. till he he hath pawned his horses to mine host of the Garter 「(金がなくなった) フォルスタッフがガーター亭の主人に馬を担保にして金を借りるようになるまで」pawn は質に入れること。mine は、聞き手の関心をひくために挿入された虚辞で特に意味はない。

87. chariness of our honesty 「用心して守っている私たちの操」

90. goodman 「夫」

92. that, I hope, is an unmeasurable distance 「夫が嫉妬することはありえないと思う」前行を受けて、that はペイジと嫉妬の距離を指しており、それが「計り知れないほど隔たっていること」が意図されている。

Mistress Ford   You are the happier woman.

Mistress Page   Let's consult together against this greasy knight. Come hither.   95

[They talk apart]

Ford   Well, I hope it be not so.

Pistol   Hope is a curtal dog in some affairs.
   Sir John affects thy wife.

Ford   Why, sir, my wife is not young.

Pistol   He woos both high and low, both rich and poor,   100
   Both young and old, one with another, Ford.
   He loves the gallimaufry. Ford, perpend.

Ford   Love my wife?

Pistol   With liver, burning hot. Prevent,
   Or go thou, like Sir Actaeon he,   105
   With Ringwood at thy heels.
   O, odious is the name!

Ford   What name, sir?

Pistol   The horn, I say. Farewell.
   Take heed, have open eye, for thieves do foot by night.   110
   Take heed, ere summer comes, or cuckoo-birds do sing.
   Away, Sir Corporal Nim!
   Believe it, Page: he speaks sense.

[Exit]

Ford   *[Aside]*   I will be patient. I will find out this.

Nim   *[To Page]*   And this is true. I like not the humour of   115
   lying. He hath wronged me in some humours. I should have
   borne the humoured letter to her, but I have a sword and it
   shall bite upon my necessity. He loves your wife. There's the
   short and the long. My name is Corporal Nim. I speak and I
   avouch. 'Tis true. My name is Nim, and Falstaff loves your   120
   wife. Adieu. I love not the humour of bread and cheese.
   Adieu.

97. curtal dog 「尻尾を短く切った犬」ピストルの比喩の意味は不明。不自然なことの喩えか。

100-113. ピストルはよく韻文を語るが、韻律は不規則なことが多い。

101. one with another 「どれもこれも同じで見境なく」

102. gallimaufry 「いろいろなものの寄せ集め」

102. perpend 「よく考えて下さい」

105. Sir Actaeon アクタイオンは、ギリシャ・ローマ神話に登場する若者。森に狩りに出かけた際に、偶然ダイアナの水浴を目撃し、その罰として鹿に変身させられ、自らの猟犬に追われることになる。イングランドの騎士の敬称であるサーを前に付すことで、アクタイオンがイングランド人化する。寝取られ亭主の額には角が生えるというのは定番の嘲弄であり、鹿の角にかけて、寝取られ亭主になりそうなフォードをアクタイオンになぞらえてからかっている。

106. Ringwood 「猟犬リングウッド」リングウッドは猟犬の名前として人気があり、シェイクスピアと同時代の詩人アーサー・ゴールディング（Arthur Golding）も、オウィディウスの『変身物語』を英訳する際に、アクタイオンの猟犬の名前に用いている。

110. foot 「出歩く」

111. cuckoo-birds 「カッコウ鳥」カッコウは、自分の雛を別の鳥に育てさせることから、寝取られ亭主（cuckold）への嘲弄に用いられた。

113. speaks sense 「分別のあることを話す」

117. borne bear（持って行く、運ぶ）の過去分詞。

117-18. it shall bite upon my necessity 「必要があれば俺の剣が黙っちゃいない」my は虚辞で、それ自体に意味はない。ニムは、情事の使い走りという卑しい仕事はしないという、武人としての誇りを大仰な言葉で示している。

118-19. the short and the long 「事の次第」手っ取り早く説明する際の決まり文句（Tilley）。

121. I love not the humour of bread and cheese 「武士は食わねど高楊枝だ」気質を表す当時の流行語である humour はニムの口癖だが、粋がって使っているので、その意味が必ずしもはっきりしないことが多い。おそらく、humour of bread and cheese は、プライドを捨ててただ生きるためだけの仕事をすることを指していると思われる。

[Exit]

PAGE   The 'humour' of it, quoth 'a! Here's a fellow frights English out of his wits.

FORD   I will seek out Falstaff.   125

PAGE   I never heard such a drawling, affecting rogue.

FORD   If I do find it — well.

PAGE   I will not believe such a Cathayan, though the priest o'th'town commended him for a true man.

FORD   'Twas a good sensible fellow — well.   130

[Mistress Page and Mistress Ford come forward]

PAGE   How now, Meg?

MISTRESS PAGE   Whither go you, George? Hark you.

[They talk apart]

MISTRESS FORD   How now, sweet Frank, why art thou melancholy?

FPRD   I melancholy? I am not melancholy. Get you home, go.   135

MISTRESS FORD   Faith, thou hast some crotchets in thy head now. — Will you go, Mistresss Page?

MISTRESS PAGE   Have with you. — You'll come to dinner, George?

[Enter Mistress Quickly]

[Aside to Mistress Ford]   Look who comes yonder. She shall be   140
our messenger to this paltry knight.

MISTRESS FORD   *[Aside to Mistress Page]*   Trust me, I thought on her. She'll fit it.

MISTRESS PAGE   You are come to see my daughter Anne?

MISTRESS QUICKLY   Ay, forsooth, and I pray how does good   145
Mistress Anne?

MISTRESS PAGE   Go in with us and see. We have an hour's talk with you.

123. The 'humour' of it　直前のニムの台詞の humour of bread and cheese を指す。ペイジは、ニムが多用する「気質、性」（humour）に反応している。

123. quoth = said で、主語の前に置かれる。

123. 'a = he

123-24. frights English out of his wits　「英語をびっくり仰天させる」fright = frighten で、frights の前に関係代名詞の who を補う。frighten *a person* out of *a person's* wits は「人をびっくりさせる、仰天させる」の意。

125. seek out　「調べる」

126. drawling　「まどろっこしい」ニムの話し方への言及。

126. affecting　「気取った口調の」

128. a Cathayan　「カタイ人みたいな奴」カタイ（Cathay）は中国を指す古語。マルコ・ポーロの『東方見聞録』をはじめ、カタイにまつわる話は空想に基づく部分が多く、ファンタジー的な要素が強かったことから、ここでは信用できない人間といった意味で用いられている。引き続き、ペイジはニムについて話している。一方、フォードはピストルのことを考えている。2人の反応の違いに注意。

136. crotchets　「ばかげた考え」

137. Will you go ...?　「私たちといっしょにいらっしゃらない？」

138. Have with you = I'll come with you「行きましょう」

138. dinner　「昼食」dinner は正式な食事を意味し、夕食に限定されない。ここでは午餐を指す。

141. paltry　「卑劣な」

147-48. We have an hour's talk with you　慣用表現で「私たちあなたに少しばかりお話があるの」

[*Exeunt Mistress Page, Mistress Ford, and Mistress Quickly*]

PAGE   How now, Master Ford?

FORD   You heard what this knave told me, did you not?   150

PAGE   Yes, and you heard what the other told me?

FORD   Do you think there is truth in them?

PAGE   Hang 'em, slaves! I do not think the knight would offer
it. But these that accuse him in his intent towards our wives
are a yoke of his discarded men: very rogues, now they be out   155
of service.

FORD   Were they his men?

PAGE   Marry, were they.

FORD   I like it never the better for that. Does he lie at the
Garter?   160

PAGE   Ay, marry does he. If he should intend this voyage
toward my wife, I would turn her loose to him, and what he
gets more of her than sharp words, let it lie on my head.

FORD   I do not misdoubt my wife, but I would be loath to turn
them together. A man may be too confident. I would have   165
nothing lie on my head. I cannot be thus satisfied.

[*Enter Host, followed by Shallow*]

PAGE   Look where my ranting host of the Garter comes. There
is either liquor in his pate or money in his purse when he
looks so merrily. How now, mine host?

HOST   How now, bully rook? [*To Shallow*] Thou'rt a gentleman.   170
Cavaliero Justice, I say!

SALLOW   I follow, mine host, I follow. — Good even and
twenty, good Master Page. Master Page, will you go with us?
We have sport in hand.

HOST   Tell him, Cavaliero Justice, tell him, bully rook.   175

SHALLOW   Sir, there is a fray to be fought, between Sir Hugh
the Welsh priest and Caius the French doctor.

153. Hang 'em = Hang them 「まさか！」Hang は軽いののしりに用いる強意表現。

153. offer 「企てる」

155. a yoke of = a pair of

159. lie 「逗留する」

163. let it lie on my head 「それは俺の頭に生えさせるさ（＝それは俺の責任だ）」構文上では it は直前の what he gets more of her than sharp words（フォルスタッフがペイジ夫人から受け取るきつい言葉以上の何かよいこと）を指すが、同時に it には寝取られ亭主の頭に生える角も含意されている。寝取られ亭主をめぐる軽口については 105 行目注参照。

165. A man may be too confident 「男というものはとかく自信を持ちすぎる傾向がある」密告を聞いても余裕の態度を見せるペイジに対する台詞。

167. ranting 「威勢の良い」my は、聞き手の関心をひくために挿入された修辞的虚辞で、「ほら！」という程度の意味。

168. pate 「頭」

170. bully rook 「相棒」1.3.2 注参照。

171. Cavaliero 「粋な伊達男」cavalier（騎士）をスペイン語風に発音した語。スペイン語では cavallero。ガーター亭の主人は同種の語をフォルスタッフに対しても用いる。後出の 185 行目注参照。

172-73. Good even and twenty 「こんにちは、みなさん」even = evening だが、午後の挨拶として用いられた。

174. sport 「お楽しみ」

Ford   Good mine host o'th'Garter, a word with you.

Host   What sayst thou, my bully rook?

[They talk apart]

Shallow   *[To Page]*   Will you go with us to behold it? My   180
merry host hath had the measuring of their weapons, and, I
think, hath appointed them contrary places, for, believe me, I
hear the parson is no jester. Hark, I will tell you what our
sport shall be.

[They talk apart]

Host   Hast thou no suit against my knight, my guest cavalier?   185

Ford   None, I protest. But I'll give you a pottle of burnt sack
to give me recourse to him, and tell him my name is Brook,
only for a jest.

Host   My hand, bully. Thou shalt have egress and regress —
said I well? — and thy name shall be Brook. It is a merry   190
knight. — Will you go, mynheers?

Shallow   Have with you, mine host.

Page   I have heard the Frenchman hath good skill in his
rapier.

Shallow   Tut, sir, I could haue told you more. In these times   195
you stand on distance, your passes, stoccadoes, and I know
not what. 'Tis the heart, Master Page, 'tis here, 'tis here. I
have seen the time with my long sword, I would have made
you four tall fellows skip like rats.

Host   Here, boys, here, here! Shall we wag?   200

Page   Have with you. I had rather hear them scold than fight.

[Exeunt Page, Host, and Shallow]

Ford   Though Page be a secure fool and stands so firmly on
his wife's frailty, yet I cannot put off my opinion so easily.
She was in his company at Page's house, and what they made
there, I know not. Well, I will look further into't, and I have   205

178. a word with you = I want a word with you「ちょっと話がある」

179. bully rook　「相棒」1. 3. 2 注参照。ガーター亭の亭主がよく使う語。

181. hath had the measuring of their weapons　「立会人を務めることになった」1. 4. 109 注参照。

182. contrary　「異なる」

183. the parson is no jester　「あの牧師（エヴァンズ）は本気だ」jester は、ここではふざける人といった程度の意味。

184. sport　「娯楽、楽しみ」

185. guest cavalier　「騎士の客人」フォルスタッフを指す。

186. I protest　「断言する」

186. a pottle of burnt sack　「あたたかいサック酒を一瓶」pottle は半ガロン（4 パイントに相当）サイズの酒器、burnt sack はサックワイン（シェリー酒の一種）を温めて、砂糖やスパイスを加えたもの。サック酒については、7 行目注参照。

187. Brook　フォードが用いる偽名　⇒後注

189. My hand　「了解だ」You have my hand（承知する）の省略。

189. egress and regress　「出入り自由」egress（出入権）も regress（復帰権）も法律用語。亭主はふざけて 2 つを並べて、自由に出入りする権利を与えている。

191. mynheers　「皆さん」オランダ語で gentlemen の意。

196. stand on ...　「…を重視する」

196. distance / passes / stoccadoes　それぞれ順に「決闘者がとる距離」「（前足を突き出して行う）突き」「急な突き」を意味する剣術用語。

197-98. I have seen the time with my long sword　「かつては長剣で評判をとったこともある」重量のある長剣は時代遅れとなった。

199. you　聞き手の関心をひくために挿入された虚辞で、特に意味はない。

200. wag　「行く」

201. Have with you = I'll come with you「一緒に行きましょう」

202. secure　「自信過剰な」

202-03. stands so firmly on his wife's frailty　「女房の道徳的な脆さをえらく自信ありげに評価している」stand on については、196 行目の注参照。

204-05. what they made there　「そこで 2 人が何をしていたのか」

a disguise to sound Falstaff. If I find her honest, I lose not my labour. If she be otherwise, 'tis labour well bestowed.

Exit

[ACT II, SCENE II]

Enter Falstaff [and] Pistol

FALSTAFF   I will not lend thee a penny.

PISTOL   Why then, the world's mine oyster, which I with sword will open.

FALSTAFF   Not a penny. I have been content, sir, you should lay my countenance to pawn. I have grated upon my good friends   5
for three reprieves for you and your coach-fellow Nim, or else you had looked through the grate like a gemini of baboons. I am damned in hell for swearing to gentlemen my friends you were good soldiers and tall fellows. And when Mistress Bridget lost the handle of her fan, I took't upon mine honour   10
thou hadst it not.

PISTOL   Didst not thou share? Hadst thou not fifteen pence?

FALSTAFF   Reason, you rogue, reason. Think'st thou I'll endanger my soul gratis? At a word, hang no more about me. I am no gibbet for you. Go, a short knife and a throng, to   15
your manor of Pickt-hatch, go! You'll not bear a letter for me, you rogue? You stand upon your honour? Why, thou unconfinable baseness, it is as much as I can do to keep the terms of my honour precise. Ay, ay, I myself sometimes, leaving the fear of God on the left hand, and hiding mine   20
honour in my necessity, am fain to shuffle, to hedge, and to lurch; and yet, you, rogue, will ensconce your rags, your cat-a-mountain-looks, your red-lattice phrases, and your bold beating oaths, under the shelter of your honour! You will not do it, you?   25

PISTOL   I do relent. What would thou more of man?

206. sound 「調べる」

206. honest 「貞淑な」

206. lose 「無駄にする」

207. well bestowed 「十分に報われた」

〔2. 2〕あらすじ……………………………………………………………………

　ガーター亭のフォルスタッフのもとにクウィックリーがやってきて、フォード夫人とペイジ夫人からの伝言を伝える。フォルスタッフが悦に入っていると、ブルックに変装したフォードがやってきて、フォード夫人への片思いを告白した上で、フォルスタッフに夫人を誘惑するようにけしかける。

……………………………………………………………………………………………

4-5. lay ... pawn 「俺の家臣であることを担保にして借金する」countenance は「支援、引き立てること」、pawn は「質（に入れること）」を意味する。

5. grated upon 「無理を言って困らせた、泣きついた」

6. coach-fellow 「相棒」ピストルとニムを馬車（coach）を引く 2 頭の馬に喩えている。

7. grate 「鉄格子」

7. gemini 「双子」

9. tall 「勇敢な」

10. handle of her fan　貴婦人の扇子の柄は、銀細工など高価な材質だった。

10. took't upon mine honour 「俺の名誉にかけて誓った」

13. Reason 「当然だ」reason = with reason

14. gratis　ラテン語で for nothing in return の意。「何の見返りもなしに」

15. a short knife and a throng 「人混みの中ですりでもしながら」金の入った巾着を切るのに使われた short knife は「すり」の隠語。

16. your manor of Pickt-hatch 「お前の領地のロンドンの下町」忍び返しを施した格子窓を意味する pickt-hatch（＝ piked hatch）は、売春宿が並ぶ界隈を指す隠語だった可能性がある。manor は貴族の領地の意だが、ここでは皮肉で用いられている。

17. stand upon 「大事にする」

18. unconfinable 「計り知れない」

21. am fain to ... 「喜んで…する」

21-22. shuffle / hedge / lurch　順に「だます」「嘘をつく」「盗む」

22. ensconce 「（何かの威を借りて）隠す」

22-23. cat-a-mountain-looks 「野良猫のような面」

23. red-lattice 「飲み屋」red-lattice（赤い格子窓）の居酒屋が多かった。

24. beating oaths 「口汚いののしり言葉」

26. What ... man? 「これ（＝降参すること）以上何を望むというんだ」

[Enter Robin]

ROBIN   Sir, here's a woman would speak with you.

FALSTAFF   Let her approach.

[Enter Mistress Quickly]

MISTRESS QUICKLY   Give your worship good morrow.

FALSTAFF   Good morrow, good wife.   30

MISTRESS QUICKLY   Not so, an't please your worship.

FALSTAFF   Good maid, then.

MISTRESS QUICKLY   I'll be sworn, as my mother was the first
  hour I was born.

FALSTAFF   I do believe the swearer. What with me?   35

MISTRESS QUICKLY   Shall I vouchsafe your worship a word or
  two?

FALSTAFF   Two thousand, fair woman, and I'll vouchsafe thee
  the hearing.

MISTRESS QUICKLY   There is one Mistress Ford, sir — I pray   40
  come a little nearer this ways. I myself dwell with Master
  Doctor Caius.

FALSTAFF   Well, on. Mistress Ford, you say —

MISTRESS QUICKLY   Your worship says very true. I pray your
  worship come a little nearer this ways.   45

FALSTAFF   I warrant thee nobody hears — *[indicating Pistol and
  Robin]* mine own people, mine own people.

MISTRESS QUICKLY   Are they so? God bless them, and make
  them his servants!

FALSTAFF   Well, Mistress Ford — what of her?   50

MISTRESS QUICKLY   Why, sir, she's a good creature. Lord,
  Lord, your worship's a wanton! Well, heaven forgive you, and
  all of us, I pray.

FALSTAFF   Mistress Ford, come, Mistress Ford.

MISTRESS QUICKLY   Marry, this is the short and the long of it: 55

31. an't = if it

33-34. I'll be sworn, as my mother was the first hour I was born. 「私を産ん
だ時の母と同様、私は生娘ですとも」生娘（処女）は出産しないので、論理的
にはおかしい。陽気なクウィックリーの軽口。

35. What with me? = What do you want with me?「俺に何か用か」

38-39. I'll vouchsafe thee the hearing. 「聞いてしんぜよう」vouchsafe は
「与える」の意。クウィックリーに合わせて、過度に丁寧な言葉を使っている。

41. this ways = this way「こちらに」

43. on = go on「続けろ」

48. God bless them, and make them his servants! 「（ピストルとニムに）神の
ご加護がありますように、神の僕となれますように！」his は God を指す。

52. wanton 「色男」

54. come 「さあさあ、ほら」クウィックリーに話を続けるように促している。

55. the short and the long 「事の次第」手っ取り早く説明する際の決まり文句
（Tilley）。

you have brought her into such a canaries, as 'tis wonderful.
The best courtier of them all, when the court lay at Windsor,
could never have brought her to such a canary. Yet there has
been knights, and lords, and gentlemen, with their coaches; I
warrant you, coach after coach, letter after letter, gift after   60
gift, smelling so sweetly, all musk, and so rushling, I warrant
you, in silk and gold, and in such alligant terms, and in such
wine and sugar of the best and the fairest, that would have
won any woman's heart; and, I warrant you, they could never
get an eye-wink of her. I had myself twenty angels given me   65
this morning, but I defy all angels in any such sort, as they
say, but in the way of honesty. And, I warrant you, they could
never get her so much as sip on a cup with the proudest of
them all, and yet there has been earls, nay, which is more,
pensioners, but, I warrant you, all is one with her.   70

FALSTAFF   But what says she to me? Be brief, my good she-
Mercury.

MISTRESS QUICKLY   Marry, she hath received your letter, for
the which she thanks you a thousand times, and she gives you
to notify, that her husband will be absence from his house   75
between ten and eleven.

FALSTAFF   Ten and eleven.

MISTRESS QUICKLY   Ay, forsooth; and then you may come and
see the picture, she says, that you wot of. Master Ford, her
husband, will be from home. Alas, the sweet woman leads an   80
ill life with him: he's a very jealousy man. She leads a very
frampold life with him, good heart.

FALSTAFF   Ten and eleven. Woman, commend me to her. I will
not fail her.

MISTRESS QUICKLY   Why, you say well. But I have another   85
messenger to your worship. Mistress Page hath her hearty
commendations to you too; and let me tell you in your ear,
she's as fartuous a civil modest wife, and one, I tell you, that

56. canaries 「困った事態」クウィックリーは同じ語をこの台詞で連発するが、quandary（窮地）と言うべきところを、発音が似ている canary（スペイン産の白ワイン）と言い間違えていると思われる。マラプロピズムの例。マラプロピズムについては、1. 1. 216 注参照。

57. the court lay at Windsor 「宮廷人の一行がウィンザー城に滞在した」 ⇒ 後注。

61. musk 「ムスクの香り」ムスクはジャコウジカの分泌物で、香水の材料に用いられる。官能的で甘い香りに特徴がある。

61. rushling クウィックリー特有の古風な言い回しで「さらさらと音がする」。高価な衣装が動くたびに立てる衣ずれの音か。

62. in such alligant terms 「とても優雅な言葉で」elegant（優雅な）と言うべきところを、発音が似ている Alicante（スペインのアリカンテ産の白ワインで 16 世紀は Allegant とも言われた）とまじったことばに間違えている。56 行目と同じくマラプロピズムの例。

62-63. in such ... the fairest 「最高級で最高品質のワインと砂糖といった具合で」

65. eye-wink 「流し目」wink が現代のウィンク、すなわち、合図のために片目をまばたきする動作を指すようになるのは 19 世紀以降のことなので、ここではおそらく誘うような一瞥^{いちべつ}を表す。

66. defy 「（受け取りを）拒否する」

66. angels 「エンジェル金貨」1. 3. 45 注参照。

66. in any such sort 「そんなやり方では」sort = manner

70. pensioners 「終身年金者」何らかの功績により王室から年金を受けることは名誉なことではあったが、伯爵以上の身分であるかのように言うのはクウィックリーの勘違い。

70. all is one with her 「彼女にとっては全て同じこと」

71-72. she-Mercury 「伝令の女神」マーキュリーはローマ神話に登場する伝令役の神。ギリシャ神話ではヘルメスと呼ばれる。she- を付すと、その女性版の意。

74-75. gives you to notify 「あなたに知らせる」

75. absence = absent　エヴァンズと同様、クウィックリーの台詞でも、方言の一形態として、文法とは異なる用法がしばしば見られる。

79. wot 「知っている」

81. jealousy = jealous

82. frampold 「不愉快な」

82. good heart 「かわいそうな人」共感や同情を示す際に発した言葉。

88. fartuous 正しくは virtuous「身持ちのよい」と言うべきところを fatuous（愚かな）あるいは fart（屁）と混同して言い間違えている。マラプロピズムの例。

88. civil 「礼儀正しい」

will not miss you morning nor evening prayer, as any is in
Windsor, whoe're be the other. And she bade me tell your 90
worship that her husband is seldom from home, but she
hopes there will come a time. I never knew a woman so dote
upon a man. Surely I think you have charms, la! Yes, in truth.

FALSTAFF Not I, I assure thee. Setting the attraction of my
good parts aside, I have no other charms. 95

MISTRESS QUICKLY Blessing on your heart for't!

FALSTAFF But I pray thee tell me this: has Ford's wife and
Page's wife acquainted each other how they love me?

MISTRESS QUICKLY That were a jest indeed! They have not so
little grace, I hope. That were a trick indeed! But Mistress 100
Page would desire you to send her your little page, of all
loves. Her husband has a marvellous infection to the little
page, and truly Master Page is an honest man. Never a wife
in Windsor leads a better life than she does. Do what she will,
say what she will, take all, pay all, go to bed when she list, rise 105
when she list, all is as she will. And truly she deserves it; for
if there be a kind woman in Windsor, she is one. You must
send her your page, no remedy.

FALSTAFF Why, I will.

MISTRESS QUICKLY Nay, but do so, then; and, look you, he 110
may come and go between you both. And in any case have a
nay-word, that you may know one another's mind, and the
boy never need to understand anything, for 'tis not good that
children should know any wickedness. Old folks, you know,
have discretion, as they say, and know the world. 115

FALSTAFF Fare thee well; commend me to them both. There's
my purse: I am yet thy debtor. — Boy, go along with this
woman.

[Exeunt Mistress Quickly and Robin]

This news distracts me.

PISTOL This punk is one of Cupid's carriers. 120

89. will ... prayer 「朝の祈りも夕の祈りも怠ることはない」you は、「ほら」と相手に何かを強調するために挿入される与格代名詞。

90. whoe'er be the other 「誰であろうと」the other は前行の any を指す。

93. charms 「魔力」

95. good parts 内面的か、身体的か、いずれを指すのかは不明だが「魅力的なところ」

96. Blessing on your heart for't! 「それはまたなんて素晴らしい！」for't ＝ for it で、it はフォルスタッフの直前の台詞を指す。(God's) Blessing on your heart は神の加護を祈る表現。

99. That were a jest indeed! 「まさか、ご冗談を！」驚きを表す慣用表現。were は仮定法で、would be と同じ。

99-100. They have not so little grace 「あの方達はそんな下品ではありません」grace は品性を表す。not little は「実に多くの」を意味するが、間に so が挿入されているので、上記のように訳出した。

100. trick 「冗談」前行の jest と同じ意味。

101. page 「小姓」身の回りの世話をする使用人で、通常は少年が務める。

101-02. of all loves 「お願いですから」必死で頼み事をする時の決まり文句。

102. has a marvellous infection to ... 「…が大好きなのです」affection（愛情）と言うべきところを infection（感染）と言い間違えている。マラプロピズムの例。マラプロピズムについては、1. 1. 216 注参照。

105. take 「支払う」

105. list 「好む」

108. no remedy 「それに限りますとも」それ以外に方法はない、という意味の慣用表現。

112. nay-word 「合い言葉」

115. discretion 「認識力」

116-17. There's my purse 「この金をどうぞ」purse は財布だけではなく、金も意味した。フォルスタッフがクウィックリーに礼金を払う理由は、コロン以下の部分で説明されている。

117. I am yet thy debtor 「あなたには今後世話になる」debtor（負債者）は比喩として用いられている。

119. distracts 「気持ちを混乱させる」

120. punk 「売春婦」フォルスタッフと夫人達の間で取り持ち役をしているクウィックリーが売春宿（の女将）になぞらえられている。

120. carriers 「使者」

Clap on more sails! Pursue! Up with your fights!
Give fire! She is my prize, or ocean whelm them all!   [*Exit*]

FALSTAFF   Sayst thou so, old Jack? Go thy ways. I'll make
more of thy old body than I have done. Will they yet look
after thee? Wilt thou, after the expense of so much money, be   125
now a gainer? Good body, I thank thee. Let them say 'tis
grossly done; so it be fairly done, no matter.

[*Enter Bardolph with sack*]

BARDOLPH   Sir John, there's one Master Brook below would
fain speak with you, and be acquainted with you, and hath
sent your worship a morning's draught of sack.   130

FALSTAFF   Brook is his name?

BARDOLPH   Ay, sir.

FALSTAFF   Call him in.

[*Exit Bardolph*]

Such brooks are welcome to me, that o'erflows such liquor.
Aha! Mistress Ford and Mistress Page, have I encompassed   135
you? Go to, *via!*

[*Enter Bardolph, with Ford disguised as Brook*]

FORD   God bless you, sir.

FALSTAFF   And you, sir. Would you speak with me?

FORD   I make bold to press with so little preparation upon
you.   140

FALSTAFF   You're welcome. What's your will? — Give us leave,
drawer.   [*Exit Bardolph*]

FORD   Sir, I am a gentleman that have spent much. My name
is Brook.

FALSTAFF   Good Master Brook, I desire more acquaintance of   145
you.

FORD   Good Sir John, I sue for yours: not to charge you, for I
must let you understand I think myself in better plight for a

121. Clap on 「（帆を）張る」以下、軍隊用語、特に海戦関連の用語が続く。

121. Up with your fights! 「防壁幕を上げろ！」fight は、戦艦で兵士を守るための盾として用いられた防御用の帆。

122. Give fire! 「砲撃せよ！」

122. prize 「戦利品」

122. whelm 「呑み込む」

123. Sayst thou so, old Jack? 「おいおいお前さん、こういうことなのか？」Jack は John の愛称。フォルスタッフは自分に呼びかけている。Sayst thou ＝ you say で、so は次の Go thy ways を指す。

123-24. make more of ... 「…をもっと評価する」

127. grossly 「ぶざまなやり方で」it は今後行おうとしていることを指すと同時に、前行で言及している自分の身体も指している。後者の場合は、grossly は巨体であることを意味する。

127. fairly 「きちんと、申し分なく」

129. fain ... 「…したがっている」

130. draught 「一杯」酒に用いる。

134. o'erflows ＝ overflows with

135. encompassed 「手中に収めた」

136. Go to, _via_! 「さあ、行け！」via は、例えば乗り手が馬に対して、あるいは戦場で上官が兵士に対して、発破をかける際に用いられたイタリア語。

139-40. make bold to press with so little preparation upon you 「大胆にも突然に訪問する」make bold ... で「大胆にも…する」、preparation は事前の準備、すなわち事前の連絡を指す。

141. What's your will? 「ご用件は？」

141. Give us leave 「二人きりにしてくれ」leave は名詞で「許し、許可」の意。人払いをする時の決まり文句。

142. drawer 「給仕人」

147. sue for yours 「こちらこそ（あなた様とお近づきになりたい）」sue for は「求める」の意。yours は your acquaintance を意味する。

148-49. plight for a lender 「経済状況」直訳すると「金貸し（lender）から見た状況（plight）」となる。

lender than you are, the which hath something emboldened
me to this unseasoned intrusion; for they say, if money go   150
before, all ways do lie open.

FALSTAFF   Money is a good soldier, sir, and will on.

FORD   Troth, and I have a bag of money here troubles me.
[*He sets it down*]   If you will help to bear it, Sir John, take
half, or all, for easing me of the carriage.   155

FALSTAFF   Sir, I know not how I may deserve to be your porter.

FORD   I will tell you, sir, if you will give me the hearing.

FALSTAFF   Speak, good Master Brook. I shall be glad to be
your servant.

FORD   Sir, I hear you are a scholar — I will be brief with you   160
— and you have been a man long known to me, though I had
never so good means as desire to make myself acquainted
with you. I shall discover a thing to you, wherein I must very
much lay open mine own imperfection. But, good Sir John,
as you have one eye upon my follies as you hear them   165
unfolded, turn another into the register of your own, that I
may pass with a reproof the easier, sith you yourself know
how easy it is to be such an offender.

FALSTAFF   Very well, sir. Proceed.

FORD   There is a gentlewoman in this town: her husband's   170
name is Ford.

FALSTAFF   Well, sir.

FORD   I have long loved her, and, I protest to you, bestowed
much on her, followed her with a doting observance,
engrossed opportunities to meet her, fee'd every slight   175
occasion that could but niggardly give me sight of her, not
only bought many presents to give her, but have given largely
to many to know what she would have given. Briefly, I have
pursued her as love hath pursued me, which hath been on the
wing of all occasions. But whatsoever I have merited, either   180
in my mind or in my means, meed I am sure I have received

150. unseasoned intrusion 「突然の訪問」season は、味付けを施すという意味もあるが、ここでは折り合いをつけるといった意味を表す。unseasoned は、今回の訪問が突然で、事前に調整されていなかったことを意味する。

152. will on = will go on 「突き進む」主語は同じ行の money。

154. bear 「持つ」

155. easing me of the carriage 「私をこの重荷から解放してくれること」重荷 (carriage) は金を指す。

160. scholar 「学識のある人」

162. means 「機会」

164. lay open 「露呈する」

166. register 「一覧にした記録」

167. sith = since 「～なので」

168. offender 「罪人」

173. protest 「断言する」

174. a doting observance 「夢中になって付き従うこと」

175. engrossed 「かき集めた」engross は「かき集める、独占する」の意で、*OED* II.4.b にこの箇所が用例として引証されている。

175. fee'd 「金を払ってでも利用した」fee（料金を支払って雇う）の過去形。

177. largely 「惜しみなくたっぷりと」

178. what she would have given = what she would like to be given 「彼女が欲しがっているもの」

180. whatsoever I have merited 「どんな功徳を積もうが」merit は神の恩寵に与れるように振る舞うことを意味する。whatsoever は whatever の強意形。

181. means 「財力」

none, unless experience be a jewel, that I have purchased at
an infinite rate, and that hath taught me to say this:

    'Love like a shadow flies when substance Love pursues,

    Pursuing that that flies, and flying what pursues.'   185

FALSTAFF   Have you received no promise of satisfaction at her
hands?

FORD   Never.

FALSTAFF   Have you importuned her to such a purpose?

FORD   Never.   190

FALSTAFF   Of what quality was your love, then?

FORD   Like a fair house built on another man's ground, so that
I have lost my edifice by mistaking the place where I erected
it.

FALSTAFF   To what purpose have you unfolded this to me?   195

FORD   When I have told you that, I have told you all. Some say
that though she appear honest to me, yet in other places she
enlargeth her mirth so far that there is shrewd construction
made of her. Now, Sir John, here is the heart of my purpose.
You are a gentleman of excellent breeding, admirable   200
discourse, of great admittance, authentic in your place and
person, generally allowed for your many warlike, courtlike,
and learned preparations.

FALSTAFF   O, sir!

FORD   Believe it, for you know it. [*Pointing to the bag*] There is   205
money. Spend it, spend it, spend more, spend all I have. Only
give me so much of your time in exchange of it as to lay an
amiable siege to the honesty of this Ford's wife. Use your art
of wooing, win her to consent to you. If any man may, you
may as soon as any.   210

FALSTAFF   Would it apply well to the vehemency of your
affection that I should win what you would enjoy? Methinks
you prescribe to yourself very preposterously.

FORD   O, understand my drift. She dwells so securely on the

183. infinite rate 「途方もない料金」

184. flies 「逃げる」

184. substance 「金」substance（実体）と shadow（影）の洒落にもなっている。

189. Have you importuned her to such a purpose? 「そんな結果になるぐらい、彼女にしつこく迫ったのでは」そんな結果（such a purpose）は、フォード扮するブルックが直前の台詞で語っているフォード夫人のつれない態度を指す。

191. quality 「本質」

197. appear honest 「身持ちが堅い（夫以外の男性にはなびかない）様子を見せる」

198. shrewd construction 「よくない噂」construction は解釈を意味する。shrewd は、噂や評判を形容する際には「批判的な」の意で用いられた（*OED* 3.b）。

201. of great admittance 「偉い方々の家に出入りを許されている」

201-02. authentic in your place and person 「身分においても人柄においても立派な」

202. generally allowed for ... 「…のことで世間に認められている」

203. preparations 「功績」

208. amiable siege 「恋の包囲攻撃」siege は軍隊用語。

208. honesty 「貞節の美徳」honesty のジェンダー化された用法については 1. 3. 41-42 注を参照。

209-10. If any man may, you may as soon as any. 「もし誰かが彼女をものにできるとすれば、それはあなたですとも」may の後に win her を補って読む。

211. apply well 「合致している、適っている」主語の it は that 以下を指す。

213. prescribe to yourself very preposterously 「見当違いの薬を自分に処方する」preposterously は「本末転倒に」の意。片思いを病に喩えるのは定番の比喩。

214. drift 「目的」

214. dwells so securely on ... 「…を理由に自信満々に構えている」

excellency of her honour that the folly of my soul dares not   215
present itself. She is too bright to be looked against. Now,
could I come to her with any detection in my hand, my
desires had instance and argument to commend themselves. I
could drive her then from the ward of her purity, her
reputation, her marriage vow, and a thousand other her   220
defences, which now are too too strongly embattled against
me. What say you to't, Sir John?

FALSTAFF   Master Brook, I will first make bold with your
money. [*He takes the bag*] Next, give me your hand. And last,
as I am a gentleman, you shall, if you will, enioy Ford's wife.   225

FORD   O good sir!

FALSTAFF   I say you shall.

FORD   Want no money, Sir John; you shall want none.

FALSTAFF   Want no Mistresse Ford, Master Brook; you shall
want none. I shall be with her, I may tell you, by her own   230
appointment. Even as you came in to me, her assistant or go-
between parted from me. I say I shall be with her between ten
and eleven, for at that time the jealous rascally knave her
husband will be forth. Come you to me at night: you shall
know how I speed.   235

FORD   I am blest in your acquaintance. Do you know Ford,
sir?

FALSTAFF   Hang him, poor cuckoldly knave! I know him not.
Yet I wrong him to call him poor. They say the jealous
wittolly knave hath masses of money, for the which his wife   240
seems to me well-favoured. I will use her as the key of the
cuckoldly rogue's coffer, and there's my harvest-home.

FORD   I would you knew Ford, sir, that you might avoid him if
you saw him.

FALSTAFF   Hang him, mechanical salt-butter rogue! I will stare   245
him out of his wits. I will awe him with my cudgel. It shall
hang like a meteor o'er the cuckold's horns. Master Brook,

216. She is too bright to be looked against. 「彼女は眩しすぎて直視できない」

217. could I ... = If I could ...　仮定法。

217. detection 「弱み」

218. instance 「前例」フォルスタッフがフォード夫人との情事に成功すれば、フォード夫人は貞淑ではないという前例を得られることを指す。

218. commend themselves 「自分の欲望を売り込む」themselves は my desires を指す。

219. ward of her purity 「自分は純潔であるという防御」同格を表す of。

220-21. other her defences = other of her defences「彼女の他の言い訳」

221. embattled 「(防備が) 張り巡らされている」求愛する自分とそれを拒む夫人の攻防が戦いの比喩で説明されている。

224. give me your hand 「握手をしましょう」

228. Want no money 「あなたが金に不自由することがないように致します」You shall を補う。shall は話者の意思を表す。

231-32. go-between 「取り持ち役」

234. be forth 「外出する」

235. speed 「成功する」

236. I am blest in your acquaintance. 「あなたと知り合えたのは天のお恵みです」

238. Hang him 「ちぇ、あんなやつ」軽いののしりの言葉。

239. I wrong him to call him poor 「哀れなと言っては失礼だな」wrong は動詞で「〜に悪いことをする」

240. wittolly 「寝取られ亭主の」wittol (寝取られ亭主) に -ly が付され、形容詞として用いられている。

241. well-favoured 「魅力的」

242. coffer 「金庫」

245. mechanical salt-butter rogue 「しょっぱいバターのようにさもしい奴」フォルスタッフ流の悪口。フランダース地方から輸入される塩気のあるバターは、国産バターよりも安く、風味が劣ると考えられていた。mechanical は、手仕事で生計を立てる人々に対する蔑視的表現。

245-46. stare him out of his wits 「正気をなくすぐらいにらみつけてやる」

246. awe 「畏れさせる」

246. cudgel 「こん棒」

247. meteor 「彗星」不吉な前兆と考えられた。

247. cuckold's horns 「寝取られ亭主の角」2. 1. 105 注参照。

thou shalt know, I will predominate over the peasant, and
thou shalt lie with his wife. Come to me soon at night. Ford's
a knave, and I will aggravate his style. Thou, Master Brook,   250
shalt know him for knave and cuckold. Come to me soon at
night.   [*Exit*]

FORD What a damned epicurian rascal is this! My heart is
ready to crack with impatience. Who says this is improvident
jealousy? My wife hath sent to him, the hour is fixed, the   255
match is made. Would any man have thought this? See the
hell of having a false woman! My bed shall be abused, my
coffers ransacked, my reputation gnawn at, and I shall not
only receive this villainous wrong, but stand under the
adoption of abominable terms, and by him that does me this   260
wrong. Terms! Names! Amaimon sounds well; Lucifer, well;
Barbason, well; yet they are devils' additions, the names of
fiends. But cuckold? Wittol? — Cuckold! the devil himself
hath not such a name. Page is an ass, a secure ass. He will
trust his wife, he will not be jealous. I will rather trust a   265
Fleming with my butter, Parson Hugh the Welshman with
my cheese, an Irish-man with my aquavitae bottle, or a thief
to walk my ambling gelding, than my wife with herself. Then
she plots, then she ruminates, then she devises. And what
they think in their hearts they may effect, they will break   270
their hearts but they will effect. God be praised for my
jealousy! Eleven o'clock the hour: I will prevent this, detect
my wife, be revenged on Falstaff, and laugh at Page. I will
about it. Better three hours too soon than a minute too late.
Fie, fie, fie! Cuckold, cuckold, cuckold!   275

Exit

248. predominate 「圧倒する」

248. peasant 「田舎者」

249. Ford's = Ford is

250. aggravate his style 「もっとひどい呼び名にしてやろう」style は呼び名 (title) の意。ここでは、「ごろつき (knave)」の上に「寝取られ亭主」とい う不名誉な呼び名が追加されることが仄（ほの）めかされている。

253. epicurian 「ふしだらな」

254. improvident 「軽率な」

255-56. the match is made 「密会が予定されている」

259-60. stand under the adoption of abominable terms 「悪口雑言の標的に なる」terms は言葉を意味し、adoption は自分に様々な酷い呼び名がつけら れることを指す。

261-62. Amaimon / Lucifer / Barbason 「アマーモン」「ルシファー」「バーバ ソン」は、いずれも悪魔の名。

262. additions 「呼び名」

263. Wittol 「寝取られ亭主」ただし、wittol は妻の不貞を黙認する夫で、妻の 不貞に気づかない cuckold とは厳密には区別される。

264. secure 「暢気（のんき）な」

264. ass 「馬鹿」

265-66. trust a Fleming with my butter 「フランダース人に自分のバターを預 ける」バターに目がないフランダース人にバターを預けることが、不用心な行 動の比喩になっている。以下の文章も同様で、trust A with B（A に B を 託 す）の文型で、それぞれの好物が列挙されている。

267. aquavitae 「ウイスキー」

267-68. a thief to walk my ambling gelding 「泥棒に御しやすい馬の散歩を任 せる」この文章は trust A to B（A を信用して B を委ねる）の文型。 ambling は馬のゆっくりした歩き方（アンブル）を指す。

270. effect 「実行する」動詞で用いられている。

274. about = set about「取りかかる、やってみる」

274. Better three hours too soon than a minute too late. 直訳すると「1分遅 れるよりも、3時間早すぎるほうがよい」という諺。日本語なら「先手必勝」 の意に近い。

275. Fie, fie, fie! 「くそ、くそ、くそ！」強い怒りと嫌悪感を示す言葉。

[ACT II, SCENE III]

Enter Caius [and] Rugby

CAIUS   Jack Rugby!

RUGBY   Sir?

CAIUS   Vat is the clock, Jack?

RUGBY   'Tis past the hour, sir, that Sir Hugh promised to meet.

CAIUS   By gar, he has save his soul, dat he is no come. He has   5
pray his Pible well dat he is no come. By gar, Jack Rugby, he
is dead already, if he be come.

RUGBY   He is wise, sir. He knew your worship would kill him if
he came.

CAIUS   By gar, de herring is no dead so as I vill kill him. [*He*   10
draws his rapier] Take your rapier, Jack, I vill tell you how I vill
kill him.

RUGBY   Alas, sir, I cannot fence.

CAIUS   Villainy! Take your rapier.

RUGBY   Forbear. Here's company.   15

[Caius sheathes his rapier]
[Enter Page, Shallow, Slender, and Host]

HOST   God bless thee, bully doctor!

SHALLOW   God save you, Master Doctor Caius!

PAGE   Now, good Master Doctor!

SLENSER   Give you good morrow, sir.

CAIUS   Vat be all you, one, two, tree, four, come for?   20

HOST   To see thee fight, to see thee foin, to see thee traverse, to
see thee here, to see thee there, to see thy pass, thy punto, thy
stock, thy reverse, thy distance, thy montant. Is he dead, my
Ethiopian? Is he dead, my Francisco? Ha, bully? What says
my Aesculapius, my Galen, my heart of elder, ha? Is he dead,   25
bully stale? Is he dead?

CAIUS   By gar, he is de coward jack priest of de vorld. He is

あらすじ・・・

　キーズは、決闘相手のエヴァンズが現れず、怒っている。その様子をガーター亭の亭主、ペイジ、シャロー、スレンダーの一行は面白がっている。ガーター亭の亭主は、ペイジ達をエヴァンズが待つフロッグモアへと行かせ、自分はキーズを伴い別ルートで同じ場所に向かう。

・・・

5. dat　キーズのフランス語訛りの英語では that を表し、ここでは仮定を示す if の意味。次行の dat も同じ用法。

6. Pible　Bible が訛って発音されている。

10. de herring is no dead so as I vill kill him.　完全に死んでいることを示す慣用表現 as dead as a herring を踏まえた台詞で、「私の手にかかれば、（まな板の）ニシン同様、完全に息の根を止めるのだが」となる。de は the が訛って発音されている。

11. vill　will が訛って発音されている。以下頻出。

14. Villainy　抽象名詞だが、キーズは「悪党（villain）」の意で用いている。

16. bully doctor!　「よう、お医者さん！」bully は親しみを表す呼びかけ。

21. foin　「突く」以下、剣術用語が続く。

21. traverse　「前後左右に動く」

22. pass　「突き」

22. punto　「剣先による突き」thy pass と同じ意味。

22-23. thy stock　「突き」

23. thy reverse　「バックハンドでの突き」

23. distance　「構えの姿勢」相手と少し距離をおく技。

23. montant　「上向きの正面突き」

24. Ethiopian　「エチオピア人」キーズの肌の色への揶揄か。『夏の夜の夢』にも、ハーミアが同様に罵られる場面がある。

24. Francisco　男性名ではなく、主人が勝手に作った語で「フランス人」の意。

25. Aesculapius　「アイスクラーピウス」古代ギリシャ・ローマ神話の医術の神。

25. Galen　「ガレノス」古代ギリシャの医学者。

25. heart of elder　「ニワトコの勇士」樫の木の中心部は堅固であることから、a heart of oak は剛の者を意味した。ここではそれをもじり、樫の木に比べて柔らかいニワトコの木（elder）に変えることで、軟弱なキーズをからかっている。

26. bully stale　「よう、小便小僧さん」stale は尿の意味。医者は検尿することから、キーズをあてこすっている。

27. he is de coward jack priest of de vorld　「彼はこの世で最も臆病な牧師野郎だ」jack は knave や rascal と同様、身分の低い者をごろつきとして蔑んで呼ぶ言葉。

not show his face.

HOST Thou art a Castalion king-urinal! Hector of Greece, my boy! 30

CAIUS I pray you bear witness that me have stay, six or seven, two tree hours for him, and he is no come.

SHALLOW He is the wiser man, Master Doctor. He is a curer of souls, and you a curer of bodies. If you should fight, you go against the hair of your professions. Is it not true, Master 35 Page?

MASTER PAGE Master Shallow, you have yourself been a great fighter, though now a man of peace.

SHALLOW Bodykins, Master Page, though I now be old and of the peace, if I see a sword out, my finger itches to make 40 one. Though we are justices and doctors, and churchmen, Master Page, we have some salt of our youth in us. We are the sons of women, Master Page.

PAGE 'Tis true, Master Shallow.

SHALLOW It will be found so, Master Page. — Master Doctor 45 Caius, I am come to fetch you home. I am sworn of the peace. You have showed yourself a wise physician, and Sir Hugh hath shown himself a wise and patient churchman. You must go with me, Master Doctor.

HOST Pardon, guest Justice. [*To Caius*] A word, Mounseur 50 Mockwater.

CAIUS Mockvater? Vat is dat?

HOST Mockwater, in our English tongue, is valour, bully.

CAIUS By gar, then I have as much Mockvater as de Englishman. Scurvy jack-dog priest! By gar, me vill cut his 55 ears.

HOST He will clapper-claw thee tightly, bully.

CAIUS Clapper-de-claw? Vat is dat?

HOST That is, he will make thee amends.

CAIUS By-gar, me do look he shall clapper-de-claw me, for, by 60

29. Castalion king-urinal 「カスタリアの泉の尿大王」Castalion は意味不明だが、ギリシャ・ローマ神話の霊泉 Castalia（カスタリア）のもじりか。カスタリアは、詩を司るアポロやミューズ達が集う泉の名前で、形容詞は Castalian。

29. Hector 「ヘクトル」1. 3. 10 注参照。

31. bear witness 「(that 以下の) 証人となる」

33. curer 「治療者」

35. go against the hair of ... 「…の性分に反する」

39. Bodykins = by God's body　軽いののしりの言葉「いやはや」。

40-41. make one 「参加する」

42. salt 「気力」塩気が比喩として用いられている。

43. sons of women 男性は皆 sons of women なので、「所詮は男」といった程度の意味で用いられる一種の慣用表現。

50. guest Justice 「判事の旦那」シャローもフォルスタッフと同じく、ガーター亭に逗留している。65 行目の Master guest もシャローを指す。

51. Mockwater 「検尿さん」mock は「偽りの」を意味するので、mockwater を直訳すると「水もどき」となる。主人はキーズをからかう際に、医者の職業にかけて検尿に言及する傾向があり、ここでもその連想が作用している。

54. By gar 「絶対に」By God が訛っている。

55. Scurvy 「卑劣な」

55. jack-dog 「雑種犬のような」

55. me vill cut = I will cut　主語の I を目的格の me で代用するキーズ特有の英語は以下も続く。

57. clapper-claw 「切り裂く」

57. tightly 「深く」

59. make thee amends 「あなたに対して罪を償う」

60. me do look he shall ... 「あいつが…するよう見届けるぞ」me の用法については 55 行目の注参照。look = look that で、「確認する、見届ける」の意。shall は話者の意思を表す。

gar, me vill have it.

HOST   And I will provoke him to't, or let him wag.

CAIUS   Me tank you for dat.

HOST   And moreover, bully — but first, [*Aside to the others*]
Master guest, and Master Page, and eke Cavaliero Slender,   65
go you through the town to Frogmore.

PAGE   [*Aside to Host*]   Sir Hugh is there, is he?

HOST   [*Aside to Page*]   He is there. See what humour he is in.
And I will bring the doctor about by the fields. Will it do
well?   70

SHALLOW   [*Aside to Host*]   We will do it.

PAGE, SHALLOW, AND SLENDER   Adieu, good Master Doctor.
[*Exeunt Page, Shallow, and Slender*]

CAIUS   By gar, me vill kill de priest, for he speak for a jackanape
to Anne Page.

HOST   Let him die. Sheath thy impatience; throw cold water   75
on thy choler. Go about the fields with me through Frogmore.
I will bring thee where Mistress Anne Page is, at a farmhouse
a-feasting, and thou shalt woo her. Cried game! Said I well?

CAIUS   By gar, me dank you vor dat. By gar, I love you, and I
shall procure-a you de good guest: de earl, de knight, de   80
lords, de gentlemen, my patients.

HOST   For the which, I will be thy adversary toward Anne
Page. Said I well?

CAIUS   By gar, 'tis good. Vell said.

HOST   Let us wag, then.   85

CAIUS   Come at my heels, Jack Rugby.

Exeunt

62. wag　「立ち去る」

63. Me tank you for dat　キーズのフランス語風の英語で、正しくは I thank you for that の意。

65. eke ...　「…も」

65. Cavaliero　「粋な伊達男」2. 1. 171 注参照。

66. Frogmore　「フロッグモア村」ウィンザーの近郊にある村の名前。

68. humour　「気分」

69. by the fields　「野原を通って」

69-70. Will it do well?　「これでいいですか？」do は「十分である」を意味する自動詞で、it will do（それで結構だ）というように、it や that を主語として用いられることが多い。

73. jackanape　「ろくでなし」スレンダーを指す。

75. Let him die　「あいつのことは放っておきなさい」直前のキーズの台詞を踏まえた表現。殺すのではなく、今はとにかく自然に任せよ、というニュアンス。

78. a-feasting　「ご馳走になっている」

78. Cried game!　「行けっ！」競技などで発破をかける際に用いられた表現。

81. lords　「貴族の男性」

82. adversary　ガーター亭の亭主は、本来は advocate（支持者）と言うべきところを間違って adversary（敵）と言ってしまっている。マラプロピズムの例。英語力のないキーズをからかうために、わざと逆の意味の言葉を使っている可能性もある。マラプロピズムについては、1. 1. 216 注参照。

86. Come at my heels　「私のすぐ後についてこい」1. 4. 55 注参照。

[ACT III, SCENE I]

Enter Evans [with a Bible in one hand and a drawn rapier in the other and] Simple [carrying Evans' gown]

EVANS   I pray you now, good Master Slender's servingman, and friend Simple by your name, which way have you looked for Master Caius, that calls himself Doctor of Physic?

SIMPLE   Marry, sir, the Petty-ward, the Park-ward, every way; old Windsor way, and every way but the town way.   5

EVANS   I most fehemently desire you you will also look that way.

SIMPLE   I will, sir.   [*Going aside*]

EVANS   Pless my soul, how full of cholers I am, and trempling of mind! I shall be glad if he have deceived me. How   10
melancholies I am! I will knog his urinals about his knave's costard when I have good oportunities for the 'ork. Pless my soul!

   [*Sings*]   To shallow rivers, to whose falls
              Melodious birds sings madrigals.   15
              There will we make our peds of roses
              And a thousand fragrant posies.
              To shallow —

Mercy on me! I have a great dispositions to cry.

   [*Sings*]   Melodious birds sing madrigals.   20
              Whenas I sat in Pabylon —
              And a thousand vagrom posies.
              To shallow, *etc*.

SIMPLE   Yonder he is coming, this way, Sir Hugh.

EVANS   He's welcome.   25

   [*Sings*]   To shallow rivers, to whose falls —

Heaven prosper the right! What weapons is he?

SIMPLE   No weapons, sir. There comes my Master, Master Shallow, and another gentleman, from Frogmore, over the

〔3.1〕あらすじ··

　エヴァンズとキーズは、ガーター亭の亭主によって自分たちがだまされていた
ことを知り、亭主の取りなしによって仲直りをする。一行は亭主に先導されて、
酒場へと繰り出す。

···

1. good Master Slender's servingman　「スレンダーさんの使用人の君」good
は、dear と同様、呼びかけに用いる敬称。この場合は、シンプルに呼びかけ
ているので、Slender ではなく、servingman を形容。

4. Petty-ward / Park-ward　いずれもウィンザーの街中の区域の名前で、「リト
ル・パーク」と「グレート・パーク」。ward は区画を表す語。

5. old Windsor　「旧市街」フロッグモア村の南にある村。

5. every way but the town way　「街道を除く全ての道」

6. fehemently　「強く」vehemently が正しい。エヴァンズのウェールズ方言に
より、v が f で発音されている。

9. Pless / trempling　いずれもエヴァンズの訛りのため、b が p で発音されて
いる。Pless (= Bless) my soul は、強い感情を表す表現で「おやおや」。

11. melancholies　「憂鬱」直前に「苛立っている (full of cholers)」と言って
いるので、気質の点では矛盾している。

11. knog　「叩き割る」knock が訛って発音されている。

11. urinals　「睾丸」

12. costard　「頭」

12. 'ork = work　具体的には、前行で言及されている行為を指す。

14 SD.　⇒後注

14. To shallow rivers, to whose falls　「小川のせせらぎに合わせて、滝音に合
わせて」sing to ...「…に合わせて歌う」の前置詞が倒置で先頭に置かれてい
る。

17. posies　「花束」

19. Mercy on me!　「ああ、どうしたことだ！」驚きなど、強い感情を表す表現。

19. dispositions to cry　「泣きたい気分」

21. Whenas I sat in Pabylon　「バビロンに座っていると」Pabylon は、バビ
ロン (Babylon) が訛って発音されたもの。バビロンは、ユダヤ人が捕囚と
なった古代王国で、その歴史は旧訳聖書に描かれている。エヴァンズの歌は途
中で変わり、この 1 行だけは、旧訳聖書「詩篇」の 137 番の一節。　⇒後注

22. vagrom　「さすらいの」vagrant が訛って発音されたもの。本来の歌詞の
「かぐわしい (fragrant)」と取り違えも生じており、マラプロピズムの一種。

27. Heaven prosper the right!　「天よ、正しき人を守りたまえ！」

stile, this way.   30

EVANS   Pray you, give me my gown or else keep it in your arms.

[Enter Page, Shallow, and Slender]

SHALLOW   How now Master Parson? Good morrow, good Sir
   Hugh. Keep a gamester from the dice, and a good student
   from his book, and it is wonderful.

SLENDER   Ah, sweet Anne Page!   35

PAGE   God save you, good Sir Hugh!

EVANS   God pless you from his mercy sake, all of you!

SHALLOW   What, the sword and the word? Do you study them
   both, Master Parson?

PAGE   And youthful still, in your doublet and hose this raw   40
   rheumatic day?

EVANS   There is reasons and causes for it.

PAGE   We are come to you to do a good office, Master Parson.

EVANS   Fery well. What is it?

PAGE   Yonder is a most reverend gentleman who, belike having   45
   received wrong by some person, is at most odds with his own
   gravity and patience that ever you saw.

SHALLOW   I have lived fourscore years and upward. I never
   heard a man of his place, gravity, and learning, so wide of his
   own respect.   50

EVANS   What is he?

PAGE   I think you know him: Master Doctor Caius, the
   renowned French physician.

EVANS   Got's will and his passion of my heart! I had as lief you
   would tell me of a mess of porridge.   55

PAGE   Why?

EVANS   He has no more knowledge in Hibbocrates and Galen,
   and he is a knave besides, a cowardly knave, as you would
   desires to be acquainted withal.

PAGE   *[To Shallow]*   I warrant you, he's the man should fight   60

30. stile 「踏み超し段」家畜の通行を防ぐ目的で牧場の通過点に設けられた段差のある柵。

31. or else 「あるいは」

32. Master Parson 「牧師さん」parson は教区牧師の意。

33. gamester 「ギャンブラー、賭博師」

36. God save you 「神のご加護がありますように」慣用的な挨拶の表現。

37. God pless you from his mercy sake 「慈悲深い神の祝福がありますように」bless が pless と訛って発音されており、本来は for と言うべきところが from になっている。いずれもエヴァンズ特有の方言。

38. What 疑問詞ではなく、驚きを表す間投詞で「なんと」。

38. the word 「神の言葉」聖書を指す。

40. doublet 「ダブレット」身体にぴったりフィットした男性用の上着。

40. hose 「レギンス」現代のレギンスによく似たタイトなズボンで、男性が着用した。

40. raw 「ずきずきと痛む」

41. rheumatic day 「リューマチ病みの年齢」

43. We are come 「私たちはやってきた」過去分詞を伴って完了を表す be 動詞の古い用法。

43. do a good office 「役に立つ」

45. reverend 「立派な」

45. belike 「おそらく」

45-46. having received wrong 「侮辱を受けた」wrong は名詞。

46-47. is ... saw 「かつてないぐらいに、本来の冷静さや忍耐と葛藤している」at odds with ... で「…と戦う」

48. fourscore years and upward 「80歳とさらに少し」score = 20

49-50. wide of his own respect 「興奮の余りに我を忘れている」wide of ... で「…から外れている」の意。

54. Got's will and his passion of my heart! 「ええい、くそっ、腹が立つ！」God's will! God's passion! Passion of my heart! といった、強い感情を表現するののしり言葉が融合されている。

54. had as lief ... 「…の方がましだ」

55. mess of porridge 「シチュー」現代英語では porridge はシリアルで作るお粥を意味するが、エリザベス朝は野菜や肉を煮込んだシチューを指した(*OED*)。

57. Hibbocrates 「ヒポクラテス」古代ギリシャの医学者 Hippocrates が訛って発音されている。

57. Galen 「ガレノス」古代ギリシャの医学者。

60. I warrant you 「ぜったいに」warrant は「断言する、保証する」の意で、I warrant you は、何かを強く主張する際に用いられた慣用表現。

with him.

SLENDER   O sweet Anne Page!

SHALLOW   It appears so by his weapons.

[*Enter Host, Caius and Rugby*]

Keep them asunder; here comes Doctor Caius.

[*Evans and Caius prepare to fight*]

PAGE   Nay, good Master Parson, keep in your weapon.   65

SHALLOW   So do you, good Master Doctor.

HOST   Disarm them, and let them question. Let them keep
their limbs whole and hack our English.

[*Shallow and Page take Caius' and Evans' rapiers*]

CAIUS   I pray you let-a me speak a word with your ear. Verefore
vill you not meet-a me?   70

EVANS   [*Aside to Caius*]   Pray you use your patience. — [*Aloud*]
In good time.

CAIUS   By gar, you are de coward, de jack dog, John ape.

EVANS   [*Aside to Caius*]   Pray you, let us not be laughing-
stocks to other men's humours. I desire you in friendship,   75
and I will one way or other make you amends. — [*Aloud*] I
will knog your urinal about your knave's cogscomb.

CAIUS   *Diable*! Jack Rugby, mine host de Jarteer, have I not stay
for him to kill him? Have I not, at de place I did appoint?

EVANS   As I am a Christians soul, now look you, this is the   80
place appointed. I'll be judgement by mine host of the
Garter.

HOST   Peace, I say, Gallia and Gaul, French and Welsh, soul-
curer, and body-curer!

CAIUS   Ay, dat is very good, excellent.   85

HOST   Peace, I say. Hear mine host of the Garter. Am I politic?
Am I subtle? Am I a Machiavel? Shall I lose my doctor? No;

65. keep in your weapon 「武器をしまっておく」in は鞘の中を指す。

67. question 「話し合う」question は「互いに関して問いただす」という意の動詞として用いられている。

67-68. Let them keep their limbs whole and hack our English 「身体は無傷にさせて、我らが英語をズタズタにしてもらう」エヴァンズとキーズの訛った英語への揶揄。hack は「切り刻む」の意。

69. Verefore Wherefore（なぜ）が訛って発音されている。

72. In good time 「十分間に合っている」この時点では、エヴァンズはもはや本気でキーズと決闘する気はないが、周囲に対してはその素振りを見せているので、この語はキーズを挑発するように語られる。

73. By gar ＝ By God「絶対に」

73. de jack dog, John ape 「このクソ犬野郎、クソ猿」jack は「ごろつき」の意。一方、Jack は John の愛称でもあるので、jack dog の類義語として John ape と口走っている。de は the が訛って発音されている。

74-75. laughing-stocks 「物笑いの種」

75. humours 「気まぐれ」

76. one way or other 「何らかの形で」

77. knog 「叩き割る」knock が訛って発音されている。11-12 行目と同じ表現。

77. urinal 「睾丸」

77. cogscomb coxcomb（頭）が訛って発音されている。

78. *Diable* 「こん畜生め！」diable は devil のフランス語で、ののしり言葉として用いられている。

78. stay 「待つ」

80. As I am a Christians soul 「キリスト教徒として誓って言うが」

81-82. I'll be judgement by mine host of the Garter. 「ガーター亭の亭主が証言してくれるだろう」judgement は「証言」の意で、直前に given を補って読む。

83. Peace 「黙れ」

83. Gallia and Gaul 「ガリアとゴール」ガリアもゴールも、古代にケルト人が定住した地域の名称で、フランスの雅称としても用いられた。すなわち、どちらもフランスを指しているが、文脈上はキーズの出身地であるフランスとエヴァンズの出身地であるウェールズを指す必要があり、矛盾している。もっとも、ケルト人ということで、ウェールズ人もフランス人も区別なくひとまとめにされていると解釈することもできる。

86. politic 「如才ない」

87. subtle 「器用な、要領がいい」

87. a Machiavel 「マキャヴェリのような策略家」

he gives me the potions and the motions. Shall I lose my
parson, my priest, my Sir Hugh? No, he gives me the proverbs
and the no-verbs. [*To Caius*] Give me thy hand, terrestrial — 90
so. [*To Evans*] Give me thy hand, celestial — so. Boys of art, I
have deceived you both. I have directed you to wrong places.
Your hearts are mighty, your skins are whole, and let burnt
sack be the issue. [*To Page and Shallow*] Come, lay their swords
to pawn. [*To Caius and Evans*] Follow me, lads of peace, follow, 95
follow, follow.

[Exit]

SHALLOW   Trust me, a mad host. Follow, gentlemen, follow.
SLENDER   O sweet Anne Page!

[Exeunt Shallow, Slender, and Page]

CAIUS   Ha, do I perceive dat? Have you make-a de sot of us,
ha, ha?   100
EVANS   This is well. He has made us his vlouting-stog. I desire
you that we may be friends, and let us knog our prains
together to be revenge on this same scall, scurvy, cogging
companion, the host of the Garter.
CAIUS   By gar, with all my heart. He promise to bring me   105
where is Anne Page. By gar, he deceive me too.
EVANS   Well, I will smite his noddles. Pray you follow.

[Exeunt]

[ACT III, SCENE II]

Enter Robin [, followed by] Mistress Page

MISTRESS PAGE   Nay, keep your way, little gallant. You were
wont to be a follower, but now you are a leader. Whether had
you rather, lead mine eyes, or eye your master's heels?
ROBIN   I had rather, forsooth, go before you like a man than
follow him like a dwarf.   5
MISTRESS PAGE   O, you are a flattering boy. Now I see you'll be

88. potions 「薬」　**88. motions** 「下剤」

89. proverbs 「説教」

90. no-verbs 「意味不明の言葉」エヴァンズの奇妙な語り口への揶揄か。

90-91. terrestrial / celestial ガーター亭の亭主は、キーズとエヴァンズを握手させる際に、医者の手と牧師の手をそれぞれ「この世の」と「あの世の」と形容している。医者は人間の身体を、牧師は人間の霊魂を扱う。

91. art 「学識」

93. hearts 「勇気」

93-94. burnt sack 「あたたかいサック酒」2.1.186 注参照。

94. issue 「結末」

94-95. lay their swords to pawn 「剣を質屋に質入れする」エヴァンズとキーズの決闘が中止になって、剣が不要になったことを意味している。

95. lads of peace 「平和の申し子たち」lad は「若い男」を意味する語で、ここでは 91 行目の boys of art と同じように用いられている。

97. Trust me 「いいとも」

99. make-a de sot of us 「私たちを馬鹿にする」sot は fool と同じ意味。

101. vlouting-stog 「笑い物」flouting stock が訛って発音されている。

102. knog our prains 「我々の知恵を絞る」knock our brains が訛って発音されている。knock は「叩いて動かす」の意。

103. scall 「卑劣な」

103. scurvy 「あさましい」

103. cogging 「いかさまをする」

107. smite 「殴る」

107. noddles 「頭」文法上は単数形であるべき語が複数形になるのもエヴァンズの方言の特徴。

〔3. 2〕あらすじ…………………………………………………………………………
　街中でペイジ夫人に遭遇したフォードは、夫人がフォルスタッフの小姓ロビンを連れてフォード夫人を訪問する途中であることを知って、猜疑心に駆られる。フォードは、密会の現場を押さえるべく、来合わせたペイジとキーズとエヴァンズを伴い、帰途につく。シャローとスレンダーは、アンへの求婚に向かう。
……………………………………………………………………………………………

1. keep your way 「先に行く」

1-2. were wont to ... 「以前は …したものだった」

2-3. Whether had you rather ...? Which would you prefer と同じ意味。

3. eye your master's heels 「主人の後ろ姿を目で追う」eye は動詞で用いられている。

a courtier.

[*Enter Ford*]

FORD Well met, Mistress Page. Whither go you?

MISTRESS PAGE Truly, sir, to see your wife. Is she at home?

FORD Ay, and as idle as she may hang together, for want of 10
company. I think if your husbands were dead you two would
marry.

MISTRESS PAGE Be sure of that — two other husbands.

FORD Where had you this pretty weathercock?

MISTRESS PAGE I cannot tell what the dickens his name is my 15
husband had him of. — What do you call your knight's name,
sirrah?

ROBIN Sir John Falstaff.

FORD Sir John Falstaff?

MISTRESS PAGE He, he. I can never hit on's name. There is 20
such a league between my goodman and he! Is your wife at
home indeed?

FORD Indeed she is.

MISTRESS PAGE By your leave, sir. I am sick till I see her.

[*Exeunt Mistress Page and Robin*]

FORD Has Page any brains? Hath he any eyes? Hath he any 25
thinking? Sure, they sleep; he hath no use of them. Why, this
boy will carry a letter twenty mile as easy as a cannon will
shoot point-blank twelve score. He pieces out his wife's
inclination. He gives her folly motion and advantage. And
now she's going to my wife, and Falstaff's boy with her. A 30
man may hear this shower sing in the wind. And Falstaff's
boy with her! Good plots they are laid, and our revolted
wives share damnation together. Well, I will take him, then
torture my wife, pluck the borrowed veil of modesty from the
so-seeming Mistress Page, divulge Page himself for a secure 35
and wilful Actaeon, and to these violent proceedings all my

8. Whither 「どこへ」

10. as idle as she may hang together 「これ以上はないぐらい退屈している」
hang together ＝ manage

10-11. for want of company 「話し相手がいないので」want ＝ lack

13. other 「別の」

14. weathercock 「風見鶏」ロビンを指す。

15-16. I cannot tell what the dickens his name is my husband had him of.
「うちの主人がいったい誰からこの子を譲り受けたのか、その名前がわからな
い」what the dickens ＝ what the devil で強意表現。had him of ＝ got
him from で him はロビンを指す。

20. hit on's name 「彼の名前を思い出す」hit on は「思いつく」。on's ＝ on
his

20-21. There is such a league 「随分と仲がよい」league は交わりやつきあい
の意。

21. goodman 「夫」

24. By your leave 「では、失礼します」leave は許可を意味する名詞。By
your leave は、立ち去る際の決まった挨拶として用いられた。

28. point-blank 「まっすぐ（ぶれずに）」

28. twelve score 「240 ヤード」score は 20 を表すので、12 × 20 ＝ 240。

28. pieces out 「助長する」piece out は、布を継ぎ合わせて長くすること。

29. inclination 「欲望」

29. motion 「刺激」

29. advantage 「機会」

30-31. A man may hear this shower sing in the wind. 「この様子を、嵐の前
の風のように受けとめる人もいるだろう」this は、前文で述べられているこ
とを指しており、大雨（shower）の到来を知らせる風に喩えられている。

32. Good plots they are laid 「上手い計画を立てたものだ」plots と they は同
格。

32. revolted 「不実な」

33. damnation 「地獄に落ちてしかるべき大罪」

35. so-seeming 「貞淑に見せかけている」so は前行の modesty を指す。

35. divulge Page himself for ... 「ペイジが…であると吹聴する」

35. secure 「暢気な」

36. wilful 「強情な」

36. Actaeon 「アクタイオン」2. 1. 105 注参照。アクタイオンは純潔の守護神
ダイアナの裸身を見た罪により鹿に変身させられる悲運の若者だが、鹿の角と
かけて、寝取られ亭主の比喩として用いられている。

36. violent proceedings 「酷い仕打ち」

neighbours shall cry aim. [*A clock strikes*] The clock gives me
my cue, and my assurance bids me search. There I shall find
Falstaff. I shall be rather praised for this than mocked, for it
is as positive as the earth is firm that Falstaff is there. I will   40
go.

[*Enter Page, Shallow, Slender, Host, Evans, Caius and Rugby*]

SHALLOW, PAGE, etc.   Well met, Master Ford.

FORD   Trust me, a good knot. I have good cheer at home, and
I pray you all go with me.

SHALLOW   I must excuse myself, Master Ford.   45

SLENDER   And so must I, sir. We have appointed to dine with
Mistress Anne, and I would not break with her for more
money than I'll speak of.

SHALLOW   We have lingered about a match between Anne Page
and my cousin Slender, and this day we shall have our answer.   50

SLENDER   I hope I have your good will, father Page.

PAGE   You have, Master Slender. I stand wholly for you. But
my wife, Master Doctor, is for you altogether.

CAIUS   Ay, by gar, and de maid is loue-a me; my nursh-a
Quickly tell me so mush.   55

HOST   [*To Page*]   What say you to young Master Fenton? He
capers, he dances, he has eyes of youth, he writes verses, he
speaks holiday, he smells April and May. He will carry't, he
will carry't; 'tis in his buttons, he will carry't.

PAGE   Not by my consent, I promise you. The gentleman is of   60
no having. He kept company with the wild Prince and Poins.
He is of too high a region; he knows too much. No, he shall
not knit a knot in his fortunes with the finger of my substance.
If he take her, let him take her simply. The wealth I have waits
on my consent, and my consent goes not that way.   65

FORD   I beseech you heartily, some of you go home with me to
dinner. Besides your cheer, you shall have sport: I will show

37. cry aim 「声援を送る」弓術大会で観客が競技者に「命中しろ」と声援を送ったことに由来する表現。前行の to these violent proceedings が cry aim の目的格。

38. assurance 「確信」

40. positive 「明白な」

43. a good knot 「陽気なご一行」

43. cheer 「ご馳走」

47. break with her ＝ break my promise to her「彼女との約束を破る」

47-48. for more money than I'll speak of 「数え切れないほどの大金をもらったとしても」

49. have lingered about ... 「…のことでぐずぐずしている」

50. cousin 「親類」

51. good will 「好意」

53. altogether 「まったく」

54. nursh-a 「家政婦」nurse が訛って発音されている。

56. What say you to ... 「…のことをどう思う」

57. capers 「陽気に踊る」

58. speaks holiday 「陽気に話す」

58. carry't ＝ carry it「上手くやる」アンへの求愛を指す。

59. 'tis in his buttons 「きっと成功する」

61. having 「資産」

61. the wild Prince and Poins 「不良の王子とポインズ」『ヘンリー四世 第一部・第二部』では、後にヘンリー五世となるハル王子の放埓な生活が描かれ、その不良仲間としてフォルスタッフ、バードルフ、ピストル、ニム、ポインズが登場する。

62. region 「社会的身分」

62. knows too much 「世慣れしすぎている」

62-63. he shall not knit a knot in his fortunes with the finger of my substance 「あの男に、私の財産という指でもって自分の身代に結び目を作るようなことは断じてさせない」shall は話者の意思を示す。substance は「財産」。「自分の身代に結び目を作る」(knit a knot in his fortunes) は「自分の身代をしっかりと堅固なものにする」の意。

64. take her simply 「（持参金なしで）ただ彼女だけと一緒になる」

64-65. waits on ... 「…にかかっている」

67. sport 「娯楽」

you a monster. Master Doctor, you shall go. So shall you, Master Page, and you, Sir Hugh.

SHALLOW   Well, fare you well. — [*Aside to Slender*] We shall 70
have the freer wooing at Master Page's.

[*Exeunt Shallow and Slender*]

CAIUS   Go home, John Rugby. I come anon.

[*Exit Rugby*]

HOST   Farewell, my hearts. I will to my honest knight Falstaff,
and drink canary with him.   [*Exit*]

FORD   [*Aside*]   I think I shall drink in pipe-wine first with him. 75
I'll make him dance. — Will you go, gentles?

PAGE, CAIUS, AND EVANS   Have with you to see this monster.

Exeunt

〔ACT III, SCENE III〕

Enter Mistress Ford [and] Mistress Page

MISTRESS FORD   What John! What Robert!

MISTRESS PAGE   Quickly, quickly! Is the buck-basket —

MISTRESS FORD   I warrant. — What, Robin, I say!

[*Enter John and Robert with a buck-basket*]

MISTRESS PAGE   Come, come, come.

MISTRESS FORD   Here, set it down.   5

MISTRESS PAGE   Give your men the charge. We must be brief.

MISTRESS FORD   Marry, as I told you before, John and Robert,
be ready here hard by in the brew-house, and when I suddenly
call you, come forth, and, without any pause or staggering,
take this basket on your shoulders. That done, trudge with it 10
in all haste, and carry it among the whitsters in Datchet
Mead, and there empty it in the muddy ditch close by the
Thames side.

MISTRESS PAGE   [*To John and Robert*]   You will do it?

70. fare you well = farewell「さようなら」別れぎわの挨拶。

72. anon 「あとで」

73. my hearts 「皆さん」sweetheart や my heart など、heart は愛情をこめて呼びかける際に用いられた。

74. canary 「カナリーワイン」スペイン領カナリー諸島産の白ワイン。甘口でデザートに供される。

75. drink in pipe-wine 「樽から注いだワインを飲む」pipe は洒落になっており、酒樽の意味以外に、笛などの管楽器も意味することから、次行のダンスへの言及に繋がる。

76. gentles = gentlemen「皆さん」

77. Have with you = I'll come with you「一緒に行きましょう」

〔3. 3〕あらすじ……………………………………………………………………………
　フォード夫人は、誘いに乗ってやって来たフォルスタッフを迎え入れる。するとそこへ、ペイジ夫人がやってきて、妻の不貞を疑うフォードが仲間と共に間もなく帰宅することを告げる。フォード夫人とペイジ夫人は、計画通りにフォルスタッフを洗濯かごに潜ませて、使用人に川まで運ぶように指示を与える。嫉妬に狂うフォードは家捜しを始め、その異様な剣幕で周囲を呆れさせる。
………………………………………………………………………………………………

1. What 「ねえ、ちょっと」誰かに呼びかける際の表現。

2. buck-basket 「洗濯かご」洗濯する前の汚れ物（buck）を入れるためのかご。

6. charge 「指示」

7. Marry 「いいかい」by Mary（聖母マリア様にかけて）に由来し、何かをきっぱりと言う際に用いる強意表現。

8. hard 「じっと集中して」

8. by 「そばに」

8. brew-house 「酒倉」母屋とは区別された、酒の醸造のための離れを指す。

9. staggering 「のろのろすること」

10. trudge 「しっかりと歩く」重い物を運んでいる時など、その重さに負けずに頑張って歩く様子を指す。

11. whitsters 「洗濯屋」whitener（洗濯物を漂白する業者）と同じ。

11-12. Datchet Mead 「ダチェット広場」ウィンザーの街とテムズ川の間に位置する。mead = meadow（草原）

MISTRESS FORD   I ha' told them over and over; they lack no   15
direction. — Be gone, and come when you are called.

[Exeunt John and Robert]

[Enter Robin]

MISTRESS PAGE   Here comes little Robin.

MISTRESS FORD   How now, my eyas-musket? What news with
you?

ROBIN   My master, Sir John, is come in at your back door,   20
Mistress Ford, and requests your company.

MISTRESS PAGE   You little Jack-a-Lent, have you been true to
us?

ROBIN   Ay, I'll be sworn. My master knows not of your being
here, and hath threatened to put me into everlasting liberty if   25
I tell you of it; for he swears he'll turn me away.

MISTRESS PAGE   Thou'rt a good boy. This secrecy of thine
shall be a tailor to thee, and shall make thee a new doublet
and hose. — I'll go hide me.

MISTRESS FORD   Do so. — Go tell thy master I am alone.   30

[Exit Robin]

Mistress Page, remember you your cue.

MISTRESS PAGE   I warrant thee. If I do not act it, hiss me.

MISTRESS FORD   Go to, then. *[Exit Mistress Page]* We'll use this
unwholesome humidity, this gross watery pumpion. We'll
teach him to know turtles from jays.   35

[Enter Falstaff]

FALSTAFF   Have I caught thee, my heavenly jewel? Why now let
me die, for I have lived long enough. This is the period of my
ambition. O this blessed hour!

MISTRESS FORD   O sweet Sir John!

FALSTAFF   Mistress Ford, I cannot cog; I cannot prate, Mistress   40
Ford. Now shall I sin in my wish: I would thy husband were

15. ha' = have

16. direction 「指示」

18. eyas-musket 「ハイタカの雛」

21. requests your company 「あなたへの面会を希望している」

22. Jack-a-Lent 「人形のジャック」大斎節（Lent）の期間に子供の娯楽のために設置された人形で、石投げの的として用いられた。

22. true 「忠実な」

25. put me into everlasting liberty 「僕を永久に自由の身にする」とは、すなわち解雇を意味する。

26. turn me away 「僕をクビにする」

27. Thou'rt = Thou art = Thou are

28. doublet 「ダブレット」身体にぴったりフィットした男性用の上着。

29. hose 「レギンス」現代のレギンスによく似たぴったりしたズボン。

29. go hide me = go and hide myself

31. cue 「（登場するタイミングを認識するために役者が用いる）合図」

32. hiss 「（観客が下手な役者に対して）野次る」

34. unwholesome humidity 「気色悪い湿気の塊」

34. pumpion 「カボチャ」

35. know turtles from jays 「キジバトをカケスと見分ける」turtles = turtle-doves（キジバト）はつがいでいることから、誠実な恋人の象徴とされた。一方、カケスは、華やかな色の羽毛と大きな鳴き声から、着飾った娼婦の比喩に用いられた。

37. period 「到達点」

40. cog 「でまかせを言って媚びる」

40. prate 「調子よくべらべらしゃべる」

41. sin 「罪を犯す」ここでは動詞として用いられている。

dead. I'll speak it before the best lord. I would make thee my lady.

MISTRESS FORD I your lady, Sir John? Alas, I should be a pitiful lady. 45

FALSTAFF Let the court of France show me such another. I see how thine eye would emulate the diamond. Thou hast the right arched beauty of the brow that becomes the ship-tire, the tire-valiant, or any tire of Venetian admittance.

MISTRESS FORD A plain kerchief, Sir John. My brows become 50 nothing else, nor that well neither.

FALSTAFF Thou art a tyrant to say so. Thou wouldst make an absolute courtier, and the firm fixture of thy foot would give an excellent motion to thy gait in a semicircled farthingale. I see what thou wert if Fortune, thy foe, were — not Nature 55 — thy friend. Come, thou canst not hide it.

MISTRESS FORD Believe me, there's no such thing in me.

FALSTAFF What made me love thee? Let that persuade thee. There's something extraordinary in thee. Come, I cannot cog, and say thou art this and that, like a many of these lisping 60 hawthorn-buds that come like women in mens apparel and smell like Bucklersbury in simple-time. I cannot. But I love thee, none but thee; and thou deserv'st it.

MISTRESS FORD Do not betray me, sir. I fear you love Mistress Page. 65

FALSTAFF Thou mightst as well say I love to walk by the Counter gate, which is as hateful to me as the reek of a lime-kiln.

MISTRESS FORD Well, heaven knows how I love you, and you shall one day find it. 70

FALSTAFF Keep in that mind. I'll deserve it.

MISTRESS FORD Nay, I must tell you, so you do, or else I could not be in that mind.

42. I'll speak it before the best lord 「どんな偉い人の前でも断言する」

45. pitiful 「みっともない」

47. emulate 「張り合う」

47. hast = has

48. arched beauty of the brow 「弓形の美しい額」日本で言うところの富士_{ふ じ}額_{びたい}。

48. becomes 「似合う」

48. ship-tire 「船の形をした髪飾り」tire は宮廷女性の間で流行したヘアアクセサリー。

49. valiant 「豪華な」

49. of Venetian admittance 「ヴェニスでも通用するような」イタリアのファッションは（現代と同様）最新流行で、イングランド人の憧れの的だった。

50. kerchief 「スカーフ」

52. make ... 「…になる」

53. firm fixture of thy foot 「あなたが足を踏みしめる様子」

54. gait 「歩き方」

54. semicircled farthingale 「半月型に広がった輪っかのドレス」

55. wert = would be

55. Fortune / Nature 神格化されている。「運命の女神」と「自然の女神」。

59. cog 「でまかせを言って媚びる」

60. lisping lisp は動詞で「舌足らずで話す」。

61. hawthorn-buds 「サンザシの蕾_{つぼみ}のような若者」

61. apparel 「洋服」

62. Bucklersbury in simple-time 「ハーブが売られる時期のバックラーズベリー通り」Bucklersbury は、ロンドンにある通りの名前で、様々な種類の薬草（simple）が売られる夏には芳香がたちこめた。

63. deserv'st = deservest = deserves

67. Counter gate 「債務者監獄の門」カウンター監獄はサザック地区にあった債務者監獄。

67. reek 「臭い煙」

71. Keep in 「絶やさない」

71. mind 「気持ち」

[Enter Robin]

ROBIN   Mistress Ford, Mistress Ford! Here's Mistress Page at   75
the door, sweating and blowing, and looking wildly, and
would needs speak with you presently.

FALSTAFF   She shall not see me. I will ensconce me behind the
arras.

MISTRESS FORD   Pray you do so; she's a very tattling woman.

[Falstaff hides himself behind the arras]
[Enter Mistress Page]

What's the matter? How now?   80

MISTRESS PAGE   O Mistress Ford, what have you done? You're
shamed, you're overthrown, you're undone forever!

MISTRESS FORD   What's the matter, good Mistress Page?

MISTRESS PAGE   O well-a-day, Mistress Ford, having an honest
man to your husband, to give him such cause of suspicion!   85

MISTRESS FORD   What cause of suspicion?

MISTRESS PAGE   What cause of suspicion? Out upon you!
How am I mistook in you!

MISTRESS FORD   Why, alas, what's the matter?

MISTRESS PAGE   Your husband's coming hither, woman, with   90
all the officers in Windsor, to search for a gentleman that he
says is here now in the house, by your consent, to take an ill
advantage of his absence. You are undone.

MISTRESS FORD   'Tis not so, I hope.

MISTRESS PAGE   Pray heaven it be not so that you have such a   95
man here! But 'tis most certain your husband's coming, with
half Windsor at his heels, to search for such a one. I come
before to tell you. If you know yourself clear, why, I am glad
of it; but if you have a friend here, convey, convey him out.
Be not amazed, call all your senses to you, defend your   100
reputation, or bid farewell to your good life forever.

75. blowing 「息切れしてあえいでいる」

75. looking wildly 「興奮した様子で」

77. ensconce me 「隠れる」ensconce は「隠す」の意。

78. arras 「タペストリー」人物や場面を描いた大判のつづれ織りで、絵画のように壁の装飾品として用いられた。

79 SD フォルスタッフがタペストリーの陰に隠れる場面では、「顕示の空間（discovery space）」や「内舞台（inner stage）」といった名称で呼ばれる部分が活用された（Styan, Wiggins）。内舞台とは、エリザベス朝の舞台の基本構造の1つで、舞台後方の奥まった部分に設けられた空間を指す。この空間は本舞台とカーテンで仕切られており、例えばこの場面のフォルスタッフのように、観客の視界から隠したり、あるいは『ロミオとジュリエット』で仮死状態のジュリエットが横たわる霊廟のように、観客に見せたりと、様々な手法で使用された。

82. you're overthrown 「あなたは破滅した」

82. you're undone 「あなたはおしまいよ」undo は「破滅させる」の意。

84. well-a-day 「ああ」悲しみや嘆きを表す。

85. to your husband ＝ as your husband

87. Out upon you! 「なんてことでしょう！」相手を非難する表現。

89. alas 「ああ」悲しみや嘆きを表す。

94. 'Tis ＝ It is

97. at his heels 「彼の後に続いて」

98. clear 「無実の」

98. why 「まあ」感情を表す強意表現。

99. friend 「愛人」

100. amazed 「うろたえる」

100. call all your senses to you 「全ての思慮分別を結集させる」

101. bid farewell 「別れを告げる」

MISTRESS FORD What shall I do? There is a gentleman, my dear friend, and I fear not mine own shame so much as his peril. I had rather than a thousand pound he were out of the house.   105

MISTRESS PAGE For shame, never stand 'you had rather' and 'you had rather'! Your husband's here at hand! Bethink you of some conveyance. In the house you cannot hide him. Oh, how have you deceived me! — Look, here is a basket! If he be of any reasonable stature, he may creep in here, and throw   110 foul linen upon him, as if it were going to bucking. Or — it is whiting time — send him by your two men to Datchet-Mead.

MISTRESS FORD He's too big to go in there. What shall I do?

[*Falstaff rushes out of hiding*]

FALSTAFF Let me see't, let me see't! O, let me see't! I'll in, I'll in! Follow your friend's counsel! I'll in!   115

MISTRESS PAGE What, Sir John Falstaff? — Are these your letters, knight?

FALSTAFF I love thee! Help me away! Let me creep in here! I'll never —

[*Falstaff gets into the basket. They cover him with clothes*]

MISTRESS PAGE [*To Robin*] Help to cover your master, boy.   120 — Call your men, Mistress Ford. — You dissembling knight!

[*Exit Robin*]

MISTRESS FORD What John! Robert! John!

[*Enter John and Robert*]

Go, take up these clothes here quickly. Where's the cowl-staff? [*John and Robert attempt to fit the cowl-staff*] Look how you drumble! Carry them to the laundress in Datchet Mead.   125 Quickly, come!

104-05. I had rather than a thousand pound he were out of the house 「あの人がこの家から出られるなら 1,000 ポンド払ってもいい」仮定法で、I had rather A than B の文型の B の部分（than a thousand pound）が前に押し出されている。主たる願望は A の部分（he were out of the house）。

106. For shame 「なんてみっともない」

106. stand そのままの状態に留まることから、ここでは「（〜などと言って）ぐずぐずする」

107. Bethink 「（of 以下のことについて）よく考える」

108. conveyance 「脱出させる手段」

110. stature 「身長」

111. foul linen 「汚れた洗濯物」

111. bucking 「洗濯」

112. whiting time 「洗濯屋が漂白を始める時間」11 行目注参照。

116. Are these your letters ペイジ夫人は自分への恋文を指して怒っている（ふりをしている）。複数形になっているのは、強い怒りの感情を表現するため。

121. dissembling 「嘘つきの」

123-24. cowl-staff 「天びん棒」大きな水桶（cowl）などを 2 人で運ぶための棒。

[*Enter Ford, Page, Caius, and Evans*]

FORD [*To his companions*] Pray you, come near. If I suspect
without cause, why then make sport at me, then let me be
your jest, I deserve it. — [*To John and Robert*] How now?
Whither bear you this?   130

JOHN To the laundress, forsooth.

MISTRESS FORD Why, what have you to do whither they bear
it? You were best meddle with buck-washing!

FORD Buck? I would I could wash myself of the buck! Buck,
buck, buck! Ay, buck! I warrant you, buck — and of the   135
season too, it shall appear.

                                          [*Exeunt John and Robert with the basket*]

Gentlemen, I have dreamed tonight. I'll tell you my dream.
Here, here, here be my keys. Ascend my chambers. Search,
seek, find out. I'll warrant we'll unkennel the fox. Let me stop
this way first. [*He locks the door*] So, now escape.   140

PAGE Good Master Ford, be contented. You wrong yourself
too much.

FORD True, Master Page. — Up, gentlemen, you shall see
sport anon. Follow me, gentlemen.   [*Exit*]

EVANS This is fery fantastical humours and jealousies.   145

CAIUS By gar, 'tis no the fashion of France. It is not jealous in
France.

PAGE Nay follow him, gentlemen. See the issue of his search.

                                          [*Exeunt Page, Caius, and Evans*]

MISTRESS PAGE Is there not a double excellency in this?

MISTRESS FORD I know not which pleases me better, that my   150
husband is deceived, or Sir John.

MISTRESS PAGE What a taking was he in, when your husband
asked who was in the basket!

MISTRESS FORD I am half afraid he will have need of washing,
so throwing him into the water will do him a benefit.   155

127. come near 「入る」

128. why 何かを強い調子で主張する時に使う表現「そうとも」

128. make sport at ... ＝ make sport of ...「…を馬鹿にする」

132. Why 128 行目と同じ用法。疑問詞ではない。「あら」

132. what have you to do 「あなたに何の関係があるのですか」＝ what's it to do with you

133. You were best meddle with buck-washing 「あなたが洗濯物の心配をしてくださるなんて結構なこと」were best ＝ would do well to で、嫌味として語られている。buck は洗濯前の汚れ物の意。

134. Buck 「牡鹿」寝取られ亭主への不安から、フォードは buck を「洗濯物」ではなく「牡鹿」の意に取り違える。牡鹿は角があることから、寝取られ亭主の隠喩となる。2.1.105 注参照。

134. wash myself of the buck 「私にかけられた牡鹿の疑いを晴らす（＝私にかけられた寝取られ亭主の疑いを晴らす)」

135-36. of the season 「角が生え替わる時期」

136. it shall appear 「今にわかるぞ」shall は話者の意思を表す。

137. tonight this past night の意で、「昨夜」。

139. unkennel the fox 狐狩りの際に獲物である「狐を巣穴から追い出す」。

140. escape 「逃げてみろ」escape if you can のニュアンスで、嫌味として語られている。

141. be contented 「気を静める」

141. wrong yourself 「自分を辱めている」

144. sport 「娯楽」

145. fantastical 「途方もない」

148. issue 「結末」

152. What a taking was he in 「あの人は、どんなに動揺したことでしょう」taking は「パニック、動揺」の意。he はかごの中のフォルスタッフを指す。

Mistress Page   Hang him, dishonest rascal! I would all of the same strain were in the same distress.

Mistress Ford   I think my husband hath some special suspicion of Falstaff's being here, for I never saw him so gross in his jealousy till now.   160

Mistress Page   I will lay a plot to try that, and we will yet have more tricks with Falstaff. His dissolute disease will scarce obey this medicine.

Mistress Ford   Shall we send that foolish carrion Mistress Quickly to him, and excuse his throwing into the water, and   165
give him another hope, to betray him to another punishment?

Mistress Page   We will do it. Let him be sent for tomorrow eight o'clock, to have amends.

[*Enter Ford, Page, Caius, and Evans*]

Ford   I cannot find him. Maybe the knave bragged of that he could not compass.   170

Mistress Page   [*Aside to Mistress Ford*]   Heard you that?

Mistress Ford   You use me well, Master Ford, do you?

Ford   Ay, I do so.

Mistress Ford   Heaven make you better than your thoughts!

Ford   Amen!   175

Mistress Page   You do yourself mighty wrong, Master Ford.

Ford   Ay, ay, I must bear it.

Evans   If there be anypody in the house, and in the chambers, and in the coffers, and in the presses, heaven forgive my sins at the day of judgement!   180

Caius   By gar, nor I too. There is nobodies.

Page   Fie, fie, Master Ford, are you not ashamed? What spirit, what devil suggests this imagination? I would not ha' your distemper in this kind for the wealth of Windsor Castle.

Ford   'Tis my fault, Master Page. I suffer for it.   185

Evans   You suffer for a pad conscience. Your wife is as honest

156-57. I would all of the same strain were in the same distress 「あの手の浮気性な人間はみんな同じように苦労すればいいんだわ」願望を表す仮定法。strain は「気質、傾向」の意。

160. gross 「(程度が) ひどい」

163. obey 「反応する」

164. foolish carrion 「ひょうきんなおばさん」carrion はここでは「だらしのない女」の意だが、それほど非難の意図はない。

166. betray him to another punishment 「彼をだましてさらに罰を与える」

167. Let him be sent 「彼に使いをやりましょう」send は何かを伝達するために使者を送ることを意味する。この場合の使いはクウィックリーを指す。

169. bragged of ... 「…について大げさなことを言った」

170. compass 「実現する、達成する」

172. use 「扱う」

177. bear 「(批判に) 耐える、(批判を) 甘んじて受ける」

178. anypody = anybody　b が p の音で発音されている。エヴァンズの方言。

179. coffers 「金庫」

179. presses 「食器棚」

182. spirit 「悪霊」

183. suggests 「そそのかす」

183-84. I would not ... Castle　I would not A for B は仮定法で、「たとえ B をもらっても A したくない」の意。ha' = have。distemper は「狂気」。

185. suffer for ... 「…のために報い (罰) を受けている」

186. pad = bad　b が p の音で発音されている。エヴァンズの方言。

186-88. as honest ... too 「5,000 人、いや 500 人に 1 人というほど貞淑な女性」

a 'omans as I will desires among five thousand, and five
hundred too.

CAIUS By gar, I see 'tis an honest woman.

FORD Well, I promised you a dinner. Come, come, walk in the   190
Park. I pray you pardon me. I will hereafter make known to
you why I have done this. — Come, wife; come, Mistress
Page. I pray you pardon me. Pray heartily pardon me.

PAGE [*To Caius and Evans*]   Let's go in, gentlemen; but, trust
me, we'll mock him. — [*To Ford, Caius, and Evans*] I do invite   195
you tomorrow morning to my house to breakfast. After, we'll
a-birding together. I have a fine hawk for the bush. Shall it be
so?

FORD Anything.

EVANS If there is one, I shall make two in the company.   200

CAIUS If there be one or two, I shall make-a the turd.

FORD Pray you, go, Master Page.

[Exeunt all but Evans and Caius]

EVANS I pray you now, remembrance tomorrow on the lousy
knave, mine host.

CAIUS Dat is good, by gar; withall my heart!   205

EVANS A lousy knave, to have his gibes and his mockeries!

Exeunt

[**ACT III, SCENE IV**]

Enter Fenton [and] Anne

FENTON I see I cannot get thy father's love;
Therefore no more turn me to him, sweet Nan.

ANNE Alas, how then?

FENTON   Why, thou must be thyself.
He doth object, I am too great of birth,
And that, my state being galled with my expense,   5
I seek to heal it only by his wealth.

187. as I will desires ＝ as I will desire to find

197. a-birding 「鳥撃ち」小銃で小鳥を狩る娯楽。

197. hawk 「ハヤブサ（sparrow-hawk）」狩猟の際に、獲物の小鳥を茂み（bush）へと追いこみ、銃で仕留めやすくするために用いられた。

200. make two 「2人目（の参加者）になる」

201. turd third（3人目）が訛って発音されている。

203. remembrance 本来は動詞 remember であるべきところに名詞が用いられているのは、エヴァンズの方言。

203. lousy 「いやな」

206. have his gibes and his mockeries 「人を馬鹿にしたり、からかったりする」

〔3.4〕あらすじ……………………………………………………………………

　ペイジ家の前で、フェントンとアンは、アンの父親ペイジのフェントンへの評価が低いことを嘆いている。そこへシャロー、スレンダー、クウィックリーが登場し、スレンダーのアンに対する求愛が始まる。ペイジ夫妻も登場し、フェントンはアンに対する自分の気持ちを2人に訴えようとするも、すげなく拒絶され、クウィックリーに指輪をアンに渡すように頼む。

………………………………………………………………………………………

2. turn me 「僕のことを話す」

2. Nan Anne の愛称。

5. state 「財産」

5. galled 「損なわれて」

Besides these, other bars he lays before me:
My riots past, my wild societies,
And tells me 'tis a thing impossible
I should love thee but as a property. 10
ANNE   Maybe he tells you true.
FENTON   No, heaven so speed me in my time to come!
Albeit I will confess thy father's wealth
Was the first motive that I wooed thee, Anne,
Yet, wooing thee, I found thee of more value 15
Than stamps in gold or sums in sealed bags.
And 'tis the very riches of thyself
That now I aim at.
ANNE   Gentle Master Fenton,
Yet seek my father's love, still seek it, sir.
If opportunity and humblest suit 20
Cannot attain it, why then — hark you hither!

                              [*They talk apart*]

[*Enter Shallow, Slender, and Mistress Quickly*]

SHALLOW   Break their talk, Mistress Quickly. My kinsman
shall speak for himself.
SLENDER   I'll make a shaft or a bolt on't. 'Slid, 'tis but
venturing. 25
SHALLOW   Be not dismayed.
SLENDER   No, she shall not dismay me. I care not for that, but
that I am afeard.
MISTRESS QUICKLY   [*To Anne*]   Hark ye, Master Slender
would speak a word with you. 30
ANNE   I come to him. [*Aside to Fenton*] This is my father's
choice.
O, what a world of vile ill-favoured faults
Looks handsome in three hundred pounds a year!
MISTRESS QUICKLY   And how does good Master Fenton? Pray

8. riots 「不品行」

8. wild societies 「悪い仲間」

9. a thing impossible 「ありえないこと」

10. but 「〜以外には」

12. speed 「成功させる」祈願文でよく用いられる。

13. Albeit ... 「…とはいえ」

16. stamps in gold 「刻印の入った金貨」

19. still 「常に」

21. hark you hither 「ここに来て、私の話を聞いて」アンは、スレンダー達が近づいてくるのに気づき、フェントンとの話を聞かれまいとしている。

22. kinsman 親戚の意だが、ここでは「甥」。

24. make a shaft or a bolt on't 「いちかばちか、ともかくやってみる」shafts（細くて長い弓）と bolts（大弓）の対比を踏まえた慣用表現（Tilley）。

24. 'Slid = by God's eyelid 軽いののしりの言葉で、「ええい」。

32. ill-favoured 「醜い」

you, a word with you.   35

[*She draws Fenton aside*]

SHALLOW   She's coming. To her, coz! O boy, thou hadst a
   father!

SLENDER   I had a father, Mistress Anne. My uncle can tell you
   good jests of him. Pray you, uncle, tell Mistress Anne the jest
   how my father stole two geese out of a pen, good uncle.   40

SHALLOW   Mistress Anne, my cousin loves you.

SLENDER   Ay, that I do, as well as I love any woman in
   Gloucestershire.

SHALLOW   He will maintain you like a gentlewoman.

SLENDER   Ay, that I will, come cut and long-tail, under the   45
   degree of a squire.

SHALLOW   He will make you a hundred and fifty pounds
   jointure.

ANNE   Good Master Shallow, let him woo for himself.

SHALLOW   Marry, I thank you for it; I thank you for that good   50
   comfort. — She calls you, coz. I'll leave you.

[*He stands aside*]

ANNE   Now, Master Slender.

SLENDER   Now, good Mistress Anne.

ANNE   What is your will?

SLENDER   My will? 'Od's heartlings, that's a pretty jest indeed!   55
   I ne'er made my will yet, I thank God. I am not such a sickly
   creature, I give God praise.

ANNE   I mean, Master Slender, what would you with me?

SLENDER   Truly, for mine own part, I would little or nothing
   with you. Your father and my uncle hath made motions. If it   60
   be my luck, so; if not, happy man be his dole! They can tell
   you how things go better than I can. You may ask your
   father; here he comes.

36. coz = cousin だが、ここでは呼びかけとして用いられている。「さあ」

36-37. thou hadst a father　シャローは、スレンダーに父親のことを思い起こさせることで、励まそうとしている。

40. pen　「（家畜を入れる）おり」

44. maintain　「養う」

44. gentlewoman　ジェントリー階級の身分を表す語で、「貴婦人」を意味する。

45. come cut and long-tail　「何があろうと」（馬や犬などの）尻尾が短く切られていようが（cut）、長かろうが（long-tail）ということに由来する諺（Tilley）。

46. degree　「身分」

46. squire　「郷士」ジェントリー階級に属し、騎士（knight）の次位に位置する身分。

48. jointure　「寡婦財産」夫の死後に妻が相続する財産で、妻の扶養のために夫によって生前に定められる。

51. comfort　「安心させる言葉」

54. will　「望み」スレンダーはこれを「遺言、遺書」と取り違えて、ちぐはぐな返答をする。

55. ’Od’s heartlings　「なんだって」by God’s heart に由来する軽いののしりの言葉。

55. pretty jest　「気のきいた冗談」

58. would　動詞で「望む、欲する」。

60. motions　「（縁組みの）申し出」

61. happy man be his dole　「その人の幸運を祈る」dole は運命の意。他人の幸運を鷹揚な態度で祝福する決まり文句（Tilley）。

[Enter Page and Mistress Page]

PAGE   Now, Master Slender. — Love him, daughter Anne. —
Why how now? What does Master Fenton here?   65
You wrong me, sir, thus still to haunt my house.
I told you, sir, my daughter is disposed of.

FENTON   Nay, Master Page, be not impatient.

MISTRESS PAGE   Good Master Fenton, come not to my child.

PAGE   She is no match for you.   70

FENTON   Sir, will you hear me?

PAGE   No, good Master Fenton.
Come, Master Shallow, come, son Slender, in.
Knowing my mind, you wrong me, Master Fenton.

                              [Exeunt Page, Shallow, and Slender]

MISTRESS QUICKLY   *[To Fenton]*   Speak to Mistress Page.

FENTON   Good Mistress Page, for that I love your daughter   75
In such a righteous fashion as I do,
Perforce, against all checks, rebukes, and manners
I must advance the colours of my love
And not retire. Let me have your good will.

ANNE   Good mother, do not marry me to yond fool.   80

MISTRESS PAGE   I mean it not. I seek you a better husband.

MISTRESS QUICKLY   That's my master, Master Doctor.

ANNE   Alas, I had rather be set quick i'th'earth,
And bowled to death with turnips.

MISTRESS PAGE   Come, trouble not yourself, good Master
Fenton.   85
I will not be your friend, nor enemy.
My daughter will I question how she loves you,
And as I find her, so am I affected.
Till then, farewell, sir. She must needs go in.
Her father will be angry.   90

FENTON   Farewell, gentle mistress. — Farewell, Nan.

66. wrong me 「私に迷惑をかける」wrong は動詞。

67. is disposed of 「嫁ぐ先が決まっている」

76. In such a righteous fashion as I do 「ご覧の通りのきちんとした方法で」

77. against all checks, rebukes, and manners 「どんな制約も叱責もしきたりもものともせずに」

78. colours 「軍旗」進軍の際に先頭でかざす。

79. good will 「承認」

80. yond fool 「あそこにいる馬鹿」

83. be set quick i'th'earth 「生き埋めにされる」quick は「生きている」の意。

84. (be) bowled to death with turnips 「蕪にぶち当たって死にそうになる」

87. question 「問いただす」

88. as I find her, so am I affected 「彼女が望むように、私も望む」affect は受身で「気持ちを動かされる」の意。

91. gentle mistress 「奥様」gentlewoman と同じく、身分を表す語。ここではペイジ夫人への呼びかけとして用いられている。

[*Exeunt Mistress Page and Anne*]

MISTRESS QUICKLY   This is my doing now. 'Nay', said I, 'will
  you cast away your child on a fool and a physician? Look on
  Master Fenton.' This is my doing.

FENTON   I thank thee, and I pray thee, once tonight,   95
  Give my sweet Nan this ring. There's for thy pains. [*He gives
  her a ring and money*]

MISTRESS QUICKLY   Now heaven send thee good fortune!

[*Exit Fenton*]

A kind heart he hath. A woman would run through fire and
water for such a kind heart. But yet I would my Master had
Mistress Anne; or I would Master Slender had her; or, in   100
sooth, I would Master Fenton had her. I will do what I can
for them all three, for so I have promised, and I'll be as good
as my word — but speciously for Master Fenton. Well, I must
of another errand to Sir John Falstaff from my two mistresses.
What a beast am I to slack it!   105

Exit

[ACT III, SCENE V]

Enter Falstaff

FALSTAFF   Bardolph, I say!

[*Enter Bardolph*]

BARDOLPH   Here, sir.

FALSTAFF   Go, fetch me a quart of sack; put a toast in't.

[*Exit Bardolph*]

Have I lived to be carried in a basket like a barrow of
butcher's offall, and to be thrown in the Thames? Well, if I be   5
served such another trick, I'll have my brains ta'en out and
buttered, and give them to a dog for a new year's gift. The
rogues slighted me into the river with as little remorse as they

95. once tonight 「今夜いつか適当な時に」

96. There's for thy pains 「ほら、これは君の尽力への御礼だ」心付けを渡す合図。

99. such a kind heart 「ああいう優しい男性」heart は brave heart（勇士）のように、限定詞を伴うと「人」の意で用いられる。

100-01. in sooth 「実際には」

103. speciously specially（特に）と言うべきところを言い間違えている。マラプロピズムの例。マラプロピズムについては 1.1.215 注参照。

103-04. I must of another errand 「もう1つのお使いに行かなければならない」must は自動詞で「行かなければならない」。of = on

105. slack 「うっかり忘れる、おろそかにする」

〔3.5〕あらすじ………………………………………………………………………
　ガーター亭で酒をあおって憂さを晴らしているフォルスタッフのもとをクウィックリーが訪れ、もう一度会いたいというフォード夫人の伝言を伝える。続いてフォード扮するブルックがやって来て、事の顛末を聞く。フォルスタッフがいそいそとフォード夫人のもとへ出かける一方、怒り狂うフォードは、今度こそ逢い引きの現場をおさえようと決意を新たにする。
………………………………………………………………………………………

3. a quart of sack 「1クォートのサックワイン」1クォートは2パイント（約1リットル）なので結構な分量。サックワインはスペインやカナリア諸島で生産された白ワイン。2.1.7 注参照。熱いトーストをサック酒やビールに浸して食べる習慣があった。

4. barrow 「手押し車一杯分の分量」

5. offall 「臓物」

7. buttered 「バターで炒めて」

7. a new year's gift 当時は、（クリスマスではなく）元旦に贈り物を交換する風習が宮廷にあった。

8. slighted me into the river slight は「軽く扱う」の意味なので、into the river との接続が悪い。そのため、slight を slide（流し込む）の過去形 slid と読み替える解釈もあるが、夫人たちがフォルスタッフを「軽く扱って川に放り込んだ」事態をフォルスタッフ特有の自由自在な言語感覚で描写しているとも考えられる。

would have drowned a blind bitch's puppies, fifteen i'th' litter!
And you may know by my size that I have a kind of alacrity   10
in sinking. If the bottom were as deep as hell, I should down.
I had been drowned but that the shore was shelvy and shallow
— a death that I abhor, for the water swells a man, and what
a thing should I have been when I had been swelled? I should
have been a mountain of mummy.   15

[Enter Bardolph with sack]

BARDOLPH   Here's Mistress Quickly, sir, to speak with you.

FALSTAFF   Come, let me pour in some sack to the Thames
water, for my belly's as cold as if I had swallowed snowballs
for pills to cool the reins. Call her in.

BARDOLPH   Come in, woman.   20

[Enter Misstress Quickly]

MISTRESS QUICKLY   By your leave, I cry you mercy. Give your
worship good morrow.

FALSTAFF   *[To Bardolph]*   Take away these chalices. Go, brew
me a pottle of sack finely.

BARDOLPH   With eggs, sir?   25

FALSTAFF   Simple of itself. I'll no pullet-sperm in my brewage.
[Exit Bardolph]

How now?

MISTRESS QUICKLY   Marry, sir, I come to your worship from
Mistress Ford.

FALSTAFF   Mistress Ford? I have had ford enough. I was   30
thrown into the ford. I have my belly full of ford.

MISTRESS QUICKLY   Alas, the day, good heart, that was not her
fault. She does so take on with her men; they mistook their
erection.

FALSTAFF   So did I mine, to build upon a foolish woman's   35
promise.

9. a blind bitch's puppies　おそらく a bitch's blind puppies「雌犬が産んだばかりの目も見えないような子犬」の意。

9. fifteen i'th' litter = fifteen in the litter で、「一度に生まれた 15 匹」。litter は（動物の）一かえりの同腹の子を指す語。

10. you may know　フォルスタッフの独白は、直接観客に対して語られている。

10-11. I have a kind of alacrity in sinking　「沈むことにかけては素早い」 alacrity は敏活の意を表す名詞。

11. If = Even if

11. down　動詞で「下にたどり着く」。

12. but that ...　「…でなかったら」

12. shelvy　「傾斜がなだらかで」遠浅の状態。

15. mummy　「死体」エジプトのミイラ（mummy）はちょうどこの頃にヨーロッパに持ち帰られたが、一般的に認知されたものではなかったと思われるので、ここはより一般的な死体と解釈するのが妥当。

17. sack　「サックワイン」スペインやカナリア諸島で生産された白ワイン。2. 1. 7 注参照。

19. reins　「腎臓」腎臓を冷やすと、性欲を抑える効果があると考えられた。

21. By your leave　「失礼ながら」leave は、許可を意味する名詞。

21. I cry you mercy　「失礼致します」cry ... mercy は「…に慈悲を求める」の意。過度にへりくだっているクウィックリー特有の表現。

23. chalices　「杯」高脚付きのグラス、ゴブレット。

23-24. brew me　「私のために準備する」

24. a pottle　「1 ポットル」4 パイント（2 リットル強）に相当する。

24. finely　「上手い味がするように」

26. Simple of itself　「何も混ぜずに酒だけで」

26. I'll no ...　「…なんか欲しくない」will は「欲する」を意味する他動詞。

26. pullet-sperm　文字通り訳すと「めんどりの精液」で、ここでは卵を指す。

30. ford　フォルスタッフはフォード夫人の姓である ford を「浅瀬」の意で用い、川に沈められたことへの嫌味を言っている。

33. take on with ...　「…に怒る」

34. erection　direction（指示）と言うべきところを言い間違えている。マラプロピズムの例。erection は「勃起」の意があるため、続くフォルスタッフの台詞は性的な意味を帯びる。

MISTRESS QUICKLY   Well, she laments, sir, for it, that it would yearn your heart to see it. Her husband goes this morning a-birding. She desires you once more to come to her between eight and nine. I must carry her word quickly. She'll make   40
you amends, I warrant you.

FALSTAFF   Well, I will visit her. Tell her so. And bid her think what a man is. Let her consider his frailty, and then judge of my merit.

MISTRESS QUICKLY   I will tell her.   45

FALSTAFF   Do so. Between nine and ten, sayst thou?

MISTRESS QUICKLY   Eight and nine. sir.

FALSTAFF   Well, be gone. I will not miss her.

MISTRESS QUICKLY   Peace be with you, sir.   [*Exit*]

FALSTAFF   I marvel I hear not of Master Brook. He sent me   50
word to stay within. I like his money well. — Oh, here he comes.

[Enter Ford disguised as Brook]

FORD   God bless you, sir.

FALSTAFF   Now, Master Brook, you come to know what hath past between me and Ford's wife.   55

FORD   That, indeed, Sir John, is my business.

FALSTAFF   Master Brook, I will not lie to you. I was at her house the hour she appointed me.

FORD   And how sped you, sir?

FALSTAFF   Very ill-favouredly, Master Brook.   60

FORD   How so, sir? Did she change her determination?

FALSTAFF   No, Master Brook, but the peaking cornuto her husband, Master Brook, dwelling in a continual 'larum of jealousy, comes me in the instant of our encounter, after we had embraced, kissed, protested, and, as it were, spoke the   65
prologue of our comedy; and at his heels, a rabble of his companions, thither provoked and instigated by his

38. yearn 「深く悲しませる」

39. a-birding 「鳥撃ち」小銃で小鳥を狩る当時の娯楽。

40. carry her word 「彼女にあなたの返事を伝える」

42. bid 「〜するように（人に）命じる」

43. frailty 「弱さ」ハムレットの「弱き者、汝の名は女（Frailty, thy name is a woman）」の有名な台詞が示すように、精神的な弱さ、すなわち意思の弱さを指すことが多い。

48. miss her 「彼女の期待に背く」

49. Peace be with you 「ご機嫌よう」平安があなたと共にありますように、という意の別れ際の挨拶。

51. stay within 「（自分が訪問するのを）宿で待つ」

53. God bless you 「ご機嫌よう」

59. sped speed「首尾良くいく、成功する」の過去形。

60. ill-favouredly 「まずく、不運な結果に」

62. peaking 「こそこそと卑屈な」

62. cornuto 「寝取られ亭主」

63. 'larum = alarum = alarm「不安」

64. comes me in = comes in「入ってくる」me は聞き手の関心をひくために挿入された虚辞（心性的与格）で、特に意味はない。

64. encounter 出会うこと、すなわちここでは「逢い引き」。

65. protested 「（愛を）誓ったり」

66. at his heels 「彼（フォード）の後に続いて」

66. rabble 「群れ」

67. thither 「その頃には」フォルスタッフは、フォードがすでに嫉妬に狂った状態で部屋に入ってきたことを説明している。

distemper, and, forsooth, to search his house for his wife's
love.

FORD   What, while you were there?   70

FALSTAFF   While I was there.

FORD   And did he search for you, and could not find you?

FALSTAFF   You shall hear. As good luck would have it, comes
in one Mistress Page, gives intelligence of Ford's approach,
and, in her invention and Ford's wife's distraction, they   75
conveyed me into a buck-basket.

FORD   A buck-basket?

FALSTAFF   Yes, a buck-basket! Rammed me in with foul shirts
and smocks, socks, foul stockings, greasy napkins, that,
Master Brook, there was the rankest compound of villainous   80
smell that ever offended nostril.

FORD   And how long lay you there?

FALSTAFF   Nay, you shall hear, Master Brook, what I have
suffered to bring this woman to evil for your good. Being
thus crammed in the basket, a couple of Ford's knaves, his   85
hinds, were called forth by their mistress, to carry me in the
name of foul clothes to Datchet Lane. They took me on their
shoulders, met the jealous knave their master in the door,
who asked them once or twice what they had in their basket.
I quaked for fear lest the lunatic knave would have searched   90
it, but Fate, ordaining he should be a cuckold, held his hand.
Well, on went he, for a search, and away went I for foul
clothes. But mark the sequel, Master Brook. I suffered the
pangs of three several deaths. First, an intolerable fright to
be detected with a jealous rotten bell-wether; next, to be   95
compassed like a good bilbo in the circumference of a peck,
hilt to point, heel to head. And then, to be stopped in like a
strong distillation with stinking clothes that fretted in their
own grease. Think of that — a man of my kidney — think of
that — that am as subject to heat as butter, a man of continual   100

68. distemper 「狂気」

69. love 「恋人」

73. As good luck would have it 「まるで幸運の女神がそう望んだかのように」 it は、文章の後半、comes in 以下を指す。

74. one Mistress Page 「ペイジ夫人という人」one の後に人名が続くと、「～ という人」「某～」の意になる。

74. intelligence 「情報」

75. distraction 「動揺」

76. buck-basket 「洗濯物のかご」3.3.2 注参照。

78. Rammed 「押し込んだ」主語の they を補って読む。

79. that = so that

84. for your good 「あなたのために」good は利益の意。

86. hinds 「下男」使用人を意味する軽侮的な表現。

91. Fate 「運命の女神」 ⇒後注

91. held his hand 「フォードの（かごの中身を探そうとする）手を制した」

94. pangs of three several deaths 「3回死ぬぐらいの辛さ」several は「様々 な（different）」の意。

95. with = by

95. bell-wether 「鈴をつけた去勢羊」去勢した雄羊の首に鈴をつけて、雌羊の 先導をさせる習慣があった。ここでは、寝取られ亭主の比喩として用いられて いる。

95-96. be compassed 「折り曲げられる」

96. good bilbo 「質のいいビルボー剣」折れずにしなる弾力性のある刃は、良 質の剣の証拠とされた。

96. in the circumference of a peck 「枡ぐらいのサイズの中に」peck は、酒 などの液体や乾物を測る際に用いられた容器。circumference は周囲の長さ。

97. hilt to point, heel to head 「柄と切り先をくっつけて、踵と頭をくっつけ て」自分の巨体を細身の剣に喩えている。フォルスタッフ流のユーモラスで大 げさな話術。

97. be stopped 「詰め込まれる」

98. strong distillation 「強烈な臭いを放つ蒸留酒」

98. fretted 「腐った」

99. a man of my kidney 「俺のような男」kidney は、「気質、たち」を意味す る。

100. [am] subject to ... 「…に弱い」

100-01. a man of continual dissolution and thaw 「常にどろどろと溶けてい るような男」dissolution も thaw も溶けること、またはその状態を意味する。

dissolution and thaw. It was a miracle to 'scape suffocation. And in the height of this bath, when I was more than half stewed in grease like a Dutch dish, to be thrown into the Thames, and cooled, glowing hot, in that surge like a horseshoe. Think of that — hissing hot — think of that, 105 Master Brook!

FORD   In good sadness, sir, I am sorry that for my sake you have suffered all this. My suit, then, is desperate? You'll undertake her no more?

FALSTAFF   Master Brook, I will be thrown into Etna, as I have 110 been into Thames, ere I will leave her thus. Her husband is this morning gone a-birding. I have received from her another embassy of meeting. 'Twixt eight and nine is the hour, Master Brook.

FORD   'Tis past eight already, sir. 115

FALSTAFF   Is it? I will then address me to my appointment. Come to me at your convenient leisure, and you shall know how I speed; and the conclusion shall be crowned with your enjoying her. Adieu. You shall have her, Master Brook. Master Brook, you shall cuckold Ford.   [*Exit*] 120

FORD   Hum! Ha! Is this a vision? Is this a dream? Do I sleep? Master Ford, awake! Awake, Master Ford! There's a hole made in your best coat, Master Ford. This 'tis to be married! This 'tis to have linen and buck-baskets! Well, I will proclaim myself what I am. I will now take the lecher. He is at my 125 house. He cannot 'scape me. 'Tis impossible he should. He cannot creep into a halfpenny purse, nor into a pepperbox. But lest the devil that guides him should aid him, I will search impossible places. Though what I am I cannot avoid, yet to be what I would not shall not make me tame. If I have horns 130 to make one mad, let the proverb go with me: I'll be horn-mad.

Exit

101. 'scape = escape

104. surge 「大波」

105. hissing hot 「熱いのが（急に冷まされて）じゅっと音を立てる」

107. In good sadness 「まったく真剣に」

109. undertake ... 「…と関わり合いになる」

110. Etna 「エトナ山」シチリア島の火山。

112. a-birding 「鳥撃ち」小銃で小鳥を狩る当時の娯楽。

113. embassy 「伝言」

116. address me 「向かう」

118. speed 「成功する」

118. be crowned with ... 「…で完成される」

122-23. There's a hole made in your best coat 「お前の一張羅のコートに穴が空いている」'To pick a hole in one's coat'（コートの穴をつまむ、すなわち「人の欠点を見つける」）という諺を踏まえている（Tilley）。

124. I will proclaim myself what I am 「本当の俺はどんな人間か見せてやる」proclaim A B で、A を B であると宣言する（明らかにする）の意。例：proclaim him a traitor（彼は謀反人であると宣言する）

127. halfpenny purse 「小銭入れ」halfpenny は小さな銀貨。

127. pepperbox 「胡椒入れ」

129. Though what I am I cannot avoid 「たとえ自分の実体を避けられないとしても」Though = Even though　実体（what I am）は寝取られ亭主であることを指す。

130. what I would not 「自分がなりたくないもの」寝取られ亭主を指す。

131. let the proverb go with me 「あの諺が自分にあてはまるだろう」

131-32. be horn-mad 「角で突き刺さんばかりに怒り狂う」1.4.45 に同様の表現がある。

[ACT IV, SCENE I]

Enter Mistress Page, Mistress Quickly, [and] William

MISTRESS PAGE   Is he at Mistress Ford's already, think'st thou?

MISTRESS QUICKLY   Sure he is by this, or will be presently. But truly he is very courageous mad about his throwing into the water. Mistress Ford desires you to come suddenly.

MISTRESS PAGE   I'll be with her by and by. I'll but bring my 5 young man here to school. Look where his master comes. 'Tis a playing day, I see.

[Enter Evans]

How now, Sir Hugh, no school today?

EVANS   No. Master Slender is let the boys leave to play.

MISTRESS QUICKLY   Blessing of his heart!   10

MISTRESS PAGE   Sir Hugh, my husband says my son profits nothing in the world at his book. I pray you, ask him some questions in his accidence.

EVANS   Come hither, William. Hold up your head. Come.

MISTRESS PAGE   Come on, sirrah. Hold up your head. Answer 15 your master, be not afraid.

EVANS   William, how many numbers is in nouns?

WILLIAM   Two.

MISTRESS QUICKLY   Truly, I thought there had been one number more, because they say "Od's nouns'.   20

EVANS   Peace, your tattlings. — What is 'fair', William?

WILLIAM   *Pulcher*.

MISTRESS QUICKLY   Polecats? There are fairer things than polecats, sure.

EVANS   You are a very simplicity 'oman. I pray you peace. — 25 What is *lapis*, William?

WILLIAM   A stone.

EVANS   And what is 'a stone', William?

〔**4. 1**〕あらすじ・・・

　ペイジ夫人は、息子のウィリアムを学校に送っていく途中、フォルスタッフが
フォード夫人宅に到着したことをクウィックリーから聞かされる。そこへやって
きたエヴァンズは、休校になったことをペイジ夫人に告げる。エヴァンズは、ウィ
リアムのラテン語能力を試そうと質問する。子供を家に帰した後、ペイジ夫人は
大急ぎでフォード夫人の家へと向かう。

・・・

2. by this = by now

2. presently 「すぐに」

3. courageous mad 「めちゃくちゃに怒って」courageous は副詞的に用いら
れて、mad（激怒して）を強めている。異例の用法。

4. suddenly 「すぐに」

5. by and by 「すぐに」

5. but = just

6. his master 「彼（ウィリアム）の先生」 ⇒後注

9. is let the boys leave to play = has given the boys a holiday　エヴァンズ
特有の不正確な文法。滑稽なぎこちなさを表現するためと思われる。

10. Blessing of his heart! 「なんて素晴らしい」直訳すると「スレンダー先生
の魂に神の祝福を」。

11-12. profits nothing in the world at his book 「勉強してもいっこうに上達
しない」profit は「進歩する」、in the world は（否定詞を強調して）「全く〜
でない」、at one's book(s) は「勉強して」の意。

13. accidence 「語形変化」

15. sirrah 「ほらっ」子供、あるいは目下の者に対する呼びかけで、苛立ちを示
す。

17. how many numbers is in nouns? 「名詞にはいくつあるか」単数と複数なの
で、ウィリアムの答えは正しい。

20. 'Od's nouns 　クウィックリーは、God's wounds（「くそっ」というののし
りの言葉）を、odd nouns「奇数の名詞」と訛って発音している。以下、ク
ウィックリーが余計な口出しをして、話をまぜっかえすやりとりが続く。

21. Peace 「黙れ、静かに」

21. tattlings 「このおしゃべり」単数形でよいところを複数形にするのは、エ
ヴァンズ独自の用法。

23. Polecats 「イタチ」売春婦の意味もあったため、続く軽口が出てくる。

23. fairer 「もう少しましな、適切な」

25. You are a very simplicity 'oman 「あなたは馬鹿ですね」無知を意味する
抽象名詞 simplicity で「馬鹿」を意味するのはエヴァンズ特有の用法。'oman
= woman

WILLIAM   A pebble.

EVANS   No, it is *lapis*. I pray you remember in your prain.   30

WILLIAM   *Lapis*.

EVANS   That is a good William. What is he, William, that does
lend articles?

WILLIAM   Articles are borrowed of the pronoun, and be thus
declined: *Singulariter nominativo: hic, haec, hoc*.   35

EVANS   *Nominativo: hig, hag, hog*. Pray you mark: *genitivo huius*.
Well, what is your accusative case?

WILLIAM   *Accusativo: hinc —*

EVANS   I pray you have your remembrance, child. *Accusatiuo:
hung, hang, hog*.   40

MISTRESS QUICKLY   'Hang-hog' is Latin for bacon, I warrant
you.

EVANS   Leave your prabbles, 'oman. — What is the focative
case, William?

WILLIAM   O — *vocativo —*O.   45

EVANS   Remember, William, focative is *caret*.

MISTRESS QUICKLY   And that's a good root.

EVANS   'Oman, forbear!

MISTRESS PAGE   Peace!

EVANS   What is your genitive case plural, William?   50

WILLIAM   Genitive case?

EVANS   Ay.

WILLIAM   *Genitivo: horum, harum, horum*.

MISTRESS QUICKLY   Vengeance of Ginny's case! Fie on her!
Never name her, child, if she be a whore.   55

EVANS   For shame, 'oman!

MISTRESS QUICKLY   You do ill to teach the child such words.
[*To Mistress Page*]   He teaches him to hic and to hac, which
they'll do fast enough of themselves, and to call 'horum'.
[*To Evans*]   Fie upon you!   60

EVANS   'Oman, art thou lunatics? Hast thou no understandings

30. prain エヴァンズの方言で、b が p の音になっている。

33. articles 「冠詞」エヴァンズは、文法事項を擬人化して説明している。

34. of ＝ from

34-35. be thus declined 「次のように格変化する」

35. *Singulariter nominativo* 「単数主格」ウィリアムは、代名詞 hic を男性形、女性形、中性形で暗唱している。

36. *hig, hag, hog* hic, haec, hoc が訛って発音されている。

36. Pray you mark 「いいから注意しなさい」pray you ＝ I pray you（お願いします）　mark は「注目する」という意の動詞。

36. *genitivo huius* 「属格は（男性形、女性形、中性形いずれも）huius」

37. accusative case 「対格」

40. *hung, hang, hog* エヴァンズにより、hunc, hunc, hoc が訛って発音されている。

41. Hang-hog ラテン語を理解しないクウィックリーは、hang（吊す）と hog（豚）をつなげて、ベーコンを連想している。

41-42. I warrant you 「絶対に」warrant は「断言する」を意味する動詞で、I warrant you は挿入句として用いられた決まり文句。

43. prabbles 「うるさく騒ぐこと」brabble が訛って発音されている。

43-44. focative case エヴァンズにより「呼格（vocative case）」が訛って発音され、v が f になっている。

46. *caret* 「無し」

47. root 「根菜」クウィックリーは、ラテン語の *caret* を英語の carrot と勘違いし、さらにエヴァンズが vocative を訛って発音した focative を fuck（性交）と聞き間違え、ニンジンを性器に喩える卑猥な連想を展開する。

48. forbear 「（発言を）控える」

50. genitive case 「属格」

54. Ginny's case 「ジニーの一件なんて、クソ食らえだ」クウィックリーは文法用語である genitive case を知らないため、genitive を人名と聞き間違い、case を格ではなく「場合」と取り違えている。case は、女性器の隠語でもあった。

54. Fie on 「なんてこと」強い不快感や嫌悪感を示す表現。

58. to hic and to hac 「hic するだとか、hac するだとか」クウィックリーは、英語の this に相当するラテン語の代名詞 hic を明らかに何か卑猥な意味の動詞と考えて、妄想している。

60. Fie upon you 「あなたときたら、もう」Fie on（upon）については、54 行目の注参照。

for thy cases, and the numbers of the genders? Thou art as
foolish Christian creatures as I would desires.

MISTRESS PAGE   Prithee hold thy peace.

EVANS   Show me now, William, some declensions of your   65
pronouns.

WILLIAM   Forsooth, I have forgot.

EVANS   It is *qui, quae, quod*. If you forget your *quis*, your *quaes*,
and your *quods*, you must be preeches. Go your ways and
play, go.   70

MISTRESS PAGE   He is a better scholar than I thought he was.

EVANS   He is a good sprag memory. Farewell, Mistress Page.

MISTRESS PAGE   Adieu, good Sir Hugh.

[Exit Evans]

Get you home, boy.

[Exit William]

Come, we stay too long.   75

Exeunt

[ACT IV, SCENE II]

Enter Falstaff [and] Mistress Ford

FALSTAFF   Mistress Ford, your sorrow hath eaten up my
sufferance. I see you are obsequious in your love, and I
profess requital to a hair's breadth, not only, Mistress Ford,
in the simple office of love, but in all the accoutrement,
complement, and ceremony of it. But are you sure of your   5
husband now?

MISTRESS FORD   He's a-birding, sweet Sir John.

MISTRESS PAGE   *[Within]*   What ho, gossip Ford! What ho!

MISTRESS FORD   Step into the chamber, Sir John.

[Exit Falstaff]

[Enter Mistress Page]

162

62. thy 話に弾みをつけたり、聞き手の関心をひくために挿入された虚辞（心性的与格）なので、特に意味はない。65行目や68-69行目の your も同じ。

64. hold thy peace 「黙りなさい」peace は「沈黙」の意。

65. declensions 「語形変化」

69. preeches 「むち打ち」breech（罰としてむちで尻を打つ）が訛り、b が p で発音されている。

72. sprag memory 「頭が良くて、記憶力がある人」sprack（頭がいい）が訛って発音されている。抽象名詞を具体的な意味で用いるのは、エヴァンズ特有の用法。4. 1. 25 注参照。

〔4. 2〕あらすじ……………………………………………………………………

　フォード夫人とペイジ夫人は共謀し、フォルスタッフを、かねてからフォードが嫌悪しているブレントフォードのばあさんに変装させる。妻がフォルスタッフと浮気していると思い込むフォードは、ペイジやエヴァンズらの制止も聞かずに、嫉妬に狂い、夫人を罵倒し、2階から降りてきた老女を殴る。一行が退場したところで、フォード夫人とペイジ夫人は、いよいよ真実を夫達に話した上で、フォルスタッフにさらに仕返しをすることを目論む。

………………………………………………………………………………………

2. obsequious 「一途な」

3. requital 「お返し」同等の愛で報いることを指す。

3. to a hair's breadth 「きっちりと」

4. accoutrement 「さらに上乗せすること」

5. complement 「不足の分を補って完全にすること」

5. ceremony 「礼節を尽くした振る舞い」

7. a-birding 「鳥撃ち」小銃で小鳥を狩る当時の娯楽。

8. gossip 「友人」特に女性同士の親しい間柄で愛情をこめて用いられた語。

9. chamber 「小部屋」

MISTRESS PAGE How now, sweetheart, who's at home besides 10
yourself?

MISTRESS FORD Why, none but mine own people.

MISTRESS PAGE Indeed?

MISTRESS FORD No, certainly. [*Aside to Mistress Page*] Speak
louder. 15

MISTRESS PAGE Truly, I am so glad you have nobody here.

MISTRESS FORD Why?

MISTRESS PAGE Why, woman, your husband is in his old lines
again. He so takes on yonder with my husband, so rails
against all married mankind, so curses all Eve's daughters of 20
what complexion soever, and so buffets himself on the
forehead, crying 'Peer out, peer out!', that any madness I ever
yet beheld seemed but tameness, civility, and patience to this
his distemper he is in now. I am glad the fat knight is not here.

MISTRESS FORD Why, does he talk of him? 25

MISTRESS PAGE Of none but him, and swears he was carried
out the last time he searched for him, in a basket, protests to
my husband he is now here, and hath drawn him and the rest
of their company from their sport to make another
experiment of his suspicion. But I am glad the knight is not 30
here. Now he shall see his own foolery.

MISTRESS FORD How near is he, Mistress Page?

MISTRESS PAGE Hard by, at street end. He will be here anon.

MISTRESS FORD I am undone. The knight is here.

MISTRESS PAGE Why then you are utterly shamed, and he's 35
but a dead man. What a woman are you! Away with him,
away with him! Better shame than murder.

MISTRESS FORD Which way should he go? How should I
bestow him? Shall I put him into the basket again?

[*Enter Falstaff*]

FALSTAFF No, I'll come no more i'th'basket. May I not go out 40

12. mine own people　使用人達を指す。but は「〜以外」の意。

14. No, certainly　「絶対に他には誰もいません」No は、12 行目の none を受けた表現。

18. in his old lines　「例の発作に取り憑かれている」line は「気まぐれ、かんしゃく」の意。ここでは、特に妻の不貞を疑うフォードの猜疑心や嫉妬を指す。

19. takes on　「わめく」

20. Eve's daughters　直訳すると「イヴの娘達」だが、女性全般を指す蔑称で「女ども」。旧約聖書の「創世記」に記されるエデンの園のエピソードではイヴが林檎を最初に食べるため、イヴ、すなわち女性に原罪の責任を負わせ、女性全般をイヴの末裔として糾弾するのは、ミソジニー（女性嫌悪）の言説の定番のレトリックとなった。

20-21. of what complexion soever　「どんな顔であろうが」complexion は「顔の色つや」を意味する。

21. buffets　「（こぶしで）何度も打ちたたく」

22. Peer out　「出てこい」妻の不貞を確信しているフォードは、額に生えているはず（だと思い込んでいる）角に向かって毒づいている。寝取られ亭主には角が生えるという定番の冗談については、2. 1. 105 注参照。

22. that　「あまりに〜なので…」（so 〜 that ...）の構文になっている。

23. civility　「礼儀正しいこと」

29. sport　「娯楽、楽しみごと」ここでは、フォード達が興じていた鷹狩りを指す。

33. Hard by　「すぐ近く」

34. I am undone　「私はおしまいだわ」

35. Why　「なんてこと」疑問詞ではなく、驚きを表す間投詞。

35-36. he's but a dead man　「彼（騎士）は死んだも同然だわ」

36. Away with him　「彼を追い出しなさい」

38-39. How should I bestow him?　「あの人をどうしたらいいかしら」bestow は「処分する、片付ける」といった意味なので、フォルスタッフを物のようにぞんざいに扱う表現におかしみがある。

ere he come?

MISTRESS PAGE   Alas, three of Master Ford's brothers watch the door with pistols, that none shall issue out; otherwise you might slip away ere he came. But what make you here?

FALSTAFF   What shall I do? I'll creep up into the chimney.   45

MISTRESS FORD   There they always use to discharge their birding-pieces.

MISTRESS PAGE   Creep into the kiln-hole.

FALSTAFF   Where is it?

MISTRESS FORD   He will seek there, on my word. Neither press,   50
coffer, chest, trunk, well, vault, but he hath an abstract for the remembrance of such places, and goes to them by his note. There is no hiding you in the house.

FALSTAFF   I'll go out, then.

MISTRESS PAGE   If you go out in your own semblance, you die,   55
Sir John — unless you go out disguised.

MISTRESS FORD   How might we disguise him?

MISTRESS PAGE   Alas the day, I know not. There is no woman's gown big enough for him; otherwise he might put on a hat, a muffler, and a kerchief, and so escape.   60

FALSTAFF   Good hearts, devise something! Any extremity rather than a mischief.

MISTRESS FORD   My maid's aunt, the fat woman of Brentford, has a gown above.

MISTRESS PAGE   On my word, it will serve him. She's as big as   65
he is; and there's her thrummed hat and her muffler too. — Run up, Sir John!

MISTRESS FORD   Go, go, sweet Sir John! Mistress Page and I will look some linen for your head.

MISTRESS PAGE   Quick, quick! We'll come dress you straight.   70
Put on the gown the while.

[Exit Falstaff]

MISTRESS FORD   I would my husband would meet him in this

43. issue out 「外に出る」issue は動詞。

44. ere 「〜前に」before と同じ用法で用いられた古語。

44. what make you here? 「ここで何をしているの」2. 1. 204-5 と同じ用法。

46-47. use to discharge their birding-pieces 「猟銃を撃つ習慣がある」銃内に溜まったすすを取り除くために、煙突の中に向けて撃つ習慣があった。birding-piece は「鳥撃ち銃」。

48. kiln-hole 「オーブンの中」

50. on my word 「誓って言うが、ぜったいに」

50. press 「食器棚」

51. vault 「地下室」

51. but 口語的な用法で、驚きなど強い感情を示す。

51. abstract 「リスト、目録」

60. kerchief 女性が外出の際に帽子の下に巻いたスカーフ。

61. Good hearts 呼びかけで、「君たち」。

63. Brentford ブレントフォードはウィンザーから東に約20キロのところに位置する町。実在の場所への言及は、この作品の持ち味の1つになっており（「解説」参照）、作品の世界に対して観客に親近感を抱かせる効果を有している。四つ折本では、「ブレントフォードの太った女（the fat woman of Brentford）」が「ブレントフォードのジリアン（Gillian of Brentford）」となっているのは、転写者によるミスか。「ブレントフォードのジリアン（またはジル）」は、滑稽詩やバラッドで人気を博した陽気な未亡人キャラクターの名前。Craik、Lindley 参照。

66. thrummed 「フリンジのついた」

67. Run up フォルスタッフに、大急ぎで2階に行くよう指示している。『ロミオとジュリエット』のいわゆるバルコニー・シーンを想像するとわかりやすいが、エリザベス朝の舞台には常設の二階舞台があった。フォルスタッフが2階に逃げこむこの場面のように、芝居の途中で演者が本舞台から二階舞台に移動する場合は、舞台上に設けられた階段を使用したのか、それとも舞台の背後にある楽屋の階段が使われたのかは定かではないが、後者の可能性が高い（Chambers）。

69. look = look for

70. come dress = come and dress

167

shape. He cannot abide the old woman of Brentford. He
swears she's a witch, forbade her my house, and hath
threatened to beat her.   75

MISTRESS PAGE   Heaven guide him to thy husband's cudgel,
and the devil guide his cudgel afterwards!

MISTRESS FORD   But is my husband coming?

MISTRESS PAGE   Ay, in good sadness is he, and talks of the
basket too, howsoever he hath had intelligence.   80

MISTRESS FORD   We'll try that; for I'll appoint my men to
carry the basket again, to meet him at the door with it as they
did last time.

MISTRESS PAGE   Nay, but he'll be here presently. Let's go dress
him like the witch of Brentford.   85

MISTRESS FORD   I'll first direct my men what they shall do with
the basket. Go up; I'll bring linen for him straight.   [*Exit*]

MISTRESS PAGE   Hang him, dishonest varlet! We cannot
misuse him enough.

We'll leave a proof, by that which we will do,   90
Wives may be merry, and yet honest too.
We do not act that often jest and laugh;
'Tis old, but true: 'Still swine eats all the draff.'   [*Exit*]

[*Enter Mistress Ford with John and Robert*]

MISTRESS FORD   Go, sirs, take the basket again on your
shoulders. Your Master is hard at door. If he bid you set it   95
down, obey him. Quickly, dispatch!   [*Exit*]

JOHN   Come, come, take it up.

ROBERT   Pray heaven it be not full of knight again!

JOHN   I hope not. I had as lief bear so much lead.

[*Enter Ford, Page, Caius, Evans, and Shallow*]

FORD   Ay, but if it prove true, Master Page, have you any way   100
then to unfool me again? — Set down the basket, villain!

73. shape 「格好」文脈上、shape は外見というよりも変装した姿を指す。

79. in good sadness 「実際に、まったく」sadness = truth

80. howsoever he hath had intelligence 「どうやってその情報を得たにせよ」

86. direct 「指示する」

88. dishonest varlet 「破廉恥な悪党」

88-89. We cannot misuse him enough 「どんなひどいことをしても足りないぐらいだ」

91. honest 「貞淑な」初期近代まで、honest は多分にジェンダー化された言葉で、女性に対して用いられる場合は、性道徳の点で慎み深いことを意味した。*OED* 3b 参照。honour が男性の場合は社会的名誉を意味したのに対して、女性に用いられる場合は貞節の美徳を意味したのも、同様のジェンダー観による用法。

92. We do not act that often jest and laugh 「ふざけたり、笑ったりしても、実際に不貞を働くわけじゃありません」that は主語 We にかかる関係代名詞。

93. Still swine eats all the draff 直訳すると「鳴かない豚ほど餌をたいらげる」となる。「むっつり助平」に似た諺。

95. hard at door 「すぐ近く、戸口に」

99. I had as lief bear so much lead 「（フォルスタッフが入ったかごを担ぐなら）同じ分量の鉛を担ぐ方がましだ」had as lief ... than 〜は「〜するくらいなら…するほうがました」の意で、than 以下は省略されている。

101. unfool シェイクスピアによる造語で、*OED* ではこの箇所が初出。「馬鹿呼ばわりしたことを取り消す」の意か。フォードの台詞は but（100）で始まっており、登場する前から会話が続いていることが示唆されている。おそらく、前回と同様に今回も取り越し苦労だったら、またフォードが馬鹿にされる、とペイジにからかわれたことに対して、逆に今回こそ疑念が本当だったら（prove true）、と言い返している。しかし、浮気をされていたら、それはそれで馬鹿にされるので、フォードのこの台詞にはナンセンスな滑稽さがある。どちらの結果になっても自分が笑い物になることに、フォード自身は気づいていない。

Somebody call my wife. Youth in a basket! Oh you panderly rascals! There's a knot, a gang, a pack a conspiracy against me. Now shall the devil be shamed. — What, wife, I say! Come, come forth! Behold what honest clothes you send 105 forth to bleaching!

PAGE   Why, this passes, Master Ford. You are not to go loose any longer, you must be pinioned.

EVANS   Why, this is lunatics. This is mad as a mad dog.

SHALLOW   Indeed, Master Ford, this is not well indeed.   110

FORD   So say I too, sir. Come hither Mistress Ford!

[*Enter Mistress Ford*]

Mistress Ford, the honest woman, the modest wife, the virtuous creature, that hath the jealous fool to her husband! I suspect without cause, mistress, do I?

MISTRESS FORD   Heaven be my witness you do, if you suspect   115
me in any dishonesty.

FORD   Well said, brazen-face, hold it out! — Come forth, sirrah!

[*He opens the basket and begins pulling out clothes*]

PAGE   This passes.

MISTRESS FORD   Are you not ashamed? Let the clothes alone.   120

FORD   I shall find you anon.

EVANS   'Tis unreasonable. Will you take up your wife's clothes? Come, away.

FORD   [*To John and Robert*]   Empty the basket, I say!

MISTRESS FORD   Why, man, why?   125

FORD   Master Page, as I am a man, there was one conveyed out of my house yesterday in this basket. Why may not he be there again? In my house I am sure he is. My intelligence is true, my jealousy is reasonable. [*To John and Robert*] Pluck me out all the linen.   130

103. knot 「一団、一味」同じ行の gang や pack も同様の意味。

104. Now shall the devil be shamed 「白黒はっきりさせて、悪党をこらしめてやる」shall は話者の意思を示す。「真実を語れば、悪魔も恥じ入る（Speak the truth and shame the devil)」という諺を踏まえた表現（Tilley)。

104. What 「おい！」呼びかける際の間投詞。

107. this passes 「これはひどすぎる」フォードの行動は許容範囲を超えている（passes）という意。119行目でも繰り返されている。

107-08. You are not to go loose any longer 「これ以上騒ぎ立てるのはやめるんだ」

113. to = as

117. hold it out 「そうやって頑固に言い張るんだな」hold out は「（意見などを）押し通す」の意。

122. unreasonable 「常軌を逸している」

128. My intelligence 「自分が得ている情報」

129. me 動詞の語勢を強めるために挿入された虚辞（心性的与格）で、特に意味はない。

MISTRESS FORD If you find a man there, he shall die a flea's death.

PAGE Here's no man.

SHALLOW By my fidelity, this is not well, Master Ford. This wrongs you.   135

EVANS Master Ford, you must pray, and not follow the imaginations of your own heart. This is jealousies.

FORD Well, he's not here I seek for.

PAGE No, nor nowhere else but in your brain.

FORD Help to search my house this one time. If I find not   140
what I seek, show no colour for my extremity. Let me forever be your table-sport. Let them say of me, 'as jealous as Ford, that searched a hollow walnut for his wife's leman'. Satisfy me once more. Once more search with me.

[Exeunt John and Robert with the basket]

MISTRESS FORD What ho, Mistress Page! Come you and the   145
old woman down. My husband will come into the chamber.

FORD Old woman? What old woman's that?

MISTRESS FORD Why, it is my maid's aunt of Brentford.

FORD A witch, a quean, an old cozening quean! Have I not forbid her my house? She comes of errands, does she? We are   150
simple men; we do not know what's brought to pass under the profession of fortune-telling. She works by charms, by spells, by the figure, and such daubery as this is, beyond our element. We know nothing. — Come down, you witch, you hag, you! Come down, I say!   155

[Enter Mistress Page leading Falstaff disguised as an old woman]

MISTRESS FORD Nay, good sweet husband! — Good gentlemen, let him not strike the old woman.

MISTRESS PAGE Come, mother Pratt, come. Give me your hand.

FORD I'll pratt her! *[He beats Falstaff]* Out of my door, you   160

131-32. he shall die a flea's death 「そいつを蚤^{のみ}のように潰してみせる」shall は話者の意思を示す。die ... death の場合、die は他動詞で、「…のような最期を遂げる」の意になる。

134. fidelity 「信仰」

135. wrongs 「名誉を傷つける」

141. show no colour for my extremity 「私の極端な行動について一切の言い訳は無用だ」colour は「口実、言い訳」の意。

142. table-sport 元来 sport は遊びや娯楽を意味するので、table-sport は食卓での話の種、すなわち「笑い物」。

143. leman 「恋人」

149. quean 女性への蔑称（「あの女」）だが、「売春宿の女将」も含意されている。

153. figure 「占星術（の際に用いられる図）」

153-54. beyond our element 「我々の理解を超えて」element は自然界の意だが、ここでは比喩的に用いられている。

158. mother Pratt イギリスの童謡の題名に見られる「ハバードばあさん（old mother Hubbard）」の例が示すように、mother は老女への呼称として用いられた。唐突に言及される Pratt は、実際に存在するイギリスの姓ではあるが、おそらくここでは固有名詞ではなく「ずるい人」を意味する一般名詞 prat から連想したフォードの造語。訳すと「いんちきばあさん」。

witch, you rag, you baggage, you polecat, you runnion! Out, out! I'll conjure you, I'll fortune-tell you!

[Exit Falstaff]

MISTRESS PAGE   Are you not ashamed? I think you have killed the poor woman.

MISTRESS FORD   Nay, he will do it. — 'Tis a goodly credit for   165
you.

FORD   Hang her, witch!

EVANS   By yea and no, I think the 'oman is a witch indeed. I like not when a 'oman has a great peard. I spy a great peard under her muffler.   170

FORD   Will you follow, gentlemen? I beseech you, follow. See but the issue of my jealousy. If I cry out thus upon no trail, never trust me when I open again.

PAGE   Let's obey his humour a little further. Come, gentlemen.
[Exeunt Ford, Page, Caius, Evans, and Shallow]

MISTRESS PAGE   Trust me, he beat him most pitifully.   175

MISTRESS FORD   Nay, by th'mass, that he did not: he beat him most unpitifully, methought.

MISTRESS PAGE   I'll have the cudgel hallowed and hung o'er the altar. It hath done meritorious service.

MISTRESS FORD   What think you? May we with the warrant of   180
womanhood and the witness of a good conscience, pursue him with any further revenge?

MISTRESS PAGE   The spirit of wantonness is sure scared out of him. If the devil have him not in fee-simple, with fine and recovery, he will never, I think, in the way of waste attempt us   185
again.

MISTRESS FORD   Shall we tell our husbands how we have served him?

MISTRESS PAGE   Yes, by all means, if it be but to scrape the figures out of your husband's brains. If they can find in their   190
hearts the poor unvirtuous fat knight shall be any further

161. rag 「ばばあ」本来は「ぼろ布」を意味する rag が、侮蔑の言葉として用いられている。

161. baggage 「あばずれ女」

161. runnion 「くそばばあ」

165. credit 「名誉」フォードへの嫌味。

168. By yea and no 「たしかに」同意を表す表現。

169. peard = beard　エヴァンズのウェールズ方言では、b が p の音になる。

169. spy 「見る」本来は過去形になるところで現在形を用いるのも、エヴァンズの特長。

171. follow = follow me

172. issue 「結末、成果」

172-73. If I cry out thus upon no trail, never trust me when I open again　狩猟に関連した用語を用いて、自分を猟犬に喩えた比喩。trail は獣の臭跡を意味し、狩猟の手がかりとなる。cry out や open は、猟犬が吠えること。「もし、私が獲物の匂いもしないのにこんなに吠えているとすれば、今度私が騒いでも二度と信用しなくてもかまわん」

174. humour 「気まぐれ、酔狂」四体液に基づく「気質」の意味も入っている。1. 1. 114 注参照。

175. pitifully 「可哀想なぐらいに」

176. by th'mass 「神にかけて、全く」mass は教会の聖餐式。

177. unpitifully 「冷酷無慈悲に」ペイジ夫人が使った表現 pitifully を受けての言葉遊び。

180-81. with the warrant of womanhood and the witness of a good conscience　女らしさ（womanhood）と良心（good conscience）をそれぞれ証人（warrant / witness）とすることから、「女らしさや良心に恥じない程度で」。

184-85. have him not in fee-simple, with fine and recovery　「変更の余地がないほどに完全に我が物とする」fee-simple は「無条件相続権」を、recovery は「権利の回復」を意味する法律用語。

185. in the way of waste 「不埒な真似」前の文章に引き続き、「毀損」を表す法律用語 waste が用いられている。

188. served 「仕打ちをした」

189-90. scrape the figures 「妄想を拭い去る」figure には、動詞で「想像する、思い描く」という意味があり、ここではその名詞形。

191. poor 「さもしい」フォルスタッフへの同情は皆無なので、「可哀想な」という意味ではない。

afflicted, we two will still be the ministers.

MISTRESS FORD   I'll warrant they'll have him publicly shamed,
and methinks there would be no period to the jest, should he
not be publicly shamed.   195

MISTRESS PAGE   Come, to the forge with it, then shape it. I
would not have things cool.

Exeunt

[ACT IV, SCENE III]

Enter Host and Bardolph

BARDOLPH   Sir, the German desires to have three of your
horses. The Duke himself will be tomorrow at court, and
they are going to meet him.

HOST   What duke should that be comes so secretly? I hear not
of him in the court. Let me speak with the gentlemen. They   5
speak English?

BARDOLPH   Ay, sir. I'll call him to you.

HOST   They shall have my horses, but I'll make them pay. I'll
sauce them. They have had my house a week at command. I
have turned away my other guests. They must come off. I'll   10
sauce them. Come.

Exeunt

[ACT IV, SCENE IV]

Enter Page, Ford, Mistress Page, Mistress Ford, [and] Evans

EVANS   'Tis one of the best discretions of a 'oman as ever I did
look upon.

PAGE   And did he send you both these letters at an instant?

MISTRESS PAGE   Within a quarter of an hour.

FORD   Pardon me, wife. Henceforth do what thou wilt.   5
I rather will suspect the sun with cold

192. we two will still be the ministers 「私たちがさらに力を尽くしましょう」
minister は「僕、働き手」の意。

194. period 「区切り、休止」

194-95. should he ... shamed if が省略されて、倒置が生じている文型なので、
if he should ... shamed として読むとわかりやすい。

196. forge 「（鍛冶場の）炉」

〔4. 3〕あらすじ……………………………………………………………………………………
　バードルフは、ドイツ人が馬を3頭借りたがっている旨をガーター亭の亭主
に告げる。亭主は、彼らが既に宿を1週間貸し切りにすることになっているこ
ともあり、代金を多めに請求する計画を立てる。

………

1. the German 以下始まるドイツ人への言及は、1597 年にガーター騎士に任
命されたドイツのヴュルテンベルク公爵を想定している可能性がある。ガー
ター騎士団入りは公爵の積年の願いだったが、式典には欠席しており、この点
も第5場のキーズの台詞 'der is no duke that the court is know to come'
（73-74 行）と符合する。宮廷上演の観客向けの冗談か（Craik）。ガーター騎
士団は、創設当初より軍事的な性質を有しており、他国の王侯貴族に騎士団の
爵位を授与することは、しばしば両国の同盟関係の担保として利用された。特
に、エリザベス一世は、相次ぐ政治的難局を乗り切るためにガーター騎士団を
外交の切り札として用いたことで知られている。解説 12 ページも参照。

4. comes = that comes　関係代名詞は duke を形容する。

9. sauce them 「そいつらに高値をふっかけてやる」

9. have had my house a week at command 「俺の宿を1週間好きなように使
うことになった」

10. come off 「金を渡す、代金を支払う」

〔4. 4〕あらすじ……………………………………………………………………………………
　これまでの経緯を聞いたフォード、ペイジ、エヴァンズが、夫人達と共に登場。
今や真相を知ったフォードは自分の過ちを妻に詫び、以後は貞節を疑うことはし
ないと約束する。一行は、一連の悪ふざけの仕上げとして、真夜中にフォルスタッ
フをウィンザーの森におびき出し、妖精に変装したアンら子供達にこらしめても
らう計画を立てる。さらに、ペイジ夫妻は、この機を利用し、アンの結婚につい
てもそれぞれの策略を練る。

………

6. suspect the sun with cold 「太陽が冷たいのではないかと疑う」

Than thee with wantonness. Now doth thy honour stand
In him that was of late an heretic,
As firm as faith.

PAGE   'Tis well,'tis well. No more.
Be not as extreme in submission as in offence.   10
But let our plot go forward. Let our wives
Yet once again, to make us public sport,
Appoint a meeting with this old fat fellow,
Where we may take him and disgrace him for it.

FORD   There is no better way than that they spoke of.   15

PAGE   How, to send him word they'll meet him in the Park at
midnight? Fie, fie, he'll never come.

EVANS   You say he has been thrown in the rivers, and has been
grievously peaten as an old 'oman. Methinks there should be
terrors in him, that he should not come. Methinks his flesh is   20
punished; he shall have no desires.

PAGE   So think I too.

MISTRESS FORD   Devise but how you'll use him when he comes,
And let us two devise to bring him thither.

MISTRESS PAGE   There is an old tale goes, that Herne the
Hunter,   25
Sometime a keeper here in Windsor Forest,
Doth all the winter time at still midnight
Walk round about an oak with great ragg'd horns;
And there he blasts the trees, and takes the cattle,
And makes milch-kine yield blood, and shakes a chaine   30
In a most hideous and dreadful manner.
You have heard of such a spirit, and well you know
The superstitious idle-headed eld
Received, and did deliver to our age
This tale of Herne the Hunter for a truth.   35

PAGE   Why, yet there want not many that do fear
In deep of night to walk by this Herne's Oak.

8. of late 「最近は」

9. As firm as faith 「信仰のようにしっかりと（根づいている）」6行目の
stand にかかる。

10. Be not as extreme in submission as in offence 「罪を犯すのも、過ちを認
めるのも、やりすぎは禁物だ」submission は「過ちを認める」の意だが、
「服従」も含意されている。

12. to make us public sport 「おおっぴらに気晴らしになるようなことを我々
に提供してもらうために」make sport は「娯楽を提供する」の意。us の前
に for を補って読む。

16. send ... word 「伝える」they'll meet ... の前に that を補って読む。

16. Park 「御猟園」王室の勅許により狩猟目的で各地に設けられていた。こう
した私有地が一般庶民の娯楽に開放されて、現代の「公園」という概念が普及
するのは 18 世紀以降である。

17. Fie 否定的に驚きを表す間投詞。「まさか」

19. peaten ＝ beaten　エヴァンズのウェールズ方言では、b が p の音になる。

20. that 結果を表す so that と同じ用法。

23. how you'll use him 「彼をどんな目に遭わせるか」use は「扱う、対応す
る」の意。

25. Herne the Hunter 以下語られる森番ハーンにまつわる民話は、おそらく
シェイクスピアによる創作と推測される。そのためスペリングも定まっておら
ず、四つ折本では Herne は一貫して Horne と綴られている（Lindley）。5. 1.
11 でフォルスタッフがブルックに逢い引きの場所として伝える「ハーンの樫
の木」がリトル・パークと呼ばれるウィンザーの猟園に実在したが、Craik が
指摘するように、おそらくこの作品が人気を博した結果、後から命名された可
能性が高い。

26. Sometime ＝ formerly「昔は」

26. keeper 「森番」

26. Forest 「御猟林」16行目の Park と同じく、王室の猟場。「森番（keeper）」
によって管理されていた。

27. still 形容詞で「静かな」。

29. blasts 「枯らす」

29. takes 「殺す」

30. milch-kine 「乳牛」

32. spirit 「亡霊」妖精や亡霊など、異界の存在を指す際に広く用いられた。

33. idle-headed eld 「馬鹿な昔の人々」

36. Why 「いやはや」疑問視ではなく、強い感情を表す間投詞。

36. there want not many that ... 「…する人には事欠かない、…する人はたく
さんいる」 want は「欠く」の意。

But what of this?

MISTRESS FORD   Marry this is our device:
That Falstaff at that oak shall meet with us,
Disguised like Herne, with huge horns on his head.   40

PAGE   Well, let it not be doubted but he'll come,
And in this shape. When you have brought him thither,
What shall be done with him? What is your plot?

MISTRESS PAGE   That likewise have we thought upon, and
thus:
Nan Page, my daughter, and my little son,   45
And three or four more of their growth we'll dress
Like urchins, oafs, and fairies, green and white,
With rounds of waxen tapers on their heads,
And rattles in their hands. Upon a sudden,
As Falstaff, she, and I are newly met,   50
Let them from forth a sawpit rush at once
With some diffused song. Upon their sight,
We two in great amazedness will fly.
Then let them all encircle him about,
And fairy-like to pinch the unclean knight,   55
And ask him why, that hour of fairy revel,
In their so sacred paths he dares to tread
In shape profane.

MISTRESS FORD   And till he tell the truth,
Let the supposed fairies pinch him sound,
And burn him with their tapers.

MISTRESS PAGE   The truth being known,   60
We'll all present ourselves, dis-horn the spirit,
And mock him home to Windsor.

FORD   The children must
Be practised well to this, or they'll ne'er do't.

EVANS   I will teach the children their behaviours, and I will be
like a jackanapes also, to burn the knight with my taber.   65

41-42. let it not be doubted but he'll come, / And in this shape. 「彼がその格好でやってくるのは間違いないと想定するとしよう」but の後に that を補って読む。but は「ただ、たしかに」という意の強意副詞。

46. their growth 「同じような寸法」

47. urchins / fairies いずれも「妖精、精霊」を指す言葉。

49. rattles 「がらがらと音が鳴る物」

51. sawpit 「木挽き穴」材木を切るための穴。

52. diffused song 「調子の外れた不穏な歌」

55. pinch 男女関係においてだらしがない人間が罰として妖精につねられる話は、イギリスの民話にしばしば登場し、シェイクスピアと同時代の文学作品にも散見される。例えば、1580 年代に活躍した劇作家ジョン・リリーの喜劇『エンディミオン』には、恋に溺れて女王の命に背いた隊長が妖精の一群に取り囲まれ、「青く赤くなるまで」身体中をつねられる場面がある。

56. revel 「宴、祝宴」

59. supposed fairies 「にせものの妖精達」

59. sound 副詞で「十分に」

61. dis-horn the spirit 「（フォルスタッフが扮している）ハーンの亡霊の角を取る」もちろん、ここには寝取られ亭主の角の比喩も含意されている。2. 1. 105 参照。

64-65. I will be like a jackanapes also 「私もいたずら小僧になって」

FORD   That will be excellent. I'll go buy them vizards.

MISTRESS PAGE   My Nan shall be the Queen of all the Fairies,
Finely attired in a robe of white.

PAGE   That silk will I go buy. — [*Aside*] And in that time
Shall Master Slender steal my Nan away   70
And marry her at Eton. [*To Mistress Page and Mistress Ford*]
                              ﹅ Go, send to Falstaff straight.

FORD   Nay, I'll to him again in name of Brook;
He'll tell me all his purpose. Sure he'll come.

MISTRESS PAGE   Fear not you that. — [*To Page, Ford, and
Evans*]   Go get us properties
And tricking for our fairies.   75

EVANS   Let us about it. It is admirable pleasures, and fery
honest knaveries.

                              [*Exeunt Page, Ford, and Evans*]

MISTRESS PAGE   Go, Mistress Ford,
Send quickly to Sir John, to know his mind.

                              [*Exit Mistress Ford*]

I'll to the Doctor. He hath my good will,   80
And none but he, to marry with Nan Page.
That Slender, though well-landed, is an idiot.
And he my husband best of all affects.
The Doctor is well moneyed, and his friends
Potent at court. He, none but he, shall have her,   85
Though twenty thousand worthier come to crave her.

                              [*Exit*]

[ACT IV, SCENE V]

Enter Host [*and*] *Simple*

HOST   What wouldst thou have, boor? What, thick-skin?
Speak, breathe, discuss; brief, short, quick, snap.

69. go buy = go and buy

71. Eton テムズ川を挟んでウィンザーの反対側に位置する町。現在は、名門パブリックスクールのイートン校で知られる。

71. send 「使いを送る」79行目の send も同じ用法。

72. I'll to him = I'll go to him　動詞が省略されている。

74. properties 「小道具」具体的には、48行目の tapers や 49行目の rattles を指す。

75. tricking 「衣装」

76. Let us about it 「取りかかろう」

76. fery = very　エヴァンズの方言では、v が f の音で発音される。

80. good will 「承諾」次行の to 以下へと続く。

83. he = him　同じ行の動詞 affects（好む）の目的語。

〔4.5〕あらすじ‥‥‥‥‥‥‥‥‥‥‥‥‥‥‥‥‥‥‥‥‥‥‥‥‥‥‥‥‥‥‥‥‥‥‥‥

　スレンダーの従僕のシンプルが、主人の使いでガーター亭を訪れ、先ほど見かけたブレントフォードの占い師の女性にスレンダーのアンへの求愛の成否を占ってほしいと要望を伝える。現れたフォルスタッフが上手くごまかしてシンプルを帰すと、今度はクウィックリーが現れ、フォード夫人とペイジ夫人からの伝言を伝える。最初は渋っていたものの、フォルスタッフは再び話を聞くためにクウィックリーを部屋に通す。

‥‥‥

1. boor 「田舎者」

1. thick-skin 皮膚が厚くて、感覚が鈍いことから、「のろま」

2. breathe 「言葉を発する」

2. snap 「さっさと」直前の3つの単語（brief, short, quick）と同じく副詞として用いられている。

SIMPLE   Marry, sir, I come to speak with Sir John Falstaff
from Master Slender.

HOST   There's his chamber, his house, his castle, his standing-   5
bed and truckle-bed. 'Tis painted about with the story of the
Prodigal, fresh and new. Go, knock and call. He'll speak like
an Anthropophaginian unto thee. Knock, I say.

SIMPLE   There's an old woman, a fat woman, gone up into his
chamber. I'll be so bold as stay, sir, till she come down. I   10
come to speak with her, indeed.

HOST   Ha? A fat woman? The knight may be robb'd. I'll call.
— Bully knight! Bully Sir John! Speak from thy lungs
military. Art thou there? It is thine host, thine Ephesian,
calls.   15

FALSTAFF   [*Within*]   How now, mine host?

HOST   Here's a Bohemian Tartar tarries the coming down of
thy fat woman. Let her descend, bully, let her descend. My
chambers are honourable. Fie! Privacy? Fie!

[*Enter Falstaff*]

FALSTAFF   There was, mine host, an old fat woman even now   20
with me, but she's gone.

SIMPLE   Pray you, sir, was't not the wise woman of Brentford?

FALSTAFF   Ay, marry, was it, mussel-shell. What would you
with her?

SIMPLE   My master, sir, Master Slender, sent to her, seeing her   25
go thorough the streets, to know, sir, whether one Nim, sir,
that beguiled him of a chain, had the chain or no.

FALSTAFF   I spake with the old woman about it.

SIMPLE   And what says she, I pray, sir?

FALSTAFF   Marry, she says that the very same man that   30
beguiled Master Slender of his chain cozened him of it.

SIMPLE   I would I could have spoken with the woman herself.
I had other things to have spoken with her too, from him.

5-6. standing-bed 「天蓋付きのベッド」天蓋を支える4本の支柱が付いているベッド。

6. truckle-bed 「ウィール付きベッド」車輪がついた低めのベッドで、天蓋付きのベッドのような大きめのベッドの下に収納できるようになっていた。

6-7. 'Tis painted about with the story of the Prodigal 「（その部屋は）放蕩息子の物語がぐるっと壁に描かれている」部屋の壁に絵画（版画）またはタペストリーがかけられている様子を示す。the Prodigal は、新約聖書の「ルカの福音書」第15章で語られる放蕩息子（prodigal son）のたとえ話を指す。放蕩の限りを尽くして、父からもらった財産を使い果たした息子が、自らの不品行を悔い改めた末に実家に戻り、慈悲深い父に許される。この物語は、改悛（かいしゅん）と赦しをめぐるキリスト教の重要な教義をわかりやすく説いた寓意であり、絵画や文学の主題やモティーフとして用いられることも多い。Astington によると、印刷出版版が発展した近代初期イングランドでは、聖書の有名な箇所を描いた版画が市場に流通し、民家の内装にも用いられた。

8. Anthropophaginian 「食人族」

10. I'll be so bold as stay 「遠慮なくここで待つとしよう」stay は「待つ」の意。ノックせずにただ待つのは大胆な（bold）行動ではまったくないが、気弱なくせに精一杯強がってみせているシンプルの滑稽さが表れている。

13. Bully 「よう、お前さん」bully は親しみをこめて仲間を呼ぶ際の呼びかけ。

14. Ephesian 「エフェソス人」新約聖書の「エフェソスの信徒への手紙」で、聖パウロにより飲酒など堕落した生活への戒めを受ける民を想起させる。

17. a Bohemian Tartar 「ボヘミアから来たタタール人みたいな野郎」タタール人は猛者として知られたアジア北東部の遊牧民族。ボヘミアはタタール人と関係性はなく、単にエキゾチックな印象を与えるために言及されている。軟弱なスレンダーにははなはだ似つかわしくない形容をあえて試みる亭主のナンセンスな冗談。

17. tarries 原形は tarry で「待つ」。

18-19. My chambers are honourable 「俺の宿はきちんとした宿屋だぞ」亭主は、フォルスタッフが女性を部屋に連れ込んでいることをからかっている。

22. wise woman 「占いの女性」中世ヨーロッパの町や村には、薬草の知識に詳しく、占いの技に長けた wise woman と呼ばれる女性がいた。

23. mussel-shell 「ムール貝の貝殻みたいな奴」シンプルへの悪態。

25. sent to her 「彼女にお伝えしたいことがあるのです」send は「使いを送る」の意。直訳すると「（私の主人、スレンダー氏が）私を彼女のもとに遣わした」となる。

26. one Nim 「ニムとかいう人」

185

FALSTAFF   What are they? Let us know.

HOST   Ay, come. Quick.   35

SIMPLE   I may not conceal them, sir.

HOST   Conceal them, or thou diest.

SIMPLE   Why, sir, they were nothing but about Mistress Anne
Page, to know if it were my master's fortune to have her or
no.   40

FALSTAFF   'Tis; 'tis his fortune.

SIMPLE   What, sir?

FALSTAFF   To have her or no. Go, say the woman told me so.

SIMPLE   May I be bold to say so, sir?

FALSTAFF   Ay, sir, like who more bold.   45

SIMPLE   I thank your worship. I shall make my master glad
with these tidings.   [*Exit*]

HOST   Thou art clerkly, thou art clerkly, Sir John. Was there a
wise woman with thee?

FALSTAFF   Ay, that there was, mine host, one that hath taught   50
me more wit than ever I learned before in my life. And I paid
nothing for it neither, but was paid for my learning.

[*Enter Bardolph*]

BARDOLPH   Out, alas, sir, cozenage, mere cozenage!

HOST   Where be my horses? Speak well of them, varletto.

BARDOLPH   Run away with the cozeners. For so soon as I came   55
beyond Eton, they threw me off from behind one of them in
a slough of mire, and set spurs and away, like three German
devils, three Doctor Faustuses.

HOST   They are gone but to meet the Duke, villain. Do not say
they be fled. Germans are honest men.   60

[*Enter Evans*]

EVANS   Where is mine host?

HOST   What is the matter, sir?

186

38. Why 疑問詞ではなく、同意や相づちなど、相手の言葉に対する様々な反応を示す間投詞。「そりゃあもちろん」

45. like who more bold もっと大胆な人間のように、の意。「もっと大胆に言ってもいいぐらいだ」

48. clerkly 「学識がある」

51. wit 「叡智」

53. mere 「正真正銘の」

54. varletto 「下郎め」varlet「下男」にイタリア語風の語尾が付されている。

56. beyond Eton 「イートンを過ぎたところで」イートンについては、4. 4. 71 注参照。

56. they threw me off from behind one of them 「3人のうちの1人の後ろに座っていた俺を振り落とした」3頭の馬を貸す際に、バードルフは添え鞍（pillion）と呼ばれる後部席に跨がっていた模様。

58. Doctor Faustuses 「フォースタス博士たち」クリストファー・マーロウの悲劇『フォースタス博士』（1592）で知られるフォースタス博士は、己の魂と肉体と引き換えに魔術を手に入れる契約を悪魔と結ぶ。材源は、中世ドイツの散文物語。

59. villain ドイツ人ではなく、バードルフに向けて言っているので、「この野郎」の意。

EVANS   Have a care of your entertainments. There is a friend
of mine come to town tells me there is three cozen-Germans
that has cozened all the hosts of Reading, of Maidenhead, of   65
Colnbrook, of horses and money. I tell you for good will,
look you. You are wise, and full of gibes and vlouting-stocks,
and 'tis not convenient you should be cozened. Fare you well.
                                                                                    [*Exit*]

[*Enter Caius*]

CAIUS   Vere is mine host de Jarteer?
HOST   Here, Master Doctor, in perplexity and doubtful   70
dilemma.
CAIUS   I cannot tell vat is dat; but it is tell-a me dat you make
grand preparation for a duke de Jamanie. By my trot, der is
no duke that the court is know to come. I tell you for good
will. Adieu.   [*Exit*]   75
HOST   [*To Bardolph*]   Hue and cry, villain, go! [*To Falstaff*]
Assist me, knight, I am undone! [*To Bardolph*] Fly, run, hue
and cry, villain! I am undone!
                                                [*Exeunt Host and Bardolph*]

FALSTAFF   I would all the world might be cozened, for I have
been cozened and beaten too. If it should come to the ear of   80
the court how I have been transformed, and how my
transformation hath been washed and cudgelled, they would
melt me out of my fat drop by drop, and liquor fishermen's
boots with me. I warrant they would whip me with their fine
wits till I were as crestfallen as a dried pear. I never prospered   85
since I forswore myself at primero. Well, if my wind were but
long enough, I would repent.

[*Enter Mistress Quickly*]

Now, whence come you?
MISTRESS QUICKLY   From the two parties, forsooth.

63. Have a care of your entertainments 「客のもてなしに注意しなさい」

64. cozen-Germans 「ペテン師のドイツ人」cozen は「だます」を意味する動詞なので、エヴァンズらしく、文法的には間違っている用語だが、意味は通じる。

65-66. Reading / Maidenhead / Colnbrook いずれも、ロンドン郊外に位置するイングランド南東部の街の名前。レディング、メイデンヘッド、コーンブルック。

66. I tell you for good will 「善意で教えてやるが」

67. look you 「気をつけろ」

67. vlouting-stocks 「人を馬鹿にするネタ」エヴァンズのウェールズ方言では、f が v の音になるので、vlout = flout（馬鹿にする）。

69. Vere is mine host de Jarteer キーズのフランス語訛りの英語で、Vere = Where、Jarteer = Garter。

70-71. doubtful dilemma 「不安でいっぱいの窮地」

72. I cannot tell vat ... キーズ流の発音に注意。w は v の音に、th [ð] が d の音になる。文法的な間違いも多いのが、キーズの台詞の特徴。

72. it is tell-a me = it tells me で、it は that（キーズは dat と発音）以下を指す強調構文。「〜を知っています」

73. By my trot By my troth（「たしかに」）が訛って発音されている。

74. is know = knows

76. Hue and cry 罪人を捕縛する際のかけ声。「泥棒め、御用だ！」

76. villain 「この野郎」癇癪（かんしゃく）を起こした亭主がバードルフに向かって悪態をついている。

83. fat 「脂肪」

83. liquor 「（防水のために）油を塗る」自分の身体が溶けて油になり、漁師の長靴の防水油として用いられる、というグロテスクだが滑稽な比喩。

85. crestfallen 「とさかの垂れた鶏のようにぐったりして」

86. since I forswore myself at primero 「賭博のごまかしがばれてからというもの」プリメロは賭博に用いられたトランプの一種。forswear myself は「偽装する」の意で、ここではごまかしが発覚したのになおも否定する状況を指す。

86-87. if my ... enough 「俺がもしも十分長生きするとすれば」wind は「息」の意。仮定法で語られており、本気で悔い改める気持はフォルスタッフにはない。四つ折本では、long enough の部分が long enough to say my prayers（たとえお祈りを言うぐらい長生きしたとしても）となっている。祈りに関する言及があった方が、普段はお祈りなどしない不真面目なフォルスタッフらしい冗談の意図は明確になるものの、シェイクスピアが書いた台詞ではなく、役者のアドリブである可能性が高い（Crane, Oliver）。

89. two parties 「2 人」party は person と同じ意味で用いられている。

FALSTAFF   The devil take one party, and his dam the other, and   90
so they shall be both bestowed. I have suffered more for their
sakes, more than the villainous inconstancy of man's
disposition is able to bear.

MISTRESS QUICKLY   And have not they suffered? Yes, I warrant;
speciously one of them. Mistress Ford, good heart, is beaten   95
black and blue that you cannot see a white spot about her.

FALSTAFF   What tell'st thou me of black and blue? I was beaten
myself into all the colours of the rainbow; and I was like to
be apprehended for the witch of Brentford. But that my
admirable dexterity of wit, my counterfeiting the action of   100
an old woman, delivered me, the knave constable had set me
i'th' stocks, i'th'common stocks, for a witch.

MISTRESS QUICKLY   Sir, let me speak with you in your chamber.
You shall hear how things go, and, I warrant, to your content.
Here is a letter will say somewhat. Good hearts, what ado   105
here is to bring you together! Sure, one of you does not serve
heaven well, that you are so crossed.

FALSTAFF   Come up into my chamber.

Exeunt

[ACT IV, SCENE VI]

Enter Fenton [and] Host

HOST   Master Fenton, talk not to me. My mind is heavy. I will
give over all.

FENTON   Yet hear me speak. Assist me in my purpose,
And, as I am a gentleman, I'll give thee
A hundred pound in gold more than your loss.   5

HOST   I will hear you, Master Fenton, and I will, at the least,
keep your counsel.

FENTON   From time to time, I have acquainted you
With the dear love I bear to fair Anne Page,

90. dam 「母親」悪魔とその母親に言及するのは、罵りの定番だった。

91. bestowed 「落ち着く、満足する」

92. inconstancy 「不実、浮気心」

95. speciously specially と言うべきところを間違えている。マラプロピズムについては、1. 1. 216 注参照。

95. good heart 「優しい人」heart は限定詞を伴って「〜な人」の意。ここでは、「(あんないい人が) かわいそうに」というニュアンス。

99-102. But that ..., the knave constable ... a witch 「〜でなければ (But that) 〜だっただろう」という仮定法の構文。

101. the knave constable 「あの警官の野郎」

101-02. set me i'th' stocks set someone in the stocks は「さらし台の刑に処す」。さらし台 (stocks) は、両足を入れる穴が空いた板状の刑具。common は、「そこら辺によくある」の意。実際、さらし台は街中に設置されて、町民の嘲弄（ちょうろう）の対象となった。

101. delivered 「救う」

105. Good hearts 95 行目と同じ用例で、対象が複数 (フォード夫人とフォルスタッフ) になっている。

106-07. serve heaven 「天国に行くために奉仕する」の意から、すなわち「善行を積む」。

107. crossed 「邪魔される」

〔4. 6〕あらすじ…………………………………………………………………………
　フェントンがガーター亭の亭主のもとを訪れ、アンからの手紙を見せながら、フォルスタッフをめぐって仕組まれている計略について説明し、その混乱の隙に乗じてペイジ夫妻がそれぞれの思惑でアンを結婚させようとしていることを明かす。フェントンは、アンの気持ちは自分にあることを語った上で、ペイジ夫妻の裏をかいてアンと結婚できるように、牧師の手配を亭主に頼む。
…………………………………………………………………………

2. give over all 「何もかもやめてしまう」「何もかも」には、亭主がフェントンから依頼されている、フェントンのアンへの求愛をこっそり応援することも含まれている。

6. at the least 「せめて、少なくとも」

7. keep your counsel 「君の秘密を守る、他言しない」

Who mutually hath answered my affection, 10
So far forth as herself might be her chooser,
Even to my wish. I have a letter from her,
Of such contents as you will wonder at,
The mirth whereof so larded with my matter
That neither singly can be manifested 15
Without the show of both. Fat Falstaff
Hath a great scene. The image of the jest
I'll show you here at large. Hark, good mine host:
Tonight at Herne's Oak, just 'twixt twelve and one,
Must my sweet Nan present the Faery Queen — 20
The purpose why, is here — in which disguise,
While other jests are something rank on foot,
Her father hath commanded her to slip
Away with Slender, and with him at Eaton
Immediately to marry. She hath consented. Now, sir, 25
Her mother, even strong against that match
And firm for Doctor Caius, hath appointed
That he shall likewise shuffle her away,
While other sports are tasking of their minds,
And at the dean'ry, where a priest attends, 30
Straight marry her. To this her mother's plot
She, seemingly obedient, likewise hath
Made promise to the Doctor. Now thus it rests:
Her father means she shall be all in white,
And in that habit, when Slender sees his time 35
To take her by the hand and bid her go,
She shall go with him. Her mother hath intended,
The better to denote her to the Doctor —
For they must all be masked and vizarded —
That quaint in green she shall be loose enrobed, 40
With ribbons pendent flaring 'bout her head;
And when the Doctor spies his vantage ripe,

11. So far ... chooser 「彼女が自分で選択できる限りにおいては」

12. to my wish 10行目の answered に続く。

14. The mirth whereof 「そこ（手紙）に書かれている楽しみごと」フォルスタッフへの計略を指す。

14. so larded with my matter 「僕の問題とあまりにも密接に関係しているので」次行の That 以下が結果を示す。

15-16. That ... both 「どちらの内容も教えないことには、1つだけを明らかにすることはできない」manifest は「明らかにする、示す」、show は「示すこと」の意。

17. great scene 「大活躍する場面」scene は演劇用語なので、これが芝居であるということを観客に認識させるメタ的な効果もある。

18. at large 「詳しく」

20. present 「～の役を演じる」

21. here 「ほらここに」フェントンは手紙を見せながら説明している。

22. something rank on foot 「しっかりと進行中の」on foot は、何か計画が着手されていることを示す熟語で、rank は強意表現として用いられている。

28. shuffle her away 「彼女を大急ぎでこっそりと立ち退かせる」

29. sports 「娯楽」

29. tasking of their minds 「他の人の関心を占めている」tasking は「～に仕事を課する」を意味する動詞の分詞形。mind は、感情が宿る心というよりも、知性や思考が働く場所なので、むしろ頭を指す。直訳すると、「彼らの頭を働かせている」となる。

30. dean'ry = deanery 英国国教会の用語で、司祭（dean）が住む住居。「牧師館」

33. thus it rests 「こういう状況なのだ」

35. habit 「服装」

38. The better to denote her to the Doctor 「キーズ医師にアンを見分けさせるのにもっとよい方法」

40. quaint in green she shall be loose enrobed 「ゆったりとした緑の衣装を美しく身につけ」quaint は「美しく」の意。アンが演じる役やその際に纏う衣装の色をめぐっては、ペイジとペイジ夫人それぞれの計略もあって、情報が混乱している。4. 4. 67-68 では、ペイジ夫人はアンには妖精の女王を演じさせ、「白い衣装（a robe of white）」を着せると語っているが、5. 5. 183-84 では、夫の計画の裏をかくために、衣装の色を緑に変更したことが明かされる。また、実際に妖精の女王に扮するのはクウィックリーである。フェントンだけが最新の正しい情報を事前に入手していたことになる。

41. pendent flaring 「ひらひらと垂れ下がっている」

42. vantage 「（アンを連れ出す）好機」

To pinch her by the hand, and, on that token,
The maid hath given consent to go with him.
HOST   Which means she to deceive, father or mother?   45
FENTON   Both, my good host, to go along with me.
And here it rests, that you'll procure the vicar
To stay for me at church,'twixt twelve and one,
And, in the lawful name of marrying,
To give our hearts united ceremony.   50
HOST   Well, husband your devise. I'll to the vicar.
Bring you the maid, you shall not lack a priest.
FENTON   So shall I evermore be bound to thee;
Besides, I'll make a present recompense.

Exeunt

50. give our hearts united ceremony 「我々の心を厳かな儀式で結び合わせる」

51. husband 「耕す」を意味する動詞で、ここでは「(計画を) きちんと実行する」の意。もちろん、フェントンが結婚して「夫」になることを見越した洒落である。

54. I'll make a present recompense 「すぐにも君に御礼をする」present は「早速の」を意味する形容詞。

⸢ACT V, SCENE I⸣

Enter Falstaff and Mistress Quickly

FALSTAFF   Prithee, no more prattling. Go. I'll hold. This is the
third time. I hope good luck lies in odd numbers. Away, go!
They say there is divinity in odd numbers, either in nativity,
chance, or death. Away!

MISTRESS QUICKLY   I'll provide you a chain, and I'll do what I   5
can to get you a pair of horns.

FALSTAFF   Away, I say. Time wears. Hold up your head, and
mince.

[*Exit Mistress Quickly*]

[*Enter Ford disguised as Brook*]

How now Master Brook! Master Brook, the matter will be
known tonight or never. Be you in the Park about midnight,   10
at Herne's Oak, and you shall see wonders.

FORD   Went you not to her yesterday, sir, as you told me you
had appointed?

FALSTAFF   I went to her, Master Brook, as you see, like a poor
old man, but I came from her, Master Brook, like a poor old   15
woman. That same knave Ford, her husband, hath the finest
mad devil of jealousy in him, Master Brook, that ever
governed frenzy. I will tell you he beat me grievously, in the
shape of a woman; for in the shape of man, Master Brook, I
fear not Goliath with a weaver's beam, because I know also   20
life is a shuttle. I am in haste. Go along with me. I'll tell you
all, Master Brook. Since I plucked geese, played truant, and
whipped top, I knew not what 'twas to be beaten till lately.
Follow me. I'll tell you strange things of this knave Ford, on
whom tonight I will be revenged, and I will deliver his wife   25
into your hand. Follow. Strange things in hand, Master
Brook. Follow.

··

　フォルスタッフがクウィックリーを送り出したところに、今度はブルックに変装したフォードが登場する。素知らぬ風を装うブルックに問われるがままに、フォルスタッフは先日自分が老女に変装させられて殴られた話をしながら、次の密会について自慢げに語り始める。

···

1. hold 「（待ち合わせの）約束を守る」

3. divinity 「聖なる力」

3-4. either in nativity, chance, or death 「生まれる時であれ、運試しをする時であれ、死ぬ時であれ」

5. chain 4. 4. 30 でペイジ夫人がハーンの亡霊が振り回す鎖に言及していることから、角と同様にフォルスタッフの変装の小道具の 1 つと予想される。

7. wears 「（時が）過ぎていく」

8. mince 「気取って小股で歩く」フォルスタッフは、密会の手引きというううしろめたいことをするクウィックリーに対して、それを気取られないようにあえて堂々と振る舞うように助言している。

20. Goliath 旧約聖書「サムエル記上」で語られるペリシテ人の巨人ゴリアテ。後にイスラエルの王となるダビデと戦い、殺される。「サムエル記上」第 17 章 7 節で、ゴリアテが揮う投げ槍の柄は「機織りの巻き棒（a weaver's beam）のように」太いと形容されている。

21. shuttle 「機の杼」機織りの道具の一種で、横糸を布の端から端まで通す際に用いられる。旧約聖書「ヨブ記」第 7 章 6 節に「わたしの一生は機の杼よりも速く」という一節があり、機の杼は人間の生の儚さの象徴になっている。

22. plucked geese 「ガチョウの羽を生きたまま引き抜いた」悪童の定番の悪戯。

23. whipped top 「コマを鞭打って回した」

26. Strange things in hand 「これから起きるすごいこと」in hand は「進行中の」の意。

Exeunt

[ACT V, SCENE II]

Enter Page, Shallow, [and] Slender

PAGE   Come, come, we'll couch i'th castle-ditch till we see the
light of our fairies. Remember, son Slender, my daughter —

SLENDER   Ay, forsooth, I have spoke with her, and we have a
nay-word how to know one another. I come to her in white
and cry 'mum', she cries 'budget', and by that we know one   5
another.

SHALLOW   That's good too. But what needs either your 'mum'
or her 'budget'? The white will decipher her well enough. It
hath struck ten o'clock.

PAGE   The night is dark. Light and spirits will become it well.   10
Heaven prosper our sport! No man means evil but the devil,
and we shall know him by his horns. Let's away. Follow me.

Exeunt

[ACT V, SCENE III]

Enter Mistress Page, Mistress Ford, [and] Caius

MISTRESS PAGE   Master Doctor, my daughter is in green.
When you see your time, take her by the hand, away with her
to the deanery, and dispatch it quickly. Go before into the
Park. We two must go together.

CAIUS   I know vat I have to do. Adieu.   5

MISTRESS PAGE   Fare you well, sir.

[Exit Caius]

My husband will not rejoice so much at the abuse of Falstaff,
as he will chafe at the Doctor's marrying my daughter. But
'tis no matter. Better a little chiding than a great deal of
heartbreak.   10

〔5. 2〕あらすじ………………………………………………………………………

　ペイジは、スレンダーが一連の騒ぎの最中にアンを連れ出す手順について確認する。

………………………………………………………………………

5. mum / budget　子供の遊戯「だんまり遊び（mumbudget）」を連想させる合い言葉。mum は「沈黙」の意。

10. spirits　「妖精」

10. become　「〜に似合う」

11. prosper　「成功させる」祈願文で語られている。

11. sport　「楽しみごと」

〔5. 3〕あらすじ………………………………………………………………………

　ペイジ夫人は、アンを連れ出して結婚するようにと、キーズに手順を言い含めている。キーズを一足先に森へと向かわせると、ペイジ夫人とフォード夫人は、好色なフォルスタッフを徹底的に懲らしめることを誓って、ハーンの樫の木へと出発する。

………………………………………………………………………

3. deanery　「牧師館」4. 6. 30 注参照。

5. vat = what　キーズのフランス語訛りの英語では、w は v の音で発音される。

7-8. not ... so much ... as 〜　「（as 以下を指して）〜すれば、あまり…ないでしょう」

7. abuse　「懲らしめること」

9. chiding　「叱責」

MISTRESS FORD   Where is Nan now, and her troop of fairies?
And the Welsh-devil Hugh?

MISTRESS PAGE   They are all couched in a pit hard by Herne's
Oak, with obscured lights, which, at the very instant of
Falstaff's and our meeting, they will at once display to the   15
night.

MISTRESS FORD   That cannot choose but amaze him.

MISTRESS PAGE   If he be not amazed he will be mocked. If he
be amazed, he will every way be mocked.

MISTRESS FORD   We'll betray him finely.   20

MISTRESS PAGE   Against such lewdsters and their lechery.
Those that betray them do no treachery.

MISTRESS FORD   The hour draws on. To the Oak, to the Oak!

Exeunt

[ACT V, SCENE IV]

Enter Evans [disguised, with others as] Fairies.

EVANS   Trib, trib fairies! Come, and remember your parts. Be
pold, I pray you. Follow me into the pit, and when I give the
watch-'ords, do as I pid you. Come, come, trib, trib!

Exeunt

[ACT V, SCENE V]

Enter Falstaffe [disguised as Herne with a buck's head upon him]

FALSTAFF   The Windsor bell hath struck twelve; the minute
draws on. Now, the hot-blooded gods assist me! Remember,
Jove, thou wast a bull for thy Europa. Love set on thy horns.
O powerful love, that in some respects makes a beast a man,
in some other a man a beast! You were also, Jupiter, a swan   5
for the love of Leda. O, omnipotent love, how near the god
drew to the complexion of a goose! A fault done first in the

13. hard by 「〜のすぐ近くの」

17. cannot choose but 「〜するより仕方ない、〜せざるを得ない」

18. If he be not amazed 「仮に驚かないにしても」If の前に Even を補って読む。

21. lewdsters 「好色な輩」

〔5. 4〕あらすじ……………………………………………………………………

　妖精に扮した牧師エヴァンズと子供達が登場。エヴァンズは妖精のように軽やかなステップで踊るように、子供達に指示する。

……………………………………………………………………………………

1. Trib エヴァンズの方言では p が b の音になるので、正しくは trip で、「軽やかに踊る」の意。

2. pold = bold

3. watch-'ords = watch words「合い言葉」

3. pid = bid「命じる」

〔5. 5〕あらすじ……………………………………………………………………

　フォルスタッフは、猟師ハーンの亡霊に扮して逢い引きの場にいそいそと向かうも、妖精に扮したクウィックリーや子供達に取り囲まれて、つねられる。フォード夫妻とペイジ夫妻からついに事の真相を聞かされたフォルスタッフは、自らの敗北を認める。そこへ、スレンダーとキーズが、アンだと思って連れ出したのが少年だったと息巻いて登場。続いて、アンとフェントンが登場し、フェントンはアンと結婚したことを告げる。騙されたのは自分だけではなかったことを知って喜ぶフォルスタッフ。一行は仲良くウィンザーへと引き上げる。

……………………………………………………………………………………

3. Jove / Europa ギリシャ・ローマ神話のエピソード。神々の王として天界に君臨するジュピター（ローマ神話では Jove あるいは Jupiter、ギリシャ神話では Zeus）は恋多き神として知られる。フェニキアの王女エウロパ (Europa) を見初めたジュピターは、白い牛に変身して近づくと、エウロパを乗せたまま海を渡り、クレタ島まで連れ去る。オウィディウスの『変身物語』参照。

5. Jupiter 3 行目の Jove と同じ神。

6. Leda 3 行目の Europa と同じく、ジュピターに愛された女性としてギリシャ・ローマ神話に登場する王女レダ。ジュピターは、白鳥に変身してレダを誘惑する。2 人の間に生まれたのが、トロイ戦争の原因として有名な美女ヘレナである。

7. complexion 「姿」ガチョウ（goose）は愚かさの象徴でもある。

7. fault 「罪」ジュピターの不貞行為を指す。ジュピターには妻ヘラがいる。

form of a beast. O Jove, a beastly fault! And then another
fault in the semblance of a fowl. Think on't, Jove, a foul fault!
When gods have hot backs, what shall poor men do? For me,   10
I am here a Windsor stag, and the fattest, I think, i'th'forrest.
Send me a cool rut-time, Jove, or who can blame me to piss
my tallow? Who comes here? My doe?

[*Enter Mistress Ford and Mistress Page*]

Mistress Ford   Sir John? Art thou there, my deer, my male
deer?   15

Falstaff   My doe with the black scut! Let the sky rain
potatoes, let it thunder to the tune of 'Greensleeves', hail
kissing-comfits and snow eryngoes. Let there come a tempest
of provocation, I will shelter me here.

[*He embraces her*]

Mistress Ford   Mistress Page is come with me, sweetheart.   20

Falstaff   Divide me like a bribed buck, each a haunch. I will
keep my sides to myself, my shoulders for the fellow of this
walk, and my horns I bequeath your husbands. Am I a
woodman, ha? Speak I like Herne the Hunter? Why, now is
Cupid a child of conscience: he makes restitution. As I am a   25
true spirit, welcome!

[*A noise of horns within*]

Mistress Page   Alas, what noise?
Mistress Ford   Heaven forgive our sins!
Falstaff   What should this be?
Mistress Ford and Mistress Page   Away, away!   30

[*The two women run off*]

Falstaff   I think the devil will not have me damned, lest the
oil that's in me should set hell on fire.

9. foul 「汚らわしい」直前の fowl（鳥）との洒落。

10. hot backs 「欲情に満ちた腰」back が指す範囲は日本語の「背中」よりも広く、肩から腰（臀部）までを指す。

12. rut-time 動物が繁殖行動を行う「繁殖期」。

12-13. piss my tallow 「俺の獣脂を小便と共に排泄する」牡鹿が交尾の後に痩せるのは、獣脂を排泄するためと言われていた。

14. my deer 「鹿」と「愛しい人（my dear）」の洒落になっている。

16-17. rain potatoes 「サツマイモを降らせる」rain は動詞。サツマイモには性欲を促す効果があると考えられていた。

17. Greensleeves 「グリーンスリーブス」2. 1. 55 でも言及される、当時の流行歌の題名。2. 1. 55 注参照。

17. hail 「（あられのように）降らせる、浴びせかける」

18. kissing-comfits 「香料入りの飴」良い香りのする果物や香辛料で作られ、口臭を消す目的があった。

18. eryngoes 「ハアザミの菓子」これも性欲促進効果があると考えられた。

19. provocation 「（性的に興奮させる）刺激」

21. bribed buck 「盗まれた牡鹿」

21. haunch 「尻」

22. sides 「脇腹」

22-23. the fellow of this walk 「森のこの辺りを管理する森番」walk は道を指す。

24. woodman 「狩人」

26. true 「誠実な、実のある」

26. spirit 4. 4. 32 と同じく「亡霊」。

31. devil will not have me damned 「悪魔はどうしても俺に地獄に落ちてほしくない」damn は他動詞で「～を地獄に落とす」。

He would never else cross me thus.

Enter [Evans as a fairy, Pistol as Hobgoblin, Mistress Quickly as the
    Queen of Fairies, Anne and others as] Fairies [with tapers]

MISTRESS QUICKLY   Fairies black, grey, green, and white,
    You moonshine revellers and shades of night,   35
    You orphan heirs of fixed destiny,
    Attend your office and your quality.
    Crier Hobgoblin, make the fairy oyes.
PISTOL   Elves, list your names. Silence, you airy toys.
    Cricket, to Windsor chimneys shalt thou leap.   40
    Where fires thou find'st unraked, and hearths unswept,
    There pinch the maids as blue as billberry,
    Our radiant Queen hates sluts and sluttery.
FALSTAFF   [*Aside*]   They are fairies; he that speaks to them
        shall die.
    I'll wink and couch; no man their works must eye.   45
EVANS   Where's Bead? Go you, and where you find a maid
    That ere she sleep has thrice her prayers said,
    Raise up the organs of her fantasy;
    Sleep she as sound as careless infancy.
    But those as sleep and think not on their sins,   50
    Pinch them, arms, legs, backs, shoulders, sides, and shins.
MISTRESS QUICKLY   About, about!
    Search Windsor Castle, elves, within, and out.
    Strew good luck, oafs, on every sacred room,
    That it may stand till the perpetual doom   55
    In state as wholesome as in state 'tis fit,
    Worthy the owner and the owner it.
    The several chairs of order look you scour
    With juice of balm and every precious flower.
    Each fair instalment, coat, and several crest   60
    With loyal blazon evermore be blest!

33. else 「そうでなければ（〜するはずがない）」仮定法になっている。

33. cross 「邪魔する」

33 SD ⇒後注

35. revellers 「浮かれ騒ぐ者達」revel は祝宴や祝宴で演じられる余興を意味する。

35. shades spirits と同じく「妖精、精霊」。『夏の夜の夢』に妖精の王として登場するオーベロンは、'king of shadows' と形容されている。

36. You orphan heirs of fixed destiny 何を意味しているのかわかりづらい語句。orphan は形容詞で、「親を持たない」妖精の特性を形容している。妖精を「親はいないが、定められた運命を継承する者達」として定義した表現か。

37. Attend = attend to「（仕事などに）精を出す」

37. quality 「本分、与えられた任務」

38. Crier Hobgoblin 「かけ声役のホブゴブリン」crier は、例えば街角で呼び売りしたり、何かお触れを大声で伝える人を指す。パックやロビン・グッドフェローという名で呼ばれることも多いホブゴブリンと総称されるいたずら好きの妖精は、他の妖精達を召集する役目を担うと考えられていた。

38. make ... oyes 「伝令を伝える」oyes は、布告などを読み上げる際に発する言葉で「聞け！」「静粛に！」の意。

39. list = listen for「注意して聞く」

39. Silence 間投詞で「静粛に！」

39. toys 「ちっぽけなもの」

41. fires thou find'st unraked 「暖炉の炎が消えていたり」rake the fire は「暖炉の火をかき立てる」

42. billberry = bilberry「コケモモ」

45. wink 「（あえて見ないために）目を閉じる」

46. Bead 妖精の名前（ビード）として言及されているが、bead は「数珠の珠、ビーズ」なので、妖精の小ささを連想させる。と同時に、エヴァンズが牧師である点を考慮すると、bead にはロザリオ（キリスト教の祈りの際に用いられる数珠）も連想させる効果もあると思われ、次行以降の祈りにも繋がる。

48. Raise up the organs of her fantasy 想像力の機能を高める、すなわちここでは「良い夢を見させる」の意。

52. About = Go about your business「（仕事に）取りかかれ」

55. perpetual doom 永遠の裁き、すなわちキリスト教の「最後の審判」で世の終わりと同義。

56. In state as wholesome as in state 'tis fit 「その位と同様に状態においても健全に」1つ目の state は「状態」で、2つ目の state は「位、身分」。

58. The several chairs of order 「ガーター勲爵士達が座る椅子」⇒後注

And nightly meadow-fairies, look you sing
Like to the Garter's compass, in a ring.
Th'expressure that it bears, green let it be,
More fertile-fresh then all the field to see.   65
And '*Honi soit qui mal y pense*' write
In em'rald tufts, flowers purple, blue, and white,
Like sapphire, pearl, and rich embroidery,
Buckled below faire knighthoods bending knee.
Fairies use flowers for their charactery.   70
Away, disperse! But till 'tis one o'clock,
Our dance of custom round about the Oak
Of Herne the Hunter let us not forget.
EVANS   Pray you, lock hand in hand, yourselves in order set.
And twenty glow-worms shall our lanterrns be,   75
To guide our measure round about the tree.
But stay! I smell a man of middle earth!
FALSTAFF   [*Aside*]   Heavens defend me from that Welsh fairy,
Lest he transform me to a piece of cheese!
PISTOL   Vile worm, thou wast o'erlooked even in thy birth.   80
MISTRESS QUICKLY   With trial-fire touch me his finger end.
If he be chaste, the flame will back descend
And turn him to no pain; but if he start,
It is the flesh of a corrupted heart.
PISTOL   A trial, come!
EVANS   Come! Will this wood take fire?   85
                            [*They burn him with the tapers*]
FALSTAFF   O, O, O!
MISTRESS QUICKLY   Corrupt, corrupt, and tainted in desire!
About him, fairies, sing a scornful rhyme,
And, as you trip, still pinch him to your time.
FARIES   [*Sing*]   Fie on sinful fantasy!   90
                       Fie on lust and luxury!
                       Lust is but a bloody fire,

62. nightly 形容詞で「夜に現れる」。

63. Like to the Garter's compass 「ガーター勲章の円形の輪のように」like to は「〜のように（like）」ガーター勲章の円環の意匠を指す。聖ジョージの赤十字を青いリボンで囲んだデザインについては図7を参照。

64. expressure that it bears 「輪が描き出す模様」it は前行の ring を指す。

66. *Honi soit qui mal y pense* ラテン語で「悪しき思いを抱く者に禍あれ」
⇒後注

67. tufts 「（房状の）花」

70. charactery 「文字を書くこと」

72. dance of custom 「恒例のダンス」

76. measure 「ダンス」

77. stay 「待つ」

77. a man of middle earth 「人間」 天国と地獄の中間の地上（middle earth）に生ける者という意。

80. o'erlooked = overlooked「呪われた」overlook は「悪い魔法をかける目で睨む」の意。

81. trial-fire 「判じのための炎」次行以降で説明されるように、火がつくかどうかを試みることによって、罪過の有無を判じる。

81. me 動詞の語勢を強めるために挿入された虚辞（心性的与格）で、特に意味はない。

83. start 「びくっとする」

85. A trial, come 「さあ、判じをやってみよう」trial については、81 行目の注参照。

88. About him = circle him round about「彼の周囲をぐるっと取り囲む」

88. rhyme 「（脚韻を踏んだ）歌」

89. trip 「軽快に踊る」

90. fantasy 「欲望」

91. luxury 「好色、淫乱」

図7 ガーター勲章のデザイン

Kindled with unchaste desire,
Fed in heart whose flames aspire,
As thoughts do blow them, higher and higher. 95
Pinch him, fairies, mutually.
Pinch him for his villany.
Pinch him, and burn him, and turn him about,
Till candles and starlight and moonshine be
      out.

[*During the song, they pinch Falstaff. Enter Caius and steals away
a boy in green; enter Slender and steals away a boy in white;
and enter Fenton and steals away Anne. After the song a noise
of hunting horns within. The Fairies run away but do not exit.
Falstaff pulls off his buck's head and rises*]

[*Enter Mistress Page, Mistress Ford, Page, and Ford*]

PAGE   Nay, do not fly! I think we have watched you now.   100
Will none but Herne the Hunter serve your turn?
MISTRESS PAGE   I pray you, come, hold up the jest no higher.
Now, good Sir John, how like you Windsor wives?

[*She points to the buck-horns*]

See you these, husband? Do not these fair yokes
Become the forest better than the town?   105
FORD   Now, sir, who's a cuckold now? Master Brook, Falstaff's
a knave, a cuckoldy knave. Here are his horns, Master Brook.
And, Master Brook, he hath enjoyed nothing of Ford's, but
his buck-basket, his cudgel, and twenty pounds of money,
which must be paid to Master Brook. His horses are arrested   110
for it, Master Brook.
MISTRESS FORD   Sir John, we have had ill luck. We could never
meet. I will never take you for my love again, but I will always
count you my deer.

96. mutually 「みんな一緒に」

100. do not fly 「逃げてはいけません」フォルスタッフに対する台詞。直前で立ち上がったフォルスタッフは、逃げようとしているところを見咎められる格好になる。

101. Will none but Herne the Hunter serve your turn? 「猟師のハンター以外の誰があなたのお役に立つでしょう？（今あなたを助けてくれるのは猟師のハンターぐらい）」反語表現。serve a person's turn は「～の役に立つ」。

102. hold up the jest no higher 例外的な high の用例だが、「これ以上冗談を続けるのをやめる」の意。

104. fair yokes 「立派な角」yoke は畑を耕す牛の首を嵌める軛<ruby>軛<rt>くびき</rt></ruby>だが、ここでは軛のように節くれだって曲がった角を指している。軛は束縛の象徴でもある。

105. Become 「～に似合う」

110. arrested 「差し押さえられた」法律用語。

113. love 「恋人」

114. deer 14行目と同様に、「鹿」と「愛しい人（my dear）」の洒落になっている。

FALSTAFF   I do begin to perceive that I am made an ass.   115

FORD   Ay, and an ox too. Both the proofs are extant.

FALSTAFF   And these are not fairies. I was three or four times
in the thought they were not fairies, and yet the guiltiness of
my mind, the sudden surprise of my powers, drove the
grossness of the foppery into a received belief, in despite of   120
the teeth of all rhyme and reason, that they were fairies. See
now how wit may be made a Jack-a-Lent when 'tis upon ill
employment!

EVANS   Sir John Falstaff, serve Got, and leave your desires,
and fairies will not pinse you.   125

FORD   Well said, fairy Hugh.

EVANS   And leave you your jealousies too, I pray you.

FORD   I will never mistrust my wife again till thou art able to
woo her in good English.

FALSTAFF   Have I laid my brain in the sun, and dried it, that it   130
wants matter to prevent so gross o'erreaching as this? Am I
ridden with a Welsh goat too? Shall I have a coxcomb of
frieze? 'Tis time I were choked with a piece of toasted cheese.

EVANS   Seese is not good to give putter. Your belly is all putter.

FALSTAFF   'Seese' and 'putter'? Have I lived to stand at the   135
taunt of one that makes fritters of English? This is enough to
be the decay of lust and late-walking through the realm.

MISTRESS PAGE   Why, Sir John, do you think, though we
would have thrust virtue out of our hearts by the head and
shoulders, and have given ourselves without scruple to hell,   140
that ever the devil could have made you our delight?

FORD   What, a hodge-pudding? A bag of flax?

MISTRESS PAGE   A puffed man?

PAGE   Old, cold, withered, and of intolerable entrails?

FORD   And one that is as slanderous as Satan?   145

PAGE   And as poor as Job?

FORD   And as wicked as his wife?

115. I am made an ass 「俺は一杯くわされた」make an ass of ～で「～を馬鹿にする」の意。ass は本来はロバを意味し、ロバは愚鈍の象徴とされた。

116. ox 角のある雄牛は、寝取られ亭主の連想から引き合いに出されている。2.1.105 注参照。

116. Both the proofs are extant 「両方の証拠が存在している」両方とは、ロバのように間抜けであることと、雄牛のように寝取られ亭主にされたことの2つを指している。 ⇒後注

119. sudden surprise of my powers 「とっさのことに理解力を奪われること」surprise は「不意打ち攻撃、奇襲」の意。

120. foppery 「愚行」

120. received belief 「完全に信じ込むこと」次行の that 以下に続く。

120-21. in despite of the teeth of all rhyme and reason 「理性に反しているにもかかわらず」in despite of one's teeth (～の反対をものともせず) と neither rhyme or reason (さっぱりわけがわからない) を組み合わせた表現。

122. wit 「知力」

122. Jack-a-Lent 「物笑いの種」人形のジャックについては 3.3.22 注参照。

125. pinse = pinch エヴァンズの英語の訛り。

131. wants matter to ... 「…する能力を欠く」

131. o'erreaching 「ぺてん」overreach は「だます」を意味する動詞。

132. a Welsh goat ウェールズは山羊の牧畜で知られていたこともあるが、おそらくエヴァンズは、たとえば下半身が山羊である森の精ファウヌスのような、山羊に関係した扮装をしていた可能性がある。

132-33. coxcomb of frieze 「粗いウールで作られた道化帽」coxcomb は道化が被る鶏の冠のような形をした帽子を指す。

133. toasted cheese 「こんがり焼いたチーズ」はウェールズ名物。

134. Seese ... putter それぞれ cheese と butter が訛って発音されている。

137. late-walking 直前に lust があるので、「夜遊び」の意。

138. Why 疑問詞ではなく、間投詞。「いいですか」といった意味。

138-41. do you ... delight? think that ... の構文に、(even) though ... hell「たとえ…としても」が挿入されている。

139-40. by the head and shoulders 「強引に」

140. without scruple 「何のためらいもなく、平気で」

142. hodge-pudding ごたまぜの材料で作ったデザート菓子。

144. intolerable entrails 「我慢できないほど大きい腹」

146. Job 旧約聖書「ヨブ記」の主要人物。相次ぐ苦難に見舞われる。それでも神を恨まない信心深いヨブに対して、ヨブの妻は信仰を捨てて死ぬことを勧める。「ヨブ記」第2章9節参照。

EVANS   And given to fornications, and to taverns, and sack, and wine, and metheglins, and to drinkings, and swearings and starings, pribbles and prabbles?   150

FALSTAFF   Well, I am your theme. You have the start of me. I am dejected. I am not able to answer the Welsh flannel. Ignorance itself is a plummet o'er me. Use me as you will.

FORD   Marry, sir, we'll bring you to Windsor, to one Master Brook, that you have cozened of money, to whom you should   155 have been a pander. Over and above that you have suffered, I think to repay that money will be a biting affliction.

PAGE   Yet be cheerful, knight. Thou shalt eat a posset tonight at my house, where I will desire thee to laugh at my wife that now laughs at thee. Tell her Master Slender hath married her   160 daughter.

MISTRESS PAGE   [Aside]   Doctors doubt that. If Anne Page be my daughter, she is, by this, Doctor Caius' wife.

[Enter Slender]

SLENDER   Whoa ho, ho, father Page!

PAGE   Son, how now? How now, son? Have you dispatched?   165

SLENDER   Dispatched? I'll make the best in Gloucestershire know on't. Would I were hanged, la, else!

PAGE   Of what, son?

SLENDER   I came yonder at Eton to marry Mistress Anne Page, and she's a great lubberly boy. If it had not been i'th'church,   170 I would have swinged him, or he should have swinged me. If I did not think it had been Anne Page, would I might never stir! And 'tis a post-master's boy!

PAGE   Upon my life, then, you took the wrong.

SLENDER   What need you tell me that? I think so, when I took   175 a boy for a girl. If I had bene married to him, for all he was in woman's apparel, I would not have had him.

PAGE   Why, this is your own folly. Did not I tell you how you

148. given to ... 「…にふけっている」

148. sack 「サックワイン」2.1.7 注参照。

149. metheglins 「メゼグリン」スパイスを配合したウェールズ産の蜂蜜酒。普通は単数のところ複数形になっているのは、エヴァンズ特有の英語。

149-50. swearings and starings 「悪態をついたり、にらみつけたり」傲慢不遜な態度の典型として成句のようにセットで使われている。

150. pribbles and prabbles 「むだなおしゃべり」1.1.47-48 注参照。

151. theme 「話の種、話題」自分が皆の物笑いのネタにされていることを指す。

151. have the start of ... 「…より先んじる、有利な立場にいる」

152. Welsh flannel 「ウェールズの雑巾」flannel は皿洗い用布巾。エヴァンズへの悪口。

153. Ignorance itself is a plummet o'er me フォルスタッフらしい凝った比喩。エヴァンズが「無知（ignorance）」として擬人化され、さらに「重り（plummet）」に喩えられている。plummet は水深を測る際に用いられた道具。「無知な野郎が重りになって俺のこと（あるいは、俺の馬鹿さ加減）を探っていやがる」といった意味。

154. Marry 「いいか」by Mary（聖母マリア様にかけて）に由来し、何かをきっぱりと言う際に用いる強意表現。

158. posset 「ミルク酒」1.4.7 注参照。

162. Doctors doubt that 「それはどうかしらね」見識者である学者（doctors）であれば、違う見解を持っている、という意味で用いられた諺のような成句。もちろん、キーズの職業（医者）への連想も意図されている。

165. dispatched 「首尾よく実行した」

166-67. I'll make the best in Gloucestershire know on't make は使役動詞で、make ... known で「…に知らせる」。「グロスター州で一番偉い人にこのことを知らせてやる」

170. lubberly 「粗野な」

171. swinged 「殴り倒した」

173. post-master's boy 「早馬屋で働いている少年」post-master は、郵便物を運ぶのに用いられた早馬（posting horses）を管理する厩舎（きゅうしゃ）の親方を指す。post-master's boy は、その厩舎で働く徒弟の少年のこと。

176. for all ... 「たとえ…であっても」

should know my daughter by her garments?

SLENDER I went to her in white, and cried 'mum', and she   180
cried 'budget', as Anne and I had appointed. And yet it was
not Anne, but a postmaster's boy.

MISTRESS PAGE Good George, be not angry. I knew of your
purpose, turned my daughter into greeen, and indeed she is
now with the Doctor at the deanery, and there married.   185

[Enter Caius]

CAIUS Vere is Mistress Page? By gar, I am cozened. I ha'
married *un garçon*, a boy, *un paysan*, by gar, a boy. It is not
Anne Page. By gar, I am cozened.

MISTRESS PAGE Why? Did you take her in green?

CAIUS Ay, by gar, and 'tis a boy. By gar, I'll raise all Windsor.   190

FORD This is strange. Who hath got the right Anne?

[Enter Fenton and Anne]

PAGE My heart misgives me. Here comes Master Fenton.
How now, Master Fenton?

ANNE Pardon, good father. Good my mother, pardon.

PAGE Now, mistress, how chance you went not with Master
Slender?   195

MISTRESS PAGE Why went you not with Master Doctor, maid?

FENTON You do amaze her. Hear the truth of it.
You would have married her most shamefully
Where there was no proportion held in love.
The truth is, she and I, long since contracted,   200
Are now so sure that nothing can dissolve us.
Th'offence is holy that she hath committed,
And this deceit loses the name of craft,
Of disobedience, or unduteous title,
Since therein she doth evitate and shun   205
A thousand irreligious cursed hours

180. her in white　二つ折本では、この箇所と 184 行目、189 行目で、なぜか白と緑が逆になっており、第 4 幕 4 場や第 4 幕第 6 場で与えられる情報と齟齬を来している。二つ折本のこの不一致の原因は定かではないが、2 つの可能性が考えられる。1 つは、印刷に使用する原稿を準備した筆耕のレイフ・クレイン（Ralph Crane）による取り違えである（Oliver, Craik）。もう 1 つの解釈は、シェイクスピア自身が間違えた可能性であり（Crane）、編者もこの考えに賛同する。複写に専念しているプロの筆耕がわざわざ白と緑の単語を取り違えるとは考えにくく、色の勘違いが生じるとすれば、それは作者の側と推測する方が自然である。そもそもアンの衣装の色の問題は複雑になっており、間違いを誘発しやすい。少なくとも元の計画ではアンが白い衣装を着ることは、第 5 幕第 2 場をはじめとして、何度も言及されている。とはいえ、アンに緑の衣装を着せることで、スレンダーを出し抜いてキーズがアンを連れ去ることを画策するペイジ夫人の裏の計略があるだけに、最終的にアンが着る衣装の色はたしかにややこしく、混乱が生じるのも無理はない。四つ折本では（白と緑に加えて）赤い衣装への言及があり、さらにややこしい混乱が生じている。ともあれ、少なくとも劇場で見る限り、アンが最終的に何色の衣装を着るのかという問題は、スレンダーとキーズがまんまとしくじり、アンとフェントンがうまく逃げるという事実の前でははとんど気にならないこともまたたしかである。

183. Good George　驚いた時に発する言葉で、「あらまあ！」。George はイングランドの守護聖人である聖ジョージを指し、「聖ジョージにかけて（by George）」に由来する表現。

185. deanery　「牧師館」4. 6. 30 注参照。

186. Vere = Where　キーズのフランス訛りの英語では、w が v の音になる。

186. By gar = By God「大変だ」

195. how chance ...?　「どうして…のか？」

197. amaze　「困らせる」

199. Where ... love　「愛情の点では全く釣り合いがとれていない状態で」

200. contracted　「婚約していた」親には内緒で、2 人の間では結婚を誓い合っていたことを指す。

201. sure　「揺るぎない」

204. unduteous title　「親に背いたと言われること」title は、前行の name と同じ意味で用いられている。

205. evitate　「避ける」

Which forced marriage would have brought upon her.

FORD   [*To Page and Mistress Page*]

Stand not amazed. Here is no remedy.

In love the heavens themselves do guide the state.

Money buys lands, and wives are sold by fate.   210

FALSTAFF   I am glad, though you have ta'en a special stand to

strike at me, that your arrow hath glanced.

PAGE   Well, what remedy? Fenton, heaven give thee joy!

What cannot be eschewed must be embraced.

FALSTAFF   When night-dogs run, all sorts of deer are chased.   215

MISTRESS PAGE   Well, I will muse no further, Master Fenton,

Heaven give you many, many merry days!

Good husband, let us every one go home,

And laugh this sport o'er by a country fire,

Sir John and all.

FORD   Let it be so, Sir John.   220

To Master Brook, you yet shall hold your word,

For he tonight shall lie with Mistress Ford.

Exeunt

209. guide the state 「支配する」

210. Money buys lands, and wives are sold by fate 土地の場合は金で買える
が、女房となると、売り手は運命なので、金では買えない、という意味。

211-12. though you have ta'en a special stand to strike at me, 「お前は特別
な場所から俺を攻撃しようとしたが」stand は狩猟の際に獲物を狙う立ち位
置を指す名詞。ta'en = taken

212. glanced 「(的から)それた」

216. muse 「文句を言う」

後 注

1. 1. 1　Sir Hugh　「サー」は騎士（Knight）の称号であるが、ここではオックスフォード大あるいはケンブリッジ大の学位を有する牧師への敬称として用いられている。Crane によると、四つ折本の表紙で「ウェールズの騎士」としてエヴァンズが紹介されているのは、おそらくこの冒頭の呼びかけを印刷業者が誤読したため。Crane は、エヴァンズの「サー」には、フォルスタッフが騎士として有する「サー」ほどの重みはない点も指摘している。

1. 1. 3　Esquire　「郷士」は、世襲貴族の下に位置する社会階層であるジェントリー（Gentry）に属する身分。近代初期においては、地方に土地を有する地主として、地方行政にも一定の役割を果たした。『英米史辞典』参照。

1. 1. 14　luces　シャローやスレンダーが自慢する紋は、カワカマスがデザインされていることから、チャールコートの貴族ルーシー家の紋章と結びつけられてきた。ルーシー家の家紋には 3 匹のカワカマスが描かれている（図 8）。チャールコートはシェイクスピアの生誕地であるストラットフォード・アポン・エイヴォンから 6 キロほど離れたところにある町。シェイクスピアが故郷を離れてロンドンに出たのは、サー・トマス・ルーシーの猟園の鹿を盗んだためであるという伝説が 18 世紀初頭からあるが、信憑性はない。Craik は、そもそもサー・トマス・ルーシーは当時ウォリックシャーに猟園を所有して

図 8　カワカマスが描かれたルーシー家の紋章

いなかったことを指摘した上で、鹿殺しの罪で糾弾されるフォルスタッフとの関連で創作されたシェイクスピア伝説という見方を提示している。

1. 1. 94　the King　本作品が執筆されたのはエリザベス朝で、時の君主はエリザベス一世（在位 1558-1603）であり、風俗など作品全体が醸し出す雰囲気もエリザベス朝のそれに近い。実際、解説で論じたように、ガーター式典への言及など、同時代のエリザベス朝の時事への言及と見られる箇所もある。しかしその一方で、この作品はシェイクスピアが 1590 年代後半に執筆した歴史劇のスピンオフ作品であることを考えれば、ここで言及される王は、ヘンリー四世（在位 1399-1413）か、ヘンリー五世（在位 1413-22）を指すと考えるのが妥当（Oliver, Wiggins）。フォルスタッフは、『ヘンリー四世』二部作で、ヘンリー五世として即位する前のハル王子の不良仲間として登場する。Crane は、本作品でのフォルスタッフが宮廷に出入りしているらしい点から、さらに踏み込んでヘンリー五世の治世と解釈している。

1. 1. 121　the Garter　Oliver によると、実際に「ガーター亭（The Garter）」という名の宿屋が 16 世紀のウィンザーに存在した。「ガーター」については、5.5.58 後注参照。飲食を提供する宿屋（inn）は、宿泊施設としてだけではなく、居酒屋、そして賭け事に興じる娯楽施設としても機能しており、町の男性達のたまり場だった。『研究社シェイクスピア辞典』の「宿屋と居酒屋」項目参照。「キングス・アームズ」や「ロイヤル・オーク」など、現在のイギリスでも王室に因んだ名前を持つパブが多く残っており、「ガーター亭」のネーミングもこうした文化に位置づけられる。

1. 3. 80　discuss ... to Ford　ニムとピストルが告げる相手をめぐっては、若干の混乱がある。ここではフォードに密告しに出かけるのがニムで、ペイジに知らせるのはピストルになっているが、実際に第 2 幕第 1 場でフォードに告げるのはピストル、ペイジに告げるのはニムである。さらにややこしいことに、版本の異同もある。四つ折本のこの箇所（80 行）では、ニムが行き先として挙げるのはペイジ、続く台詞（81 行）でピストルが挙げるのはフォードになっている。こうしたことから、統一を重視して四つ折本を採用し、80 行、81 行、そして 85 行でペイジとフォードを入れ替える編者も多い（Craik、Crane、Hibbard）。しかし、その場合は 85 行以下のニムの台詞が明らかに後に嫉妬に狂うこととなるフォードを念頭においているだけに、どうしても違和感が生じる（Melchiori）。単純な名前の取り違えなどの錯誤はシェイクスピア劇ではままあることで、「解説」で述べたように急いで執筆されたと推測される本作品にはこの種の不一致が多い。この箇所に関しては、文脈を優先し、あえてそのままとした。

2. 1. 55　Hundredth Psalm　二つ折本では「100 の聖歌（hundred Psalms）」となっているが、「詩篇」は 100 ではなく 150 の聖歌で構成されており、齟齬が生じる。おそらく Craik が指摘するように、原稿を写す際、あるいは印刷の植字の際に hundredth とすべきところを誤った上に、さらにつじつまを合わせるために Psalms と複数形に変更したものと推測される。「全地よ、主に向かって喜びの叫びをあげよ」で始まる「詩篇」の 100 番は、特に人気のある聖歌で、現代も教会の礼拝などで親しまれているが、近代初期の礼拝でどのように歌われたかは定かではない。おそらく現代ほど音楽的ではなく、詠唱に近いと思われるが、会衆がなじみのあるバラッドのメロディに合わせて聖歌を歌った可能性も指摘されている（Marsh）。

2. 1. 187　Brook　四つ折本ではブルック（Brook）となっているフォードの偽名が、二つ折本ではブルーム（Broom）に変更されている。変更の理由も時期も定かではないが、最も有力な説は、エリザベス一世の側近貴族だったコバム卿ことブルック家への揶揄を回避するためという推測である。ブルック家は、フォルスタッフの人物造型のもとになっているジョン・オールドカッスルの子孫であり、シェイクスピアが当初『ヘンリー四世　第一部』でオールドカッス

ルとして登場させたところ、第7代コバム卿ウィリアム・ブルックあるいはその息子であるヘンリー・ブルックの抗議を受けて、フォルスタッフへの変更を余儀なくされた可能性が指摘されている。寝取られ亭主にされることに怯えるフォードの偽名にブルックを用いることが、この一件に対するシェイクスピアや劇団の意趣返しだったと推測する批評家もいるが、「河」を意味するフォードと「小川」を意味する brook の単なる語呂合わせの可能性もあり、断定は難しい。ともあれ、宮廷上演の際に無用なトラブルを避けるために「ブルック」を「ブルーム」に変更し、それが以後の上演やテキストに適用された可能性は十分に考えられる（Craik, Crane）。

2.2.57　the court lay at Windsor　衛生上の理由から、複数の王宮を定期的に移動するのが当時のヨーロッパの王室の慣例だった。君主が動けば、貴族を筆頭とする一行も動くので、宮廷はたえず地理的な移動を伴っていたことになる。なかでもエリザベス一世は地方への移動を好み、ロンドンのホワイトホール宮殿（現存しない）を本拠地としつつも、イングランド各地に巡幸に出かけた。ノルマン時代に建設された中世の古城ウィンザー城は最も格式のある王宮の１つであり、ガーター騎士団の叙勲式典の開催地として有名。ハンプトン宮殿と同じく、ロンドンに比較的近い場所に位置していることもあり、巡幸の起点・終点としても活用された。

3.1.14.　SD　エヴァンズがここで歌い始める唄はシェイクスピアと同時代の劇作家クリストファー・マーロウによる恋愛抒情詩「僕のところにおいで、恋人になろう（'Come live with me and be my love'）」の一部だが、21行目のWhenas I sat in Pabylon は「詩篇」の137番の１行目。2.1.55と同様に、世俗的な歌と聖歌が入り混じっている。マーロウのこの詩は当時かなり人気を博した。歌う際に、同時代のバラッドから転用されたメロディの楽譜については、Craik, Appendix B 参照。

3.1.21.　Whenas I sat in Pabylon　元気を出そうと歌い始めるエヴァンズだが、途中で気分が滅入ったのか、哀切な歌詞と調べをもつ聖歌の一節に切り替わってしまう。旧約聖書に収められている「詩篇」の137番は、「バビロンの流れのほとりに座り（Whenas we sat in Babylon the rivers round about）」で始まり、故郷エルサレムを追われたイスラエルの民を思って嘆く詩。

3.5.91　Fate　古代ギリシャ・ローマ神話では、運命を司る神は複数存在する。まず、「運命の女神たち（Fates）」と呼ばれる３姉妹の女神は、人間が避けることのできない死と結びつけられることが多い。一方、人間のいわゆる運・不運を司る「運命の女神（Fortune）」もおり、人間の運命の計りがたさを示す存在として恐れられた。どこに進むかわからない球体に乗った盲目の女神や、（チャンスをつかみ取るという寓意との関連で）長い前髪を持つ女神として描かれるのは後者の方であり、フォルスタッフのここでの台詞で言及される「運命の女神」もこちらに近いと思われる。『ギリシア・ローマ神話大事典』の「運

命」と「フォルトゥナ」の項目参照。

4.1.6 his master グラマー・スクールと呼ばれる中等学校の就学開始年齢は7、8歳。大学と同じく、もともとは中世に聖職者養成のために設立された教育機関であるため、聖職者の公用語であるラテン語の教育が中心だった。シェイクスピアの時代には、折からの人文主義と相俟って、ギリシャ語・ラテン語など古典文学が重要視されると共に、自国語である英語の教育への関心も高まった。『英米史辞典』参照。

5.5.33 SD 二つ折本では、妖精の女王役の台詞の話者表示はクウィックリー、ホブゴブリン役の台詞の話者表示はピストルとなっているが、2人がこの余興に参加することは、フォード夫人達が具体的な計画を立てる場面(第4幕第4場)では言及されていない。そのことから、これはあくまでもクウィックリーとピストルを演じた2人の役者が、それぞれ妖精の女王とホブゴブリンの役を演じていることを示しているに過ぎないのであって、必ずしもクウィックリーとピストルがフォルスタッフをからかう余興に参加しているわけではないという点を強調する解釈もある（Craik, Crane）。しかし、エヴァンズと同様に、クウィックリーとピストルもフォード夫人達の仲間に引き入れられて、余興に参加していると考えることは十分に妥当であると思われる。特にクウィックリーは、フォード夫人とペイジ夫人の手先としてフォルスタッフを騙すだけに、最後の計略にも加担しているのはむしろ自然と言える。以下の場面で、妖精に扮する町人達の台詞は韻を踏んでいることにも留意。散文から韻文へ、そして無韻詩ではなく脚韻を有する韻文へと調子を変えることで、妖精の素早い動きを表現する同様の仕掛けは『夏の夜の夢』にも見られる。

5.5.58 The several chairs of order ガーター騎士団の騎士が着席することになっている椅子を指す。order は「騎士団」を意味する。この場面で繰り返し言及されるガーター騎士団（The Order of the Garter）の叙勲式典は現在も続くイギリス王室の儀式で、聖ジョージの祝日である4月23日にウィンザー城の聖ジョージ礼拝堂で行われ、イギリスの勲爵位の最高位として知られるガーター勲位が授与される。騎士達は礼拝堂に設置されている仕切りのついた聖歌隊席に座し、それぞれの騎士の紋章、兜、旗が頭上に掲げられた（Oliver）。

5.5.66 *Honi soit qui mal y pense* 「悪しき思いを抱く者に禍あれ」はガーター勲章のモットーで、5.5.63注で言及した青いリボンにも記されている。ガーター騎士団は1348年にエドワード三世によって創設された。おそらくはフランスとの戦争に向けて戦意高揚を図る目的があったと推測されるが、創設をめぐって人口に膾炙した艶笑譚が存在する。舞踏会で貴婦人が落としたガーター（靴下止め）を拾いあげたエドワード三世が、居並ぶ宮廷貴族のよからぬ妄想を制すべく、「悪しき思いを抱く者に禍あれ」と言い放ち、女性の名誉への崇敬を命じて騎士団を創設したという逸話である。ガーターの持ち主については、王妃とする説と、王の恋人であるソールズベリー伯夫人とする説の2つが

存在した。騎士道ロマンスに通底する女性崇拝の理念や宮廷風恋愛の要素が加味されることにより、ガーター騎士団は（その名が示唆する通り）ロマンス色を帯びることとなった。

5.5.116　Both the proofs are extant　フォルスタッフは夫ではないため、寝取られ亭主の冗談は一見するとずれているように思われるかもしれない。しかし、フォード夫人の恋人気取りでいたところ、フォード夫人には別の相手、すなわち夫がいたという点において、フォルスタッフはやはり、周知の事実に一人だけ気づいていない愚かな寝取られ亭主の立場に陥っていることになる。

[編注者紹介]

竹村はるみ（たけむら　はるみ）

1968年生まれ。京都大学文学部卒業。同大学院文学研究科博士後期課程（英米文学専攻）研究指導認定退学。京都大学博士（文学）。

姫路獨協大学を経て、現在は立命館大学文学部教授。

［著書］『グロリアーナの祝祭―エリザベス一世の文学的表象』（単著、研究社、2018年）*Spenser in History, History in Spenser: Spenser Society Japan Essays*（共編著、大阪教育図書、2018年）、『シェイクスピアと演劇文化―日本シェイクスピア協会創立50周年記念論集』（共著、研究社、2012年）、『食卓談義のイギリス文学―書物が語る社交の歴史』（共著、彩流社、2006年）、『ゴルディオスの絆―結婚のディスコースとイギリス・ルネサンス演劇』（共著、松柏社、2002年）

〈大修館シェイクスピア双書 第2集〉

ウィンザーの陽気な女房たち

©Harumi Takemura, 2022　　　　　　　NDC 932／xii, 222p／20cm

初版第1刷——2022年12月20日

編注者————竹村はるみ

発行者————鈴木一行

発行所————株式会社 大修館書店

　　　　　　〒113-8541 東京都文京区湯島2-1-1

　　　　　　電話 03-3868-2651（販売部）　03-3868-2293（編集部）

　　　　　　振替 00190-7-40504

　　　　　　［出版情報］https://www.taishukan.co.jp

装丁・本文デザイン————井之上聖子

印刷所————広研印刷

製本所————ブロケード

ISBN 978-4-469-14267-9　Printed in Japan

大修館 シェイクスピア双書 (全12巻)
THE TAISHUKAN SHAKESPEARE

お気に召すまま	*As You Like It*	柴田稔彦 編注
ハムレット	*Hamlet, Prince of Denmark*	高橋康也・ 河合祥一郎 編注
ジュリアス・シーザー	*Julius Caesar*	大場建治 編注
リア王	*King Lear*	Peter Milward 編注
マクベス	*Macbeth*	今西雅章 編注
ヴェニスの商人	*The Marchant of Venice*	喜志哲雄 編注
夏の夜の夢	*A Midsummer-night's Dream*	石井正之助 編注
オセロー	*Othello*	笹山　隆 編注
リチャード三世	*King Richard the Third*	山田昭広 編注
ロミオとジュリエット	*Romeo and Juliet*	岩崎宗治 編注
テンペスト	*The Tempest*	藤田　実 編注
十二夜	*Twelfth Night; or, What You Will*	安西徹雄 編注

大修館 シェイクスピア双書 第2集（全8巻）
THE TAISHUKAN SHAKESPEARE 2nd Series